## Praise for Katy Munger

"Casey Jones joins the ranks of smart and gutsy heroines. Don't miss her!"

—*Janet Evanovich*

"Katy Munger's trademark — a hard-boiled, plot-intensive mystery augmented by raucous humor and delivered by the brassy, wise-cracking heroine, Casey Jones."

—*Ft. Lauderdale Sun-Sentinel*

"Casey's funny and shrewd, not least about herself… she's a heroine with a difference, and someone you'd like to know better."

— *The Drood Review of Mystery*

"Casey Jones… is smart, tough, and tenacious... more complex than many other female sleuths—she's cynical, raunchy, and has none of the reticence that can be so irksome… Munger does a fine job of bringing to life the Southern backdrop."

—*Publishers Weekly*

"Prepare to meet one of the funniest, raunchiest, most enjoyable P.I.s to come along in a while."

— *Murder, Ink*

"The author has a knack for developing a far-flung cast of characters without losing sight of the myriad personalities or making fun of Southern eccentricities. And the full-figured, tough-talking Casey, with her unabashed affection for men, is a refreshing, confident sleuth."

—*Ft. Lauderdale Sun-Sentinel*

Casey Jones books by Katy Munger:

LEGWORK
OUT OF TIME
MONEY TO BURN
BAD TO THE BONE
BETTER OFF DEAD
**BAD MOON ON THE RISE**

Published by Thalia Books • 2009



ISBN 978-0-9819442-4-1
Manufactured in the United States of America
First Edition: September 2009

# Bad Moon on the Rise

***A Casey Jones Mystery***

By Katy Munger

# Chapter One

Corndog Sally and her husband, Downtown Mac, had less than a dozen teeth between them — but that didn't stop them from being the smilingest couple on Hillsborough Street. Sally sold flowers out of a little stall near the General Assembly Building while Mac puttered around the tourist-filled lawn wagging a state-of-the-art metal detector that mostly beeped for garter belt snaps from the 1950's. What were those legislators doing back in the good ole days, anyway?

Mac and Sally made a pretty good living for over sixty years. Just about everybody in Raleigh recognized them. They were happy people, and happy people are getting harder to come by in this world. In fact, Sally only stopped smiling once to my knowledge — and that was when Mac got crushed to death in the Dempsty Dumpster behind the Happy Store while tracking down loose change. I admit that some considered this an ironic way for Mac to go, but the older I get, the more I view life's ironies as its inevitabilities in disguise. They renamed the Happy Store a few weeks later, for obvious reasons, and they still keep a framed photo of Mac behind the counter out of guilt.

As for Corndog Sally, she folded up shop after Mac died. No one I knew saw her again once the last clod of dirt had been shoveled over Mac's coffin. Her whereabouts were as mysterious as her name: who on god's green earth would call someone "Corndog Sally," even here in the South where stupid nicknames are a religion?

Of course, the bigger question was what she had done to earn such a moniker. Corn dogs are neon pink hot dogs of dubious origin encased in soggy cornmeal then thrown into the deep fryer until all the additives have melted into one rubbery tube that gets a popsicle stick rammed up its ass — all so you can hold it in one hand while gripping a jumbo Pepsi in the other. I hoped to god Sally had never actually eaten one, though it would certainly explain why she was so well-preserved for her age, which had to be creeping up on ninety.

All of this, I hope, explains why I was so surprised to find Corndog Sally waiting for me on an autumn afternoon that was hotter than two foxes fornicating in a forest fire. It may as well have been July. If global warming wasn't real, our planet was having hot flashes and we all needed to buckle our seat belts.

It had been a good seven years since I had last seen Sally. Time had changed her. When I came barreling through the door, Sally, who had never so much as raised her voice in my presence before, was toe-to-toe with Bobby D. and giving him a piece of her mind that would have blistered a more sensitive man. And no wonder. Bobby was not only asking her *why* she was named Corndog Sally, he was assuming it was because she liked to eat the dang things and then he had leapfrogged over all common sense whatsoever and declared that he could beat her at a corndog-eating contest anywhere and anytime. She just had to name the time and place.

"You mind your own beeswax," Sally spat at Bobby. "And maybe you ought not to take so much pride in being a bigger glutton than the rest of us folks."

I was too astonished to say a word. She had a point about Bobby, but what had happened to the sweet, good-natured woman we all knew as Corndog Sally? We'd have to start calling her Mad Dog if she kept this sort of attitude up.

"I've been waiting for you for half an hour," she snarled once she spotted me.

I couldn't say much back to that. Corndog Sally was blacker than the tar on Hargett Street and one thing you learn in the South is that you never, ever sass a black woman over seventy. Not only does it show bad breeding, you're likely to get your ass kicked if you do. There's not a bamboo-waving ninja master on the planet who can compete with the way those little old ladies can whip a hickory switch around.

Instead, I kept my mouth shut — which, granted, is unusual for me — and showed her into my closet-sized office, which was chiefly notable for the collection of bras hanging from the doorknob. A girl should be prepared. Depending on whether I plan to be running, shooting or taking my underwear off and whirling it above my head, I like to choose between underwire, sports or the soft lace cup.

Corndog Sally didn't look as if she liked to choose between anything in the way of a bra. She sat across from me, adjusted her '70's-era Afro wig, then plopped her own waist-length babies up on the desk like she was serving them up for supper. They looked like a pair of sweet potatoes waiting to be buttered. I guess being that old lets you pretty much do whatever you damn well please with your body parts.

"What is it, Sally?" I asked.

When she didn't answer me, I tried again. "God almighty, Sally — you disappear for seven years and now you're not even going to talk to me? I haven't seen you since the funeral."

"I saw you there," she conceded. "That was right nice of you, Miss Jones."

"Call me Casey."

"Miss Jones, I want you to find my grandson." She slid a photo across the desk.

I stared at a handsome boy with a head of curly black hair. He was about fourteen or fifteen and spinning a basketball on the tip of his left index finger. He looked tall and cocky and talented. He also looked mighty light to be Sally's grandson.

"This boy is white," I pointed out.

Sally snatched the photo back. "I don't need me a detective to tell me *that.* I need you to tell me where he is."

"How can he be white?" I was unwilling to let the subject drop. When you're me, tact is a luxury reserved for cops about to either ticket me or undress me.

"He's white because his daddy was white." Sally stowed the photo away in a pocketbook the size of a sofa cushion. "Didn't they teach you nothing in high school?" She was assuming I had never clawed my way through college, which was a safe bet on her part. I am not of the upper class and it shows. If I ever walked into a Talbot's, I suspect the sales ladies would all run screaming for the exits.

Sally reconsidered her rudeness. "This picture was taken in the winter time," she explained. "He browns up real nice in the summer sun."

"When did you last see him?" I asked.

"About four or five months ago, when his momma stopped by, probably looking for money. My oldest daughter wouldn't let her in the door. For good reason."

"So he's with his mother?"

"I don't know and I don't care," Corndog Sally snapped. "I don't want you to find his momma. I want you to find him."

I didn't have to ask why she didn't want to find her daughter. Drugs are everywhere, even in Raleigh, North Carolina. You could hike up the highest mountain on the Blue Ridge and into the deepest cave you could spot, and you'd probably find a circle of droopy-eyed teenagers going through their grandmothers' pocketbooks looking for something they could either hock or sniff.

"How much money do you want to put into it?" I asked. "A missing persons case can be a money pit."

"I've got money." She clutched her handbag to her chest like I was planning to rip my fee out of her wallet right then and there.

"Fine, I just don't want to spend it all."

"Mac left me well-prepared for," she said. "I can pay whatever it takes."

"No problem. I just wanted to be sure," I said, knowing an apology was in order. "It's been seven years, you know? People were worried about you. No one knows where you've been or what you've been living on."

"I've been living on the savings from a lifetime of hard work, that's what I've been living on. And I've been raising my grandson," she said. "That is, I was until his momma came sniffing around and took him back. Probably for the welfare money."

"Oh." What else could I say?

"Just find my grandson, Miss Jones. It's important to me. He was Mac's favorite. I can't let his momma tear him down. She says she's off drugs, but that's a lie. It's always a lie. If you can't tell for yourself that a person's off drugs, if they got to keep shouting it from the rooftops, then they ain't off enough drugs to suit me. Trey's just a boy and he's a talented basketball player. The best he's ever seen, his coach says. He could be somebody. But not if he stays with his momma."

"Okay," I agreed. "I'll find him for you. Just let me have that picture back, would you?"

It had taken ten minutes to get there, but what do you know? The smile on Corndog Sally rose like the sun coming up behind Pilot Mountain on a spring morning in May.

* * *

TOO TALL JOHNSON PROVED TO BE both a disappointment and a contradiction in terms. What he had in height, he lacked in length. And in technique. He had seemed like a good idea four gin-and-tonics ago, but midnight had revealed the awful truth: not only was Too Tall too short, he was too damn quick on the draw to boot. He wouldn't even make it into the ranks of Minute Men. And, like all men, the time he'd spent in my bed was in inverse proportion to the time he now intended to spend parked on my sofa, flipping through television channels in search of post-coital sports. Men like him are why I go through a dozen Duracells a year.

"I hate to be rude," I lied as I handed him his jacket. "But you have to leave my home now."

"What?" He looked confused, an expression I had come to sense often in the dark of my bedroom.

"Go," I told him. "I need to work."

"Work?" He glanced at his watch, which he had kept on during sex, although, frankly, a stop watch would have been more appropriate.

"The advantage to being self-employed," I explained, "is that you don't have to punch a clock." My expression convinced him that I might take to punching him if he didn't hurry up and leave, so Too Tall threw his jeans and sweatshirt back on and stumbled out into the night.

I picked up the phone and called my friend Marcus Dupree, who is a night owl and can be counted on to be wide awake until the wee hours of the morn.

"Too Tall Johnson should change his name to My Johnson Is Too Short," I announced when Marcus picked up the phone. There was no need to introduce myself.

"I could have told you that," Marcus said with the authority of a man who spends too many hours hiding in the stalls of the

Durham Police Department's third floor bathroom, trying to sneak quick smokes in between other people's quick pees. "He can't stick with a case, either. His closure rate is the lowest in the entire department."

"For the record, he didn't close the deal tonight, either. Thanks for the warning."

"Why don't I just send you the sexual particulars on every man in the department?" Marcus suggested sweetly. "It would save us both a lot of time."

"I thought he was cute," I grudgingly admitted. "At first."

"You must have been in Micky's," Marcus guessed correctly, naming a dive bar on Roxboro Street that was home to a motley assortment of cops and robbers. "The lighting in there is atrocious. I almost got killed there once when I tried to pick up a man I thought was giving me the look. It turned out to be a dyke with a glass eye. She'd obviously lost the real thing in some bar room brawl. I was lucky to escape with my manhood intact."

I sighed. Marcus had all the fun.

"I need your help on a case," I told him.

"What kind of case?" Marcus asked. I heard a click as he lit up one of his girlie smokes and waited for details.

I explained about Corndog Sally and her search for her grandson. Marcus was from Durham, a good thirty miles away from Sally's old stomping grounds in Raleigh, so he didn't know who she was. But he picked up that she was as black as he was, which he approved of, and he understood immediately when I explained about her family situation.

"Drugs," he said with distaste. "I'll kill anyone who gets near my family with that shit."

I believed him. So did the dealers in Durham, who were also wary of Marcus's job as a clerk for the police department. A dozen Duprees had been born and raised within spitting distance of some of the worst blocks in town, and yet all had escaped the lure of drugs. Every single one of them. This was a miracle that makes the Shroud of Turin look like a piece of used Kleenex.

"I think the key to finding the kid is to track down his mother," I explained. "He's fifteen and never had a daddy. Dollars to doughnuts he's with her right now, trying to take care of her sorry, drug-riddled ass. Corndog Sally was taking care of the boy until about a year and a half ago."

"Why's she named Corndog?" Marcus interrupted.

"I don't know. You ask her. She'll chew me out if I do."

"Why'd she wait so long to look for him?"

"Until this past summer, she knew where he was. He was living with his mother, going to Perry County High. Sally got to see him every now and then. She said he seemed okay, but he and his mother both disappeared this past summer."

"So they've been off the grid for at least four months?"

"Yup. Sally got a phone call in August from the boy. The kid said he was fine, but wouldn't say where he was. She's heard nothing since."

"You been on the Web?" Marcus asked, knowing I'd have already searched every nook and cranny of the Internet hoping for a hint to the mother's current whereabouts.

"I have. She did some time at a women's prison for robbery about five years ago, probably trying to support her habit. Then she moved from shitty apartment to shitty apartment all over Durham for the next few years before moving out into the country. But I don't know where she is now. I've talked to just about every brother and sister she has, and they don't know either. And they don't much seem to care."

"Where are her people from?" Marcus asked. It was a traditional Southern question, asked as part of nearly every conversation, regardless of social milieu.

"Mostly Durham and Wake County. Some of them have moved to Johnston County. One or two to Perry. That's where she and the kid lived last year, but the house they rented is empty and she left no forwarding address."

"Why would anyone live in Perry County?"

This was a very good question. Perry County was a tiny slice of North Carolina, linking Wake and Johnston counties. It was known solely for its red clay and white trash.

"Beats me," I said, though I knew firsthand how limited your options are when you are poor. One man's trailer is another man's mansion.

"Did you check out the Raleigh/Durham drug houses?" Marcus asked. The only saving grace about drugs infiltrating the Triangle was that the area was still small enough that it was obvious where all the activity was taking place.

"Yes. That's how I ended up with tall, dark and dudly tonight. I've been up and down the bars on Roxboro, Mangum and even Hillsborough Street for two days now, rounding up the usual suspects. No one was sober enough to recognize the mother, though I admit it's a sorry photograph. I suspect it was taken about three tankers full of crystal meth ago. But I'm still pretty sure she hasn't been hanging out locally."

"I could call my friend in Perryville, see what he knows. Maybe she went back to her old stomping grounds there."

"Will he be up this late?" It was nearly one o'clock in the morning.

"He's working," Marcus said. "They tend to stick the gay cops on the night shift out in Perry County. When they're not running them out of town on a rail."

"Okay," I agreed, grateful for the help. "Her name is Tonya Blackburn. The kid's name is Trey. She's in her mid-thirties, small and toffee-colored. I got a couple photos of her from Sally and the most recent one shows her hair in corn rows that turn into lots of little braids."

"Well, she won't be keeping that look up if she's on the powder," Marcus predicted before he hung up. He was right. A lot of people liked to delude themselves that semi-rural America was safe from drugs. Marcus knew better, and so did I. Coke and crack may have been bumped down the line by crystal meth, but they still ruined a lot of lives. So did cheap ass heroin, ecstasy and a bunch of other crap. People were mixing and matching their drugs these days as enthusiastically as bums trying on clothes in a thrift shop. And there were always kids coming up who would try anything up to and including sniffing toilet bowl cleaner to catch a buzz. If they made self-destruction an Olympic sport, America would bring home the gold medal for sure.

I ate a bowl of leftover macaroni-and-cheese while I waited for Marcus to call me back. I knew I could depend on him. Marcus was a rarity in Southern law enforcement: he was as gay as a tree full of parrots and had crawled out of the closet at birth. As a result, he was at the epicenter of an informal network of others in police and sheriff departments across the state who were still in the closet but sometimes in need of a little moral — or computer hacking — support. I figured his friend in Perryville was part of this underground group or else Marcus would have given me his name.

He called me back about an hour later. "There are two drug houses in Perryville, and then there's another one tucked into the county just outside of town."

"Did your friend recognize Tonya's name?"

"Oh, yeah," Marcus said. "She was picked up a few times, once for being passed out on the courthouse steps, so I think it's safe to assume she's now a candidate for the short bus. But she's never been booked in Perry County. He says her kid was a basketball star at Perry County High. Played on varsity as a freshman."

"*Was* a star?" I said as hope that she'd be found easily faded.

"The kid didn't show up this semester. The coach and cheerleading squad are heartbroken. My friend thinks they've left Perry County."

"Did he have any opinions on where she might be?"

"He didn't much care," Marcus admitted. "But he was pretty sure that if she was anywhere nearby, she'd be at the drug house outside the town limits. He said she was picked up there a few times in the past during drug sweeps, but never had anything on her so she walked. That's the advantage of gobbling down every scrap of drugs the second you get your hot little hands on them, I guess."

"Thanks, Marcus. I owe you."

"I'm putting it in the bank with the rest of your IOU's," he warned me.

If Marcus Dupree ever decided to call in his chits, I'd be his slave for life.

# Chapter Two

It's not pretty being a private detective. But it's not boring, either — which was the point. At least most of the time. At the moment, staring at the parade of living cadavers slipping in and out of a rural house in the middle of Perry County, well, let me tell you: it wasn't anywhere near boring enough.

The Carolina countryside at night is like a church, hushed and filled with expectations. It belongs to the darkness, to the shadows of pine trees bending beneath the night wind, to the whisper of owl wings slipping through the silence. Empty roads stretch beneath the moon, leading over the horizon, beckoning with endless possibilities. It is a time when man becomes insignificant and benign.

Except, of course, for those nights when mankind proves it is the worst of all species, capable of debasing itself to bottomless depths while destroying all that is good in the world around it.

I had parked behind a pair of deserted mobile homes rusting among a jungle of overgrown weeds. A fallen tree had crashed across both roofs, popping the metal open like the tops of sardine cans, exposing the jagged edges of corroding walls.

Through a gap between the two structures, I could see the stoop of a dilapidated ranch house going to ruin next door. Its dirt yard was crowded with broken-down cars, refrigerators and a huge pile of scrap furniture that loomed up into the darkness like a junkyard blooming in the night. For the last two hours, at any one time, two or three cars would be parked only inches from the front steps, the passengers having moved ghostlike into the interior of the drug house, their movements hurried and furtive. Black and white, short and tall, young and old, men and women — it didn't matter. They shared a desperation and a feigned confidence that was frayed around the edges with an uncontrollable need to hurry. They scurried inside as if life and death awaited them there. And, of course, for most of them, it did.

About five o'clock in the morning, a white woman drove up in a red truck. She climbed out of the vehicle, screamed at someone in the front seat to stay put, then hurried inside for her drugs. I had visions of a Mastiff leaping from the cab to shred newcomers and decided to check out the occupant. I slipped from my car and crept closer, memorizing the truck's license plate number out of habit. As I got near, the front seat shadow morphed into two scrawny children jammed into the front cab — no child safety seats, or even seat belts, in sight. They were watching the door to the ranch house, each tiny face frozen with an unwavering gaze that would have put the most loyal dog to shame. Would their mother return?

She did. She hurried out five minutes later, slipping out the door so quickly I could not get a glimpse of her down-turned face. She was thin and dressed in a grimy tee shirt. Her blond hair hung in greasy strands to her shoulders.

"Hold it," I said as she reached the truck.

Her body froze, except for her right hand, which flew unwillingly to her back pocket. I shoved her against the side of the truck and patted her down. She'd stuck a baggie full of pills and some rock in her back pocket. Scattered among the crystals and a fistful of familiar blue and pink pills were several large white pills that I did not recognize. I patted down the rest of her pockets. She didn't have a penny left on her.

"You a cop?" she asked in a reedy voice, resigned to being either robbed or arrested and sounding as if she couldn't decide which would be worse. Her ferret-like face had a jumpiness to it and I knew she'd stopped to sample the wares inside.

"Sure am," I lied, confident I had the upper hand and could pull off just about any charade. For one thing, I outweighed her by a good seventy pounds. "Get in the truck."

"Why?" she asked.

"Get in the truck," I repeated.

She climbed in and forgot to shut the door. The dome light illuminated the lines in her face. She was thirty going on sixty. Her skin was the color of boiled turnips and her teeth as brown as tea.

The kids didn't look much better. They turned out to be a boy and a girl, almost identical with their bright blond hair, runny noses and suspicious eyes. They were dressed in oversized tee shirts and underwear. They watched me silently, expressions unchanging, as I stepped closer to the truck. I locked eyes with the little girl. Something in her face shifted and softened. She leaned forward slightly, as if secretly entreating me to take her away. How I wished that I could.

"Recognize this woman?" I asked the mother, holding a photo of Tonya Blackburn up to the light.

The woman squinted at it, confused by my failure to arrest her. Her eyes slid to my left hand, where I still held her bag of drugs, then reluctantly returned to the photo.

"I think so," she said. "She comes here sometimes. I think maybe she even works here. Can I have my stuff back now?"

"When's the last time you saw her?" I asked, holding the bag of drugs up a little higher, like it was a prize I intended to give for the right answer.

"I don't know." Her voice broke. "Maybe six months ago."

I shook my head, disgusted. Six months? She'd been coming to this hellhole for at least half a year, which meant her kids had been waiting in the front seat of that truck for their mother to return to being a mother for an awful big chunk of their lives.

I had to ask. "How long you been coming here?"

"I'm gonna quit," she said automatically.

"Where's their father? Does he know?"

She spit near my feet. The wad of saliva landed near the toe of my boot and quivered in the red clay. I stared at it for a moment, then looked back up at her. It had missed me by inches. Her eyes darted away from mine. She could not hold my gaze.

"What father?" she finally said sullenly. "Even if he knew the kids were here, he wouldn't give a damn."

"Get out of here," I told her, tired of being a witness to the wreck this stranger had made of her life. I slammed the door and slapped it with my palm. "Go."

"What about —" she bit back her words as her eyes tracked the baggie I held.

"Forget about it," I said. "Next time spend the money feeding your kids."

She tried to spit in my face again, but this time I ducked. I heard the grind of the gears being jammed into place and jumped up onto the front stoop just as she gunned the motor and backed the truck rapidly across the yard. She peeled out onto the winding blacktop and headed toward town, weaving back and forth across the center line in her drug-tinged anger.

I hated to let those kids go. But I had learned it was a bad idea to interfere in other people's lives if you were just passing through.

* * *

I STEPPED BACK INTO THE SHADOWS, hiding by a corner of the house, waiting for more druggies to come. They came all right. A pair of cars pulled up and a party of college-age kids hurried inside, as if afraid someone might see them out in the middle of nowhere. After that, a steady stream of broken-down wrecks stopped by, disgorging passengers. Inside, a drug party was in full swing. This wasn't a loud music, cut-the-rug party, I saw, as

I peered through a hole in the dirty sheet that had been draped over the living room window. People sat on the floor, leaning against the walls or lounging on ratty lumps of furniture, passing a pipe from hand to hand, breathing out tiny plumes of white smoke after holding it in for as long as they could, staring at the ceiling, staring into space, staring at each other. No one spoke. The college-age boys sipped at beers methodically, as if that small, familiar action somehow made them normal. One woman lay listlessly on her back in the middle of the room, a human coffee table, unnoticed by the others. Whatever she was doing, she damn sure wasn't tweaking. My guess was that she'd mainlined a ghetto's worth of the cheap ass black tar heroin that had recently infiltrated the state from Mexico. There had to be a good reason for the smile on her face. No one in their right mind could have managed a smile surrounded by the disintegrating human beings that ringed her.

By six o'clock, I was cold, I really had to pee and I was sick of staring at stoned-out losers. But there were too many people for me to approach any one person. I didn't want to start a stampede. I needed information, not a bunch of tweaked out, panic-stricken drug addicts trampling me in their fear.

It was close to seven o'clock before the crowd broke up, stumbling out to their trucks and cars or, in the case of the college kids, Jeeps bought by clueless parents. They were ready for the long drive home to their apartments, schools and, worst of all, assembly lines. With my luck, I'd be the one to buy the computer made later that day by one of these sleepless stoners coming down from a three-day high.

It was as if a parade of zombies had risen from the grave to march out into the world. They had a gray pallor in the morning light and moved stiffly, as if their joints ached. Their faces were blank, their eyes already dead. I hid in the shadows and thanked God I was not one of them. I had touched the madness that was drug addiction many years ago and I never again wanted to feel the unfillable hunger, never again desired to fight the pull or spend the night's darkest hours battling between craving and sleeping.

The baggie I'd confiscated was still in my back pocket. I took it out. It held a collection of dirty yellow crystals that looked like someone had both pissed and puked all over them. Very appetizing. It was crystal meth and it scared the shit out of me. I had never touched that particular drug in my life. Thank god it had come along after I had sworn off the hard stuff. But the power of it seemed overwhelming in its potential to enslave. What if I was unable to resist just a taste? Would I be hooked? Would my life unfold before me in one long, downward spiral before I even had time to catch my breath?

I emptied the crystals out onto the gravel and ground them to dust beneath my boots. I didn't ever want to find out. But I kept the pills after examining the big, white ones carefully. What the hell could they be? As for the Valium and Vicodin, well, I'm no fool. I kept them for my PMS stash. They could make that time of the month downright fun. It's hypocritical of me, I know, but I'm a big fan of better living through pharmaceuticals, so long as you don't mix your stash with bullets or booze or chase your pills down with the hard stuff.

The last of the cars finally pulled away from the house, leaving only a yellow Chevy that had seen better decades. I peered in the living room window for a final check. The comatose woman still lay sprawled in the middle of the rug and I could see the pants legs of someone sitting against the wall near my window. That was okay. I'm a big girl. I was tipping the scales at close to one hundred and eighty pounds at the moment. I could handle one conscious and one unconscious person easily, even if it came down to simply sitting on them. It was time to see if anyone left behind had spotted Tonya Blackburn or her son recently.

The door was unlocked. I pushed my way inside. The house smelled like cat piss and chemicals. Just another romantic detail of life in the fast lane. The pasteboard walls had head-sized dents in them and plastic picture frames dangled from nails hammered into the walls, the contents long-since hocked or burned for heat. I turned a corner and came nose-to-nose with a fake oil painting of a crying clown. Jesus. How could anyone stare something like that in the face while they were high? I picked my way over a stained beige carpet to the living room, expecting a crack-crazed pit bull to emerge from a closet and chomp its jaws down on my ass at any moment. Instead, a tiny calico kitten wandered out of a reeking bathroom to nudge my feet. It was red-eyed and underfed, no doubt having already inhaled enough meth to fell a 300-pound lumberjack. I'm sure some college kid found it entertaining to exhale up its little pink nose. People can be real sick when they put their minds to it.

The zoned-out woman lay in the middle of the living room floor, eyes closed, a Mona Lisa smile curling her lips. I checked her pulse, just to be sure. She had taken a lickin' but she was still tickin' so I moved on by.

A skinny black man sat hunched on a ratty sofa pushed against the far wall. A forgotten cigarette dangled from his fingertips, dribbling ashes on the carpet at his feet. He was a poster boy for fire safety. He was also staring at the television as if watching a program, but the set had long ago been smashed in — otherwise it would have been pawned — and only a jagged black hole met his gaze. Perhaps he was waiting for *Star Trek* to start.

"You're going to set the house on fire," I said, removing the cigarette from his hand. His eyes rolled up at me. They were rimmed in yellow and a red crust glued the right one halfway shut. Spittle flecked his lips and a dried line of snot snaked from a nostril across one cheek. I'd seen healthier-looking people on a slab at the morgue. Better-smelling ones, too.

He mumbled something along the lines of "Why you?"

"Wake up," I said more sharply, shoving him back against the couch. This caused a wooden leg to snap beneath the sofa and the whole left end of it fell to the floor with a clunk. The junkie sitting on it simply listed to one side like a drunken mariner going down with his ship. I had disturbed someone's home, however: a mouse darted out from under the sofa, scurried across the rug, reached the passed-out woman, then ran up her hips, across her torso and down the other side before disappearing through a far door. The kitten was sitting in the doorway but did not appear to care as the mouse ran right past it.

*Et tu, Brutus?* I thought.

"Hey, watch it."

Well, what do you know? After thirty seconds of moving his lips, the man on the couch had achieved sound.

I stared at him and he stared blankly back, having already forgotten he'd started the conversation. I wasn't going to get anywhere unless I took drastic action. I checked him out more closely. He was dressed in clothes that had not been washed for at least three weeks, but his pockets were smooth. I checked the folds and cushions of the couch, wary of hypodermic needles. When I found no weapons, or paraphernalia that night hurt me, I left him and wandered off in search of the kitchen, where I filled an old orange juice carton with water from the tap.

He was still sitting on the couch, staring at the broken television set and listing to one side when I returned.

"Hey — look!" I said. "Isn't that Shelly Winters in *The Poseidon Adventure?*" His head jerked up and I threw the water in his face. He sputtered in indignant anger. But at least he perked up.

"No call for that," he mumbled, clawing at the air like there were bats flying around his head.

"Sober up, handsome," I said. "I need to talk to you."

"You the law?"

"No. And be glad I'm not. This place is full of enough drugs to put you away for life. Hell, you're full of enough drugs to put you away for life."

"Ain't none left," he said sullenly, brushing water off his filthy shirt. "Why else you think everyone left?"

"What's she on?" I asked, nodding at the woman on the floor.

"What's it to you?" He looked around for his cigarettes and I pushed a pack on the floor toward him with the toe of my boot. "What you want from me?"

"Information." I stood as far away as possible and held up the photo of Tonya Blackburn. "Do you know this woman?"

He squinted at the photo and I held it closer. He stared at it for so long that I thought he had fallen asleep. "Do you know her?" I asked in a louder voice, doing my best to sound like I was seconds away from kicking his ass.

"Yeah, I know her," he said, taking a drag off his cigarette. He released the smoke in a long plume and watched it rise to the ceiling. "She's just some crack whore. What you want with her?"

I kicked his feet so hard that his legs flew up in the air like he was a scarecrow being tossed over a fence. I don't know why I did it. It just made me feel better.

"What you do that for?" he complained, rubbing his ankles.

"Watch your language around me," I said. "I'm a lady."

"Yeah," he said sullenly. "I can tell."

At least he was coherent enough to be sarcastic.

"How do you know her?" I demanded.

"She used to hang out here," he said. "'Til she ran out one night acting crazy."

"What are you talking about?" I moved closer, although I was still unwilling to touch him or his furniture.

"It's nothing," he said. "No business of yours."

That was when I lost it. The cat stench, the starving kitten, the drugged-out woman at my feet, the waste of human protoplasm snarling in front of me: I just had to get away from it all. And the only way to get away was to move things along.

I pulled my Colt out of my jacket pocket and stuck it in his face. He wet his pants, which was satisfying. I had his attention at last and the smell didn't make much difference.

"What you want?" he said in a tiny voice. "I got no money."

"Tell me about her," I ordered. "Everything you know."

"Everyone knows her," he said. "Her name's Scout. That's what we call her."

"I don't give a shit about her stupid drug nickname." The single most annoying thing about addicts was how they gave each other nicknames, like they were kids in a clubhouse and it made them cool. "What do you know about her? Where is she now?"

He was staring at the photo again, more alert as the effect of the drugs wore off. He noticed Tonya's son Trey in the photo. "That her son?" he said. "Guess she wasn't shitting us after all."

"Yeah, that's her son. I'm trying to find him."

"We thought she was lying." He peered at the boy some more, puzzling out what was off about the photo. "That boy's *white,*" he said indignantly.

"Congratulations, Sherlock. Now where is she?"

He shook his head. "She been gone for two, three weeks now. Like I say, she run out of here one night all freaked out."

"Start at the beginning," I ordered him. "And don't leave anything out." I nudged him with the tip of my gun just to make sure he got my point. It wasn't loaded, but he didn't know that.

"No call for that," he said, eyeing the barrel. I lowered the gun and waited. He cleared his throat, as if he were making a valedictorian speech and then told me what I needed to know:

"She used to hang out here a lot, maybe last year. Always had money, you know. Could pay for her share, you know. Even worked it a little, picking up stuff for other people, 'til people caught her taking a cut, you know, when she thought they wasn't looking. After that, she disappeared for awhile."

"When?" I asked.

"You think I keep track?" he said indignantly. I raised the gun again and he hurried to explain. "End of winter, maybe. Then she come back maybe six months ago. She walk in here like she never be gone. She got drugs again. Lots of drugs."

"She have the boy with her?" I asked.

He shook his head. "She never bring no boy here. We all think she's lying. She bring newspaper photos here sometimes, showing a bunch of boys on some basketball court and she try to say one of them is her boy, you know. No one here high enough to believe her. I tell that girl she be on crack for sure and we all laughed. She didn't like that none, you know. She used to being the big dog around here, always being the one to bring the product, you know, selling the shit and not being the one who got to scrounge for nickels and dying to be doing it. But there be plenty of times when the tables turn on her and she just a junkie like the rest of us. But she don't like no one to remind her of that."

"Go on."

"She leave again for awhile and she come back here end of this past summer, now that I think of it, with a big load of drugs to sell and flashing her cash 'til she run out again. This time she say she's never coming back, but I tell her I'll see her again soon. Nothing changes, you know. It's always the same. People leave, you know, and then they come back. Not too many leave and never come back. Lest they be dead, you know?"

"I know."

He stared at me for a second before he glanced down and, for the first time, noticed that he had wet his pants.

"Sorry," I lied. "Some of the water spilled in your lap."

He accepted this explanation with the remnants of his dignity. "Sure enough, she come back and she's into the smoke again. That girl can smoke some smoke when she gets started."

"Whereas you are a model of restraint and respectability," I observed.

"Huh?" He blinked at me.

"Go on."

"This go on for a week or so. Then one night, Choo Choo here offer her some H-2-O and she just freak the fuck out."

"Who's Choo Choo?"

"That's Choo Choo." He pointed to the woman on the floor. I definitely did not want to know why she was called Choo Choo and so I did not ask.

"Choo Choo offered her *water* and she freaked out?" I asked, sounding dubious at best.

"Choo Choo don't offer her no water. I said she offer her some H-2-0."

"That *is* water," I said impatiently.

He looked at me like I was the village idiot, savoring his superior knowledge over me. "You don't know what H-2-O is?" he asked. "Maybe you call it Double H?"

"Gee, I must have missed that when I was studying Drugs 101. That will teach me to just say 'no.'" I cocked the gun and moved it closer. "I am so not in the mood. What is Double H?"

"Double H is what Choo Choo's on," he explained, gesturing toward Sleeping Beauty. She was still alive. I knew this because she'd started to snore. Not dainty little rasps, mind you, but big honking snorts. She sounded like a pair of geese trying to outrun a jet. I stopped and stared at her in amazement. She had a hell of a pair of lungs.

"She's got that sleep acne," the man offered helpfully.

"Sleep apnea?"

He nodded. "That's it."

"Then perhaps she shouldn't be taking drugs that impair her respiratory functions?" I suggested. "What the hell is Double H?"

"The O-Train, people call it. Big white pills. If you know how to take 'em, they got a kick that lasts and lasts." He grinned, revealing rotting teeth. "Kind of like me."

"Careful, Romeo," I told him, "Don't make me throw cold water on you again."

He stuck his lower lip out. "Choo Choo here offer that girl some Double H and Scout just freak out, you know? She jump up like she been bit by a snake and she start to run for the door."

"She sees the pill and starts to run?" I asked. Christ, what the hell was in it?

He nodded, stretching his moment of importance out. "Then she get to the door and she just stop, cause she ain't got no ride, you see." He thought this was funny and cackled for awhile. I waited him out. "Then she come back in here and ask if she can borrow one of the cell phones."

"You have cell phones?" I asked in disbelief, looking around the barren room.

He spoke solemnly, as if he were on the witness stand. "Well, at any one time, we might have had us a cell phone, yes."

Yeah, like right before the run to the pawnshop, I thought.

"I let her use one," he said self-importantly. "And some dude come pick her up in a truck."

"What kind of truck?" I asked.

"Like a bread truck," he said, nodding. "You know."

"What the hell does that mean? Did it have a picture of a loaf of bread on the side of it?"

He shook his head. "No, but it was one of them big white, boxy kind of trucks. You know. Tin body, with a picture on it."

"What kind of picture?" Getting information from him was like pulling teeth, which was a step I was literally considering next if he didn't hurry it along.

"It had, you know, like drums painted on the side."

*"Drums?"*

He nodded. "You know, my people's drums."

*"Your* people's drums?" I asked slowly.

"African drums." He beat on the sofa cushion and damn if he wasn't the only black man I have ever met who clearly lacked rhythm. He had about as much finesse as a pair of jackrabbits thumping their way across a tin roof.

"You know," he insisted when I looked at him blankly. "There was a painting of them tall round drums with bells on the side of the truck and then the short ones with a gourd thingie next to it. African drums."

"Well, you are just a fount of cultural knowledge."

He smiled proudly.

"Have you seen her since?" I asked.

His smile faded. "Nope. She climbed in the truck and they drove away. Ain't seen her since."

"Who was driving?"

He shrugged. "No business of mine."

"You didn't get a look at the guy driving the truck?" I asked, knowing they'd be on the alert for cops and would check out each car that pulled into the yard.

"He was my brother," he suddenly remembered, pleased with himself.

"Your brother?" I asked incredulously.

"Yeah, you know. A brother. Black like me." He raised a feeble black power salute, then apparently forgot what he was doing in the middle of it and stared at his fist blankly, as if wondering who — or what — he had been intending to punch.

"That really narrows it down." My sarcasm was sadly wasted because, well, he was too wasted.

"He had a mean set of dreads," he added suddenly. "The long kind."

"Yeah?" That would help, at least. There weren't that many sets of serious dreadlocks in and around these parts.

"Yeah." The guy rubbed his own scruffy head in envy. "He was a big dude with some big ass dreads hanging down. I saw 'em dangling out the window and thought they were snakes at first."

I bet he had. I bet he saw snakes and dragons and gorgons and pulsating, undulating floral landscapes half the damn time.

"Knew I'd remember if I thought hard enough." He leaned back, satisfied that he had accomplished something in his greasy, smoke-filled day. Outside, the morning sun cleared the pines and a ray of sunlight leaked in under the dirty sheet that served as a curtain. I suddenly wanted very much to be out of that house and heading toward home, with the clean country air blowing the stink from my head.

"That help?" he asked, closing his eyes and inhaling deeply from his cigarette. "Worth something to you?" He held his palm out and waited, hoping for money.

I slapped him a high five instead, then wiped my palm on my pants. "Yeah, brother," I said. "That helped. You're a prince among men."

He looked disappointed, especially when I scooped up his kitten on my way out.

"Hey," he yelled after me. "Why you taking my kitten?"

"You know," I yelled back. And fled.

# Chapter Three

Marcus was deeply offended. "So you think because I happen to be black, I'm going to know every other black dude in a five-county radius?"

"No," I said. "I definitely do not. I'm just trying to catch a break. Drums, okay? Focus on the drums. Who the hell drives around in a white bread truck painted with African drums?"

"A drummer?" he suggested.

*"Marcus."*

"I will ask around," he said prissily. "Despite your lack of racial sensitivity."

"Oh, balls, Marcus. Don't give me that shit. What is really the matter here?"

"My husbear is in Germany for a month visiting his family. He did not ask me along. I'm a *schvatza*, apparently."

Marcus wasn't actually offended. He was just lonely.

"Maybe it wasn't the race thing," I suggested. "Maybe it was the gay thing?"

"That makes me feel so much better," he said acidly.

"I have a solution for you."

"What?" he asked suspiciously.

"Pussy."

"Oh, do not, under any circumstances, go there."

"No, really," I insisted. "I rescued the sweetest little kitten from the crack house. I can't keep it. I'd kill it. You know I can't even keep a house plant alive."

"That's true." Marcus was silent as he mulled it over. "How big is the monkey on its back?"

"Pretty big, I suspect. It's inhaled a lot. But it's cute as a button."

"What if it goes into withdrawal and starts clawing my leather couch?"

"Get it a box filled with catnip," I suggested. "Just let it roll around in there for a few weeks and stay stoned to the gills until it kicks the habit."

"Kittens do not have gills," he said stiffly.

"Yeah, I know that, Marcus. Now do you want the god-damned cat or not?"

"What color is it?"

"Calico. It would go with your decor."

"Okay," he agreed. "But you're buying the catnip. And I want three pounds of it. At least."

Man, he could drive a hard bargain.

* * *

MARCUS CAME THROUGH BY DINNER TIME. I drove over and swapped the kitten for information, scoring homemade chicken picatta in the process. According to Marcus, there were three possibilities in the area for who owned the truck with the drums painted on the side. One was an organization devoted to teaching school children traditional African music; another was a nationally-known percussion quartet whose founding members lived in Durham; and the third was some guy, name unknown, who was reputed to live in town and was thought to be one of the greatest living djembe drummers alive but who shunned publicity, was very religious, and may or may not live in some apartment building in some bad neighborhood, somewhere, because he didn't want to lose touch with his urban roots. I thanked Marcus for providing such specific information and was met with silence for my sarcasm, followed by an icy invitation to fresh-baked pound cake for dessert and a suggestion I help myself, as he needed to retrieve the kitten from where it was hanging by its claws from his raw silk, custom-dyed curtains.

It had to be the third guy, I reasoned, as I drove home to my apartment. Not for any reason other than that, with the way my luck was going on this case, chances were it was the most obscure choice possible.

How do you go about finding a religious hermit who drums like a god?

Of course: the churches. I could start by driving around all the black churches in Durham the next day, since it was a Sunday — though that would take all morning and then some, as there are dozens of them. I'd hit Raleigh if I found nothing in Durham. If worse came to worse, I'd give up on religion and drive around skanky apartment lots until I found a white bread truck with drums painted on its side.

I decided to do it. It wasn't like I had any other leads, and I really wanted to call Corndog Sally with some progress soon. She wasn't the type of person to ask for help, yet she had asked me for help. I felt the responsibility she had given me keenly. I had to find the boy.

* * *

I ALMOST MISSED THE TRUCK in the crush of vehicles jamming the parking lot of the Holy Redeemer Church of Christ out on Rose of Sharon Road. If I had not stopped my car to investigate a mysterious knocking, I would surely have missed it.

Pulling to a halt near the side of the lot, I determined two things: the knocking was not my transmission, but an immense and persistent rhythm coming from inside the church; and two, the bread truck was right there, parked behind a 16-passenger van that was currently disgorging a bevy of plump ladies dressed to the nines, the feathers on their hats bobbing like quail as they scurried inside the massive church doors.

All of them were black. And, no doubt, so was every other face in the place. Me? I am not just white, I am *white*: as in white trash white, with genetically pale skin that screams "all I do is watch television, eat Hostess Sno-Balls and live in a trailer park." And I was suddenly conscious of my too-blonde hair and intentionally black roots, which I wear simply to confuse people into underestimating me.

Okay. I was white. They were not. This clearly presented a problem when it came to blending in. There was nothing I could do about it. Except move fast.

The pulsating beat grew louder as I approached the front stairs. The brick stoop was capable of holding fifty people, at least, and entirely appropriate to the huge structure looming behind it. This was a church built for capacity and, judging from the sound that leaked outside, it was filled to the rafters. The doors were massive slabs of wood, but not even they could contain the music that poured out into the world: gospel music. Not your grandmother's gospel music, either. Not even your mother's gospel music. This was your funky older brother's gospel music, infused with a heavy dose of Sly and the Family Stone. Whoever was performing in there was burning down the house: I could feel the bass beat clear in the marrow of my bones and I wasn't even inside yet. Lord, but if anyone in there had a pacemaker it had to be thumping in their chest like Jack Rabbit Slim.

As I reached the top step, two doormen dressed in matching gray suits swung the front doors open for me like I was the Queen of England. A tidal wave of sound washed over me. I felt as if I had literally been lifted off my feet and rushed upward to heaven. It was the most amazing sound I have ever heard: a Niagra Falls of voices raised in chorus, fueled by passion just this side of hysteria, soaring over the music of a band that must have numbered over a dozen people to be making such a ruckus. The hair on my arms rose as adrenaline shot through my body. This was why people fell to the ground and spoke in tongues, why normally sane individuals fainted in ecstasy praising a higher power. Music like this was impossible to hear and remain unmoved. It was faith in its most robust incarnation, hope made real in sound. Alto voices, baritones, tenor, sopranos soaring above them all, guitars, drums, bells, at least two sets of keyboards — and a driving backbeat that threatened to blow out the stained glass windows above me.

The crush inside was so great, I could not see the front of the church. I began to wiggle my way through the crowd, slipping from sliver of space to space. People stepped aside willingly or looked past me. No one seemed to overtly notice I was white. They were too polite or hypnotized by the show in front of them. Some swayed along, a very few sang along, but most seemed content to watch. This was not a service, I realized, but a performance. And someone was giving it their all.

Suddenly, a contralto voice filled the air above the crowd with a note that hovered, swelled and broke, then ran up and down the scales in a spectacular display of vocal fireworks. The crowd erupted in applause and I realized that whoever the singer was, she was just getting started. She was Whitney Houston on steroids, with a hefty dose of Ethel Merman thrown in. She was my chance to reach the front, as every eye was on center stage. I weaseled through packs of families and bypassed groups of sweet-smelling men with gleaming shaved heads that shone like mahogany in the crimson-stained light pouring in through the stained glass windows.

I finally reached a cross aisle and made my way to a side area near the left wall where I'd be able to get closer to the stage at the front of the church. As I drew closer, I spotted the source of the driving backbeat that was rattling the fillings in my teeth. I stopped short, astonished. This was not something you see every day: middle-aged triplets, aligned in a row, each one dressed in a different colored pencil-legged zoot suit: purple, gray and black. Each held a Fender Bass 350 and their fingers were flying as they dipped forward and leaned backward in perfect unison, emitting a beat that rattled my breastbone like a train driving through the church.

All three of them were identical, tall and slender, with coffee-colored skin, delicate features, gleaming gold teeth winking at the crowd, eyes closed as they concentrated on the music. A crowd of young women clustered at their feet gazed upward at them with a rapture not even their mothers could muster for the Lord himself. Behind them, a huge stained glass window displayed three angels reaching out to Saint Peter. But, honey — those angels didn't have a prayer of being noticed, not with that competition nearby.

My god. Most unholy fantasies unreeled in my mind as I stared at the trifecta of perfection above me. Now, *they* were proof there was a God.

Unfortunately, when I noticed what was dominating center stage beside them, my triplet fantasy burst like a balloon in a briar patch, evaporating at the sight of what looked to be a massive Little Bo Peep. Step back, Aretha. A woman stood at center stage, several feet in front of a back-up chorus of women in glittery gowns who swayed back and forth as they held down the harmony. There must have been six of them on back-up, but they were small fry indeed compared to the lead singer. She was at least as big as my boss, Bobby D., and that was saying a lot. It meant she tipped the scales at well over three hundred pounds. But while Bobby tended to favor leisure suits and gold medallions, this woman was wearing an enormous white dress with rows of ruffles cascading down the front and flowing out behind her in a milky river of taffeta. Her hair

— if, indeed, it was hers — had been molded into an elaborate waterfall of bouncy brown curls topped by a floppy white hat exploding with ivory flowers and pink bows. Even more inexplicably, while she held a microphone in one hand, she held a beribboned staff in the other. The tool of a shepherdess calling to her flock? A giant toothpick to ensure a head start at the post-performance buffet? She was Mega-Bo Peep meets Mothra.

I could not decide, nor could I take my eyes from her. She was magnificent. She sailed across the stage like a queen, or maybe the Queen Mary, bowing and sweeping her staff toward the crowd as she sang, raising it high when her voice climbed into its upper register, lowering it when she took deep breaths. She was a one-woman symphony orchestra, conductor and all, and she had one of a handful of voices on the entire planet that could have out-belted the massive band arrayed behind her.

Which reminded me — I was on the job. My drummer was there somewhere.

I searched the lineup, peering behind the back-up singers, but found no African drummers at all. This was a thoroughly modern, electronic, totally juiced-up version of the Word. It was the Gospel according to Marshall and Fender.

Just the same, it was impossible not to respond. The whole crowd was dancing, even the little old ladies. I was busy busting out some moves I had not attempted in fifteen years, when a very large young woman, caught up in the throes of passion, trundled past and threw me against a window radiator. I caught my balance and, for the first time, noticed someone staring at me. A distinguished-looking gentleman was eyeing me with more than a modicum of suspicion from his spot at the end of a nearby row. And no wonder, I was dressed in a black pair of slacks, black tee shirt and black jacket. In other words, my look implied "cop," while his look implied he was getting ready to scream, "Cop!"

I decided to move on and make it quick.

I pushed closer to the front, veering even further to the side, through a doorway that led to backstage. Reasoning that if one wanted to find an African drummer, one should first find an African drum, I followed a man carrying musical equipment down a passageway into a large backstage room filled with performers waiting their turn to take the stage.

My man wasn't hard to spot. Most of the room was filled with a traditional gospel choir dressed in purple and gold robes, listening intently to the group still on stage. Behind them, against a far wall, stood a trio of men dressed in African robes. They were clustered tightly together, as if trying to discuss a private matter they did not want others to hear. I had been wrong in my guess about who owned the bread truck. My quarry was part of a group. And I was pretty sure I had found him. Behind three men in daishikis, a tall black man with long dreadlocks was tightening the frame on a stand of drums while listening placidly to his bandmates. Whatever disagreement the trio was having, he clearly had no stake in it.

I was across the room and at his side before he even noticed me. "Hey," I said, tapping him on the shoulder. "Could I talk to you for a minute about —"

I have never see a man move so fast and, believe me, there have been times when my men could not get out the door fast enough. This one was out the door before the words were even out of my mouth.

"Hey!" I yelled after him as he turned the corner in a flurry of bouncing dreadlocks. I started after him, but his bandmates stepped in front of me, blocking the way.

"I'm not after him," I said angrily, clawing my way through the roadblock. "I just wanted to ask him about..."

What was the use? I was white, dressed in black, and looked like I was packing. That meant I was trouble. Even the gospel choir was in on the unspoken agreement to slow me down. They shifted imperceptibly, managing to block the door without ever actually seeming to. I had to push my way past a dozen of them and it took me a solid minute just to get out the damn door. Once free, I ran down the hall toward an outer exit, cursing. I knew this would not help my karma — surely cursing in church is not a good idea, no matter what religion you belong to? But I was steamed. I meant the guy no harm. All I wanted was a few answers.

The exit door led into a side parking lot. He was going to make a run for it. I darted between two huge old Cadillacs, almost knocked down a portly man directing traffic, and nearly twisted an ankle rounding the corner of the church when I slipped on some gravel. Damn it. I recovered and poured it on. He'd be heading for his bread truck. And he had a head start. But he was not getting away from me.

God bless the elderly. My man made it to his truck, but he was going nowhere. A transportation van from the Eternal Joy Rest Home blocked his exit. The back doors had been thrown open and two skinny nurse's aids were maneuvering an enormous man in a wheelchair down the handicap ramp.

I had the drummer trapped.

"Well, hello there." I said sweetly as I slid into his front seat. "Come here often?"

"What do you want?" he said, staring grimly ahead. He was a handsome man, the kind that looks as if his family tree is groaning with the genetic fruit of generations of African and Egyptian kings. I felt outclassed just looking at him.

"Why did you run?" I asked.

"Who are you?"

"Who are you?"

"Who wants to know?"

This was getting us nowhere.

"Look," I said. "I'm a private investigator. I'm not after anything but some information."

"Information about what?"

"Tonya Blackburn."

He leapt from the car and started running again.

"Jesus Christ!" I jumped out on the gravel, my ankle twitching at the impact.

"Tell it, sister!" the fat man in the wheelchair yelled back enthusiastically at me. "Jesus saves! Jesus saves!"

I dashed around him and headed for my quarry. The nurse's aids stared after me, worried, their hearing obviously better than the old man's.

The church bordered a small farm and that's where my mystery man was headed. He darted into a small grove of gangly pine trees separating the church lot from its neighbor. Pine needles slapped at my face as I gained on him. Bad ankle or not, I could move — and this man was not getting away. He was fast reacting; I was fast pursuing. And I wanted him. Badly.

I gained a few feet when his way was blocked by a tangle of fallen pines. He slipped, regained his balance and started toward an open field that stretched out on the other side of the grove. I took the more direct route. I leapt up on a fallen trunk, took a deep breath and launched myself into the air, flying over a bush and landing squarely on the back of his shoulders. I wrapped my arms tightly around him as we tumbled to the ground. He was not getting away again.

Oh, Jesus, Mary, Mother of God, all wrapped up in a basket of breadsticks. We landed in a patch of blackberry bushes rimming a cotton field.

Do you know how prickly blackberry bushes are?! It was like being attacked by a thousand stinging bees at once. Pinpricks of pain stabbed my ankles, my arms, my face, tearing through my stretch pants to rake my legs. I screamed, but at least the torture put a crimp in our tussle. One roll through that row of bushes and onto the cotton field and we were done.

"Damn, that hurts," I said, picking briars from my eyebrows. It's all good clean fun until someone puts an eye out.

He groaned and sat up, catching his breath.

"Why did you run like that?" I demanded indignantly. The earth beneath my butt was damp.

"You're asking me why a black man ran from a cop who appeared out of nowhere and was heading right for him?" he asked sourly as he inspected one of his dreadlocks. It was studded up and down with tufts of white cotton like some sort of weird mutant candy. "Oh, man," he said in frustration. "This will take me forever to get out."

"I'll help." I was resigned to winning his cooperation. I began to pick the wisps of cotton from his hair while he plucked the briars from his robe.

"I'm not a cop," I explained. "I'm a private investigator and all I wanted to do was talk to you about Tonya Blackburn. You didn't have to run."

"I'm not going to tell you where she is," he said glumly.

"You knew I was going to ask you about Tonya, didn't you?" I sucked on a finger where a thorn had drawn blood. Pickin' cotton's no picnic, either. "How?"

"Because you're the third white person in two weeks who has come after me looking for her," he said. "And every single one of you looks like trouble."

I pulled my fake P.I. license out of my pocket and showed it to him. It looked just like the real thing, which I was not allowed to carry, seeing as how I had the small matter of a long-ago felony on my record. "Read it carefully," I said. "Did anyone else have one of these?"

He stared at it dismissively, then ratcheted up the sarcasm. "No, one of them had an actual badge."

"A badge? You're sure."

He glared at me. “Yes, unfortunately, I’m sure.”

Okay, beautiful man or not, his people skills left a lot to be desired.

“What kind of badge?” I asked, rather stupidly.

“The kind cops carry around?” he suggested sarcastically, flinging away a tuft of cotton in disgust. “Do you know how long it took to get my hair like this?”

“Sorry!” Geeze. What else did the guy want me to say? I went back to picking the cotton from his hair while we talked. “So one guy was a cop and the other was...?”

“I don’t know what the other was,” he said. “He never got close enough for me to get a good look at him. He wasn’t as fast as you.”

Was he making a joke? I smiled. This was progress. “What did they want?”

“They probably wanted to know where Tonya was,” he said. “Same as you do. I didn’t tell them. And I’m not telling you.”

“You seem to protect her pretty seriously,” I said gently.

He was silent.

“I heard you pulled her out of a drug house over in Perry County.”

He remained silent.

“What’s the story with you two?” I asked. “Why are you still trying to rescue her from herself?”

He looked away from me, studying the end of one dreadlock. It smelled faintly of coconut.

“How long have you known her?” I tried again.

“Since first grade,” he mumbled.

“Ah.” Lifetime friends are hard to come by in this day and age. It was a strong bond.

"If she owes someone money, I'm not going to help them find her," he said.

"She doesn't owe anyone money. Her mother wants to find Trey, that's all. In fact, I'd pretty much say that Sally is desperate to find Trey. She's worried sick about him and I think we both know why."

At the mention, however indirect, of Tonya's drug habit, his whole face sagged in despair. I felt bad for him. What must it be like to have watched someone transform from a bouncy, enthusiastic six-year old who had her whole life in front of her into a skeletal, lifeless, lying shell of a human being intent only on putting more poison into her bloodstream? To love someone like that, yet still remember the promise of what they might have become, was a poison in itself and a terrible sorrow unless you could make yourself stop caring. Obviously, he wasn't there yet.

"I'm really sorry," I said to him. "I know what it's like."

"You can't know what it's like," he said simply.

"Believe me, I do." I thought of all the hot Florida nights I'd spent cruising certain streets in my pick-up truck, looking for a certain car, hoping to spot the face of the person I loved and wanted so desperately to protect.

"I don't want to hurt her," I explained. "Just let me know where you last saw her, so I can get in touch with Trey."

He would not answer. He was staring down at a muddy tangle of trampled cotton plants, maybe thinking of a time long ago.

"I think Sally's dying," I said gently. "That's why she wants to find her grandson so badly." It was the first time I had said out loud what I had suspected from the start of this case.

He looked up at me. "What makes you say that?" he asked. "She's tougher than the rest of us combined."

I thought of the way Corndog Sally had sat hunched over in my office the first time she came to see me, the slight trembling in her hand. A chink in her armor, a sign that all was not well. And the tone of her voice had been so... final.

"It's just a feeling I have," I explained. "I think that's why she needs to know Trey is safe."

"Oh, man," he said, pulling his knees up against his chest. "Not Sally."

"Please," I asked. "If you tell me where I can find Trey, I'll sit here all afternoon and pick the cotton from your dreads."

He looked away. That's when I heard it: voices coming through the woods. His friends to the rescue.

"I'll give Tonya any message you want me to," I said. "I'll make sure she's safe, if only for a little while."

The voices were growing louder.

He took the plunge. "Last I heard, she was living in a trailer off Beaver Dam Road out by Salter's Creek," he said quietly. "It's a red trailer. Sort of. There's a broken awning in front of it. She might be driving an old white Chevy truck I gave her. Or she might have sold it for drugs by now. She's hiding out from someone. I don't know who. I'm afraid to ask. Probably some dealer she owes a lot of money to."

"And Trey?" I asked.

He looked away. "Oh, Trey will be with her, trying to stop her. He isn't old enough to know it's useless to try."

"When was the last time you saw her?'

He shrugged. "Maybe two weeks ago. She wasn't doing too good. Trey wanted to track down some guy he thought was his father, some white guy from Durham. Tonya didn't want Trey to meet him, said it would be a mistake. She wouldn't tell him who he was."

I was finally learning something that would lead me toward the truth. "And?" I asked.

He shrugged again. “And nothing. Tonya wouldn’t give in. She flat out refused to tell Trey who his father was.”

“Why?” I asked.

He shrugged. “Don’t know. But I can guess.”

“Well, could you tell me your guess?”

“She probably didn’t want the guy to see her the way she is now. All those years of putting that shit in her body? It shows. And if you know what she looked like before the drugs started working on her, it’s... terrible to see how much she’s changed. I think maybe she couldn’t stand seeing that in his eyes.”

“Do you know who Trey’s father is?” I asked.

He shook his head. “No. I don’t think they were together long. But I do think she really loved him.”

“What makes you say that?”

“She didn’t want him to see what she’d become.”

I hated people in that instant. I hated all the people in the world who sold drugs for money, tearing off a piece of other people’s souls for something as meaningless as cash. I hated the people who raised their kids indifferently and let them think it was okay to do that. And I hated the people who would do such a thing to themselves and to the ones who loved them.

“I’m sorry,” I said again. “Really, I am.”

He looked away. Our talk was over.

His three bandmates emerged from the woods, dressed in their daishikis like apparitions from another continent.

“Everly,” one of the men said. “What’s going on, man?”

“Oh, are you guys the Everly Brothers?” I asked and was met by resolute silence, which is exactly what I deserved for attempting a joke about the ultimate white group with the ultimate of black groups. The men just stared at me silently, shoulder to shoulder, poised as if, together, they were one well-coiled animal ready to pounce if I so much as twitched a muscle.

"It's cool," Everly said, pulling a tuft of cotton from one of his braids. "How long until we go on?"

The trio stared, not answering, still processing the scene.

"She a cop?" one of them finally asked.

"No. How long until we go on?"

"About ten minutes," one of the men answered as he blatantly checked me out from head to toe. He smiled at me hopefully, revealing even white teeth.

No way, Jose. Not the way my ass felt at that moment. It was stinging from the damp and the nettles.

"We'd better get back," Everly said suddenly. He rose and brushed the cotton and mud from his robes, pulling out a few thorns before giving up.

I clambered to my feet since no one was stepping forward to help me. I tried to be of some assistance. "The back of your hair," I explained as I plucked more tufts of white from his dreads.

"You cotton pickin' white people crack me up," one of Everly's bandmates said. His friends roared in appreciation.

Funny guys. At least when they're the ones making the jokes.

I pulled the last of the bigger cotton tufts from Everly's hair. "Thanks," I whispered into his ear.

"Just help Trey," he muttered as he turned to go. His voice broke as he said it.

# Chapter Four

I intended to head out to Perry County in search of Tonya Blackburn's trailer first thing Monday morning, but I made the mistake of stopping by my office in Raleigh first, primarily to make sure Bobby D. had at least shifted his weight to an alternate buttock over the weekend and not mummified into a mountain.

What a surprise. Not only was Bobby eating a breakfast burrito, he was doing it in front of a horrified audience of one: an immaculately dressed black woman who was so engrossed in watching bits of scrambled egg and black bean sauce dribble down Bobby D.'s front that she did not even look up when I walked in.

"Casey!" Bobby bellowed enthusiastically, spraying his desk with bits of black bean. "You've got a visitor." Cash register signs practically danced in his eyes. If she was a new client, he had a percentage cut on the way.

I didn't think he should count this particular chicken just yet. Watching Bobby D. eat had turned the woman green, which is quite a feat since she had started out as deep brown.

I didn't recognize her. She looked like she could run a Fortune 100 Company. Her blue business suit was silk and why it wasn't wrinkled was beyond me. I can't even put on silk underwear without it looking like the back end of a Shar-Pei puppy.

"Alicia McCoy," the woman said, rising to her feet. She extended a hand. Her shake was confident. "I'm Tonya Blackburn's sister."

"Oh," I said. Not the most intelligent response, but I was startled: this was the sister of a drug addict on her last legs?

"Can we talk somewhere privately?" she asked in a clipped voice. Bobby D. was noisily slurping down his Pepsi and getting ready to dive into a second breakfast burrito. His desk looked like a Rottweiler and a badger had tussled on top of it, perhaps fighting over a bag of garbage from a Mexican restaurant.

But that wasn't even the strangest sight. As I stared, aghast, at the mess, I noticed a six-foot fiberglass hot dog leaning against the wall behind Bobby. The end of it had been painted with a smiling face like those creepy cartoon wieners that dance across the movie screen begging you to eat them.

"What in god's name is that?" I asked him.

He glanced at it. "Oh, that thing? It's a..."

"Ahem." Our visitor clamped her lips in a very tight line, letting me know that I needed to deal with her now. The giant fiberglass hot dog would have to wait.

"My office," I suggested. "Coffee?"

"No thanks." She stared at Bobby wolfing down his second burrito. "I'm not thirsty. Or hungry. Or even in the mood to breathe."

Hmm... maybe she had a sense of humor?

Alas, she did not, nor did she have a heart, apparently. As soon as she entered my glorified closet of an office, she removed her cashmere coat, looked around for a place to hang it, then sat down primly in my visitor's chair, draped it over her lap, and got right to the point. "I understand my mother hired you to look for my sister," she said.

"Not really. She hired me to look for her grandson. There's a difference."

"My mother is old," the woman said, not missing a beat. "And sentimental. Her desires are misguided. We have our family to think of. I'm here to convince you to drop the case."

I wondered what pack of wolves had raised her. "I can understand your feelings, but I work for your mother and can not be influenced in what I do on this case by anyone but her."

"Do you have any idea what it has been like having Tonya in the family?" the woman asked. I noticed that her right hand was trembling with the effort of staying in control. She saw me looking and hid it under her coat.

"I can imagine," I said. "But that's all the more reason to find Trey."

"Tonya has nearly destroyed our family," the women plowed onward. "Not to mention my career, my parent's happiness, everything she has touched."

Hoo boy. I don't like to throw stones. And I know what it's like to have a lying, scheming, bloodsucking drug addict siphoning the money and goodwill out of the family tree. But somewhere down the line, this woman and Tonya Blackburn had been sisters. They had played dolls together, broken bread together, maybe even shared a bedroom together. Surely this woman, with all of her material riches, had a spark of humanity left in her for her sister?

"The best thing this family could possibly do right now is to walk away from Tonya and anyone connected to her," my visitor said when I did not respond. "She's stolen enough money and energy from my mother as it is."

Scratch the spark of humanity theory. "I know it's hard," I said, trying to be sympathetic.

"No, you don't know." Her teeth were so tightly clenched I could barely understand her. "Do you have any idea what it's like for your sister to barge into your office time and again, in front of clients and staff, dirty, ragged, smelling of urine, stinking of the streets, begging you for money, hair all wild and ratted, not caring about anything but that I give her enough for her next pipe of crack?"

"Meth," I said. "Not crack. You know? Speed, crank, crystal, tweak, ice. I think that's what she's probably on."

"Thank you for that lesson in drug terminology," the woman snapped. "Now answer my question. Do you know what it's like?"

"No, I don't," I admitted. "But I'm guessing you kept giving her money just to get rid of her and that's why she kept coming back for more."

"What choice did I have when she would approach me in front of everyone? I had to get her out the door."

"And now that she's finally gone, hopefully for good, you want her to stay away?"

"Yes. And I don't apologize for it."

I had seen it before. And a big part of me didn't blame her. Trying to help a drug addict can leave you feeling abused and very angry once you've been manipulated one time too often. And drug addicts always push it to that point. But this woman had gotten stuck in the anger phase and I could not afford for her emotions to interfere with my case.

"You know what I think?" I asked.

"What?" she said warily.

I stood up from my chair. "I think your mother is dying and she wants to see her grandson again before she goes. And I think if you had pulled your head out of your ass, you might have seen it before I did."

Okay, sometimes I'm mean.

She froze. "Why do you say that?" she asked.

I shrugged. "It's time for you to talk to your mother, not me. I have another appointment now, so I'll see you out."

She rose. "You don't know what it's been like," she said, her voice trembling.

I suddenly felt sorry for her. All the perfect outfits in the world, all the latest model cars, all the houses with too many rooms — none of them were going to stave off the sorrow she would feel when she lost her own flesh and blood. And I wasn't talking about losing her mother. I was talking about when the day came that she would lose her sister. Here was a woman, driven by whatever forces drove her, to build a life that seemed perfect from the outside looking in, trying desperately to convince herself that her life had nothing to do with her sister's, that her sister didn't matter, that when the drugs finally got to her sister — and they would — and all life was gone, that it wouldn't matter to her.

Well, I knew it would matter. You can't preempt that kind of sorrow. And when this woman finally realized that, it would be a pitiful sight.

"I'm sorry," I said as kindly as I could. "I wish I could help you, but I can't."

She didn't say anything as she put on her coat and left. She just marched past Bobby D. and slipped out the door.

"What was that all about?" Bobby asked.

"You don't want to know," I searched the debris on his desk. "Got any doughnuts?"

"Sorry. I ate them all."

"You gonna eat that, too?" I pointed to the giant fiberglass hot dog behind his desk. "Explain."

He explained. When he was done, I couldn't stop laughing.

It was the last opportunity I would have to laugh for a long, long time.

* * *

THE *YAHOO!* MAP I WAS CONSULTING had absolutely nothing whatsoever to do with reality. It was as if I was staring at a map of the other Perry County, the one on Mars. It would be tough, though, for anyone to keep up with the changing nature of these country roads, especially when a lot of them wound through private property or were rendered impassable by overflowing creeks and rivers. Perry County had seen some heavy flooding in recent years. Roads tended to disappear and appear far faster than anyone could keep up with the changes.

It took awhile, but I finally found Beaver Dam Road. It was little more than a trail that led deep into the woods. There was nothing I could do but pray for my suspension and turn onto it. About half a mile in, the road curved to the right to run alongside a manmade channel about twelve feet wide created to help alleviate flooding from the nearby New River. Brown water ran in a muddy stream through it toward some unknown larger body of water. I saw where the road had gotten its name. Remnants of beaver dams marked the sluggish water at intervals, telling me that someone was at war with the beavers. They put up a dam, man knocked it down. They put up a new dam, man knocked that one down as well.

I knew the beavers would win out in the end. They always do. Mostly because it's against state law to kill a beaver in North Carolina, although I do admit that an awful lot of beavers seem to be accidentally run over in driveways out in the hinterlands. Despite this mysterious phenomenon, the beaver population thrived.

As small as the road was, crude driveways led off the main trail at intervals, leading to isolated homes. I followed each driveway faithfully, discovering two log cabins, a hippy teepee still going strong after what must have been thirty years or more, one grungy modular home the size of a doublewide trailer and a partially built house that had been abandoned right after the foundation had been poured. Multiple cracks in the concrete showed why.

When I finally found Tonya Blackburn's trailer, I had a bad feeling right away. It was a rusted shell with a sagging awning. Bits of red paint barely clung to a rusted exterior. There were curtains on the windows and the front door was shut, but I could see that the back door was open ever so slightly— and not in a good way. It swung in the wind nonchalantly, as if man did not exist in this particular clearing. I stepped from my car, scared enough to retrieve my Colt from the glove compartment. Something rustled through the underbrush as I approached the trailer — it sounded large. I beat my palm against the trailer side a few times, the metal reverberating beneath my touch as my sharp slaps echoed inside. No answer. Suddenly, a dark shape darted out the back door, jumped off the ledge over two concrete block steps, soared past my head and scurried off through the tall grass. It was either a very fast possum or a very tanned raccoon.

Definitely not a good sign.

I knocked repeatedly on the side of the trailer, calling out Tonya's name. Still no answer. Wrapping my jacket sleeve around my hand so I wouldn't leave prints, I pushed against the back door. It swung wide, releasing a sweet, deeply decayed odor that I recognized at once. Shit. Something had died inside. Something that was a hell of a lot bigger than a mouse.

Please don't let it be the boy, I said to myself. Just don't let it be the boy.

In part to put off the inevitable grim discovery — and partly to cover my ass — I pulled a pair of surgical gloves from my knapsack and put them on. It's not like I make a habit of breaking and entering. But it's not like they take up a lot of room to carry, either. Besides, I'd searched way too many places wearing pot-holders on my hands. A death scene called for finesse.

I had a pack of watermelon bubble gum on me. Each piece had enough fake flavoring in it to fell a hippo, but at least it would mask the fetid sweetness of putrid flesh. I chewed a quick square, plugged half of each nostril with a tiny pink wad and popped another piece into my mouth. It's called improvisation.

I took a deep breath of fresh air and entered.

Something had torn through that trailer like a tornado. The furniture, what little there was, had been kicked over. Even the cheap couch was tipped on its side, its cushions ripped open so that tufts of cotton stuffing burst out like drifts of snow. Kitchen cabinet doors hung open and a counter full of bowls, pots and pans had been leveled with what looked like a single sweep of the arm, sending the contents crashing to the floor. Chairs had been turned over and cabinet drawers pulled out and dumped upside down.

I moved through the kitchen, past the wrecked living room and into a cramped hallway. How the hell did all those obese trailer residents you see screaming obscenities at each other on *Jerry Springer* even fit through these things? No wonder they were so grumpy. My butt was no prize, but it didn't need its own zip code yet either and I was barely squeezing through.

A tiny bedroom jutted off to the left. Reluctantly, I glanced inside, knowing from the overpowering odor that the source of the smell had to be in there.

Tonya Blackburn was laying face up on a bare mattress. She wore a torn blue nightgown that had slipped indifferently from her undernourished body. She was staring up at the ceiling through a face swollen with decay, the eyes milky and unseeing. The smell in the room was unbearable. She'd been dead for at least five days, I gauged. Inside her body, her organs had turned to soup. If it had been summer, I would never have been able to even recognize her. But cool nights and an open back door had preserved her just enough to convince me it was Tonya. One thin arm sprawled off the mattress and flopped toward the door, exposing an expanse of brown skin dotted with scabs and scars. Her other arm was curled against her chest. A dirty rag had been tied around the upper half of it and a needle dangled listlessly from the pockmarked skin.

Live by the sword. Die by the sword.

And, yet, there was something staged about her pose. The way the arm was cradled against her chest, and the knot so neatly tied off on her right arm. Was she left handed or had she been in the Navy? Because the knot seemed so... precise. I didn't like the looks of it. Maybe she'd been helped along by someone?

I knelt near her body, pulling my tee shirt up over my mouth to mask the smell. Something else was off. Her arms were pocked with track marks, but they were old scars, all except for a few.

I examined her body more closely and discovered a series of small bruises ringing her neck in an irregular line. Normal tissue decomposition or post-mortem bruises bearing testament to a strangling? I was no coroner, but I had watched one on TV plenty of times and, damn it, I had my suspicions.

It made me mad. After all the effort she had made to get clean, Tonya hadn't fallen off the wagon on her own — she had been pushed and then thrown under the wheels. But who would want to harm her and why?

And where was the boy?

I didn't touch anything in Tonya's room. I backed out carefully and inched my way around a pile of scattered schoolbooks and papers that led toward the end of the hallway. I stuck my head out the back door for a few gulps of fresh air before I continued on past a tiny bathroom that, apparently, had not seen running water for some time. I found a slightly larger bedroom beyond it. Unlike the rest of the trailer, the back bedroom, while disheveled, was fundamentally clean. The floors and walls looked scrubbed and the bed had been made, even if clothes, shoes, notebooks, a handheld video game and the other signs of young life were scattered across the bedspread. I checked under the bed — this one had a frame, at least — and found nothing, not even dust motes. I gave up and checked inside a tiny closet. A high school athletic jacket hung from a hanger beside a single light blue tee shirt emblazoned with a basketball and the UNC Tarheels logo. Otherwise, the closet was empty.

This was Trey's bedroom — and Trey was not in it.

That meant he might still be alive.

It also meant he might have seen his mother die. Or, worse, had something to do with her dying. I didn't know the kid, and if this was where he had been living, who knows what he might have been driven to do. If that was the case, I owed it to Sally to find him first, before the cops did, so I could determine what had really happened here in Perry County.

I knew one thing already: whatever had happened here, someone had been looking hard for something. My bet was on money or drugs. But all I could find that would lead me anywhere was a stack of what looked like old mail wrapped with a rubber band and tucked into the pocket of Trey's athletic jacket. I didn't know what a kid would be doing going around with mail in his pocket, and it was odd he had left the jacket behind; it had to be one of his most treasured possessions given how little he had. The mail was the only sign of the outside world I could find in the trailer so I took it. Maybe it would help me figure out why Tonya Blackburn and her son had ended up hiding in this godforsaken trailer in the middle of nowhere. I grabbed the mail and backed out of the bedroom. The smell inside the trailer was unbearable. I'd have to burn my clothes, I suspected, which pissed me off. A good pair of breathable black stretch pants are hard to find. Maybe I could boil them? I could use one of those jumbo deep fryers, the kind that holds gallons of oil and ends up frying more drunks than turkeys each Thanksgiving.

As I passed Tonya's bedroom, I glanced in again at the odd tableau her broken body formed. I saw a glimmer of brown beneath her right leg and stepped closer for a better look. It was a pill bottle, with several large pills inside. I took the bottle, easing it out from beneath the bag of bones and skin that had once been Tonya Blackburn. There was no label on the bottle. But then, addicts seldom buy drugs from a pharmacy. I wondered if what was in the bottle would match the brownish residue left in the head of the needle. Well, I'd leave the needle for the cops, but the pills were going with me, along with the mail.

I took a moment before I left to say a quick prayer over Tonya's body — wishing her an eternity in a place of peace, even though I wasn't exactly the praying kind and God had probably been exasperated with me for a long time now. But I thought she deserved something and it was all I could do for her.

I had not known Tonya Blackburn, and maybe she had not exactly been the best of mothers. But I was still filled with sadness as I gazed at the sorry end to her life. That people could be so unhappy, that people could hate themselves so much they would let life come to this: a body neglected and poisoned beyond recognition, sprawled on a dirty mattress in a dark metal box stuck in the middle of nowhere. It was a rejection of all that was good and clean in the world, a gradual refusal of every little thing that made life worth living until, at last, all that mattered was a smudge of brown in a spoon and the empty promise of a thin, tea-like liquid coursing through your veins.

Unexpectedly, I thought of Tonya Blackburn's sister, with her expensive clothes, fine shoes and straightened hair. Two sisters, a shared childhood and two very different fates. How close were we all to an end like this?

It made me wonder. At what point in life had Tonya Blackburn chosen the path that led her forever away from any hope of happiness? Had she known that was what she was choosing at the time? What exactly had brought her life to this? I decided I would find out.

Not for Tonya, exactly, but maybe for me.

* * *

I DROVE RECKLESSLY AWAY FROM THE TRAILER, anxious to get away as fast as I could. I pried the bubble gum out of my nostrils and tossed it into the weeds. Then I rolled the windows of my car down all the way, hoping the fresh air would sweep some of the stench from my clothes.

I was so preoccupied with getting the hell away from death I almost missed the cloud of dust lingering above one of the nearly hidden driveways snaking back from the road. Someone had turned down it recently. I slowed for a quick look. From the width of the tire tracks, it had been a truck. Well, that didn't mean much. Someone lived there or there wouldn't be a damn driveway. I peered down the rutted road and saw nothing else. I let it go and kept driving until I reached the main road and found a small gas station and grocery store near the Johnston County line. By then, I felt safe enough to pull over and examine the stack of mail I had taken from the trailer.

Why would a kid carry a stack of mail around?

I soon found out. It was Trey Blackburn's version of a scrapbook, a stack of minor achievements that represented the only pride he could find in his life. I found certificates of merit for his studies going back to grade school, a letter proving he had made the honor roll during his first semester at Perry County High, a few carefully folded letters from his now-dead grandfather Mac and Trey's birth certificate. There was no father's name listed. This was followed by a postcard of the mountains in their full autumn glory, with a messily scrawled back inscription that read, "Back home soon. Study hard and do what Coach says. I love you so much, always remember that, no matter what. – Mom." It was dated last May; I could not quite read the exact day, but the postcard itself looked to be decades old, the ink faded and the photo watercolor-like. The identifying caption was short: *The Blue Ridge Mountains boast some of the most beautiful peaks in the world. No wonder so many people love calling North Carolina home.*

The caption confirmed the age of the postcard. "I like calling North Carolina home" had not been used as a slogan by the state tourism board since the 1970's. That was well before Trey's time and my best guess was that Tonya had found it in some dust-covered rack in a store somewhere and felt the need to send her son some small token of her role as his mother.

I don't know why, but the message on the postcard made me sad. *I love you so much, always remember that, no matter what.* It was almost as if she was telling him good-bye, as if she knew something bad was going to happen.

I stowed it in my back pocket and kept going through the stack. Next up was a small wallet-sized school photo of a girl with black hair. I didn't recognize her, but she looked to be Trey's age. I also found several letters addressed to his mother and examined them closely. One was a letter congratulating her for completing a drug rehab program. The date on it was over three years old. The kid was clinging to past glory. Another was a letter from the North Carolina Parole Commission confirming that Tonya had completed the terms of her sentence. That letter was a year old, and evidence of no glory at all. But then the last letter in the pile stated that Tonya Blackburn had been accepted for re-admission to Piedmont Technical College, with full credit given for the six courses she had taken there previously.

Now that was interesting. She had been planning to return to college and complete her studies, studies that had perhaps been interrupted by a stint in jail, if the parole letter was any indication. I went back over the timeline Corndog Sally had given me. Trey had been living with Sally during the time his mother might have been in prison, I figured, then he'd had about nine months of nearly normal life living with his mother and attending Perry High before they'd pretty much gone into hiding. What had happened to cause Tonya to go on the run and take Trey with her?

I went back through the other envelopes, searching for a clue. I found one item I had not noticed before: a color photograph tucked inside a letter to Trey from his grandfather. The photo made no sense. It showed a beautiful young black girl dressed in a miniskirt and flowered blouse standing beside a white man who was sitting on a huge motorcycle, his denim jacket cut off at the top of the sleeves to reveal a very fine set of biceps. He was a handsome man, with long legs that stretched out in worn jeans to keep the motorcycle precisely balanced. He wore cowboy boots with big heels that dug into the dirt road. He wore no helmet and his black hair flowed freely to his shoulders. An equally dark handlebar mustache topped a wide grin. Mirrored sunglasses covered his eyes. He was smiling at the girl beside him with an almost joyous confidence in her proximity.

That grin looked familiar.

I peered at the photo closer, trying to place where I had seen it before. There was something about the photo, though, that prevented my brain from making the leap to recognition. Something was out of context — the man was out of context.

I knew him, but not like that. Not as a biker.

I tried to imagine what he would look like without the sunglasses. He'd have dark eyes, I knew, very dark against that smooth white skin. Sort of like....

*I couldn't breathe.*

Just like that, I could not breathe and my whole life changed. All that I thought I knew suddenly became as foreign and unfathomable as a country I'd never been in before.

I knew the man on the motorcycle. I knew him well. And as soon as I realized who he was, I knew that the beautiful black girl standing beside him had to be Tonya Blackburn before the drugs took hold. And the man on the motorcycle had to be Trey's father. Trey had inherited his smile and his eyes.

All of which explained why Corndog Sally had come to me.

* * *

"WHEW, GIRL. YOU STINK!" With his usual tact and charm, Bobby D. got right down to it. "I hope the client paid up before he died."

"It wasn't the client. And she's paid up," I said. "Have you seen my emergency overnight bag? I have got to get out of these clothes."

"Women say that to me all the time."

*"Bobby."*

"Under the coffee table." He took a noisy slurp from his Pepsi. "But if you don't mind my saying so, you need more than a change of clothes."

"I need a change of life," I said sourly as I rummaged through the bag, retrieving a pair of jeans and a tee shirt. The tee shirt was left over from my brief love affair with *Bon Jovi* in the 80's, and the art on it was downright embarrassing. Which meant I could either look like a fool or stink like a hound that had rolled in the carcass of a dead cow. I chose to look like a fool. Wouldn't you?

I peeled the smelly tee shirt off over my head and tossed it into a trashcan. "Burn that when you get a chance, would you?"

"Sorry babe." He bent over a legal pad filled with his scrawls. "I don't do trash. How else can I help?"

"You want to help? Tell me what these are." I tossed the bottle of pills I'd taken from Tonya's trailer onto his desk. For a man with hands the size of catcher's mitts, he had a surprisingly delicate touch. It took him only seconds to have them in his hand and to make the call.

"These are Happy Horse pills," he announced, staring down at the fat white pills. "Mr. Ed's, Jethro Downers, the big H-2-0, scourge of the Appalachians, your friend and mine: Hillbilly Heroin. Also known as Oxycontin. They go for over fifty bucks a pill on the street these days. They've been cracking down on this stuff." He smiled happily at them. Hopefully, too, I noted.

"No shit. How did I miss that?"

"I suspect you were too busy stinking." He stowed the pills away in his drawer. "Best let me keep these for you," he said.

"Best for who?" But I let it go. I'd flirted enough with drugs in my life. When I got that little feeling in my stomach, the one that cried, "Let's experiment with something new!" I tended to walk away as fast as I could. I'd learned that walking away meant I could keep walking away. A few Darvon during that time of the month was all my conscience would let me justify. "Be my guest," I said magnanimously, just to ensure I did not change my mind. "But you have to take out the garbage in return. And call the body in for me."

Bobby raised his eyebrows but said nothing. I knew what he was thinking: *you didn't even have the decency to call someone about the body?*

"Please? I didn't have time to deal with it and maybe there are just a few teensy things I may have taken from the scene and, well, can't you just do it anonymously?"

"If the Perry County cops find out you were there and didn't call it in, you're going to be in deep shit," he warned me.

"If the Perry County cops find out I was there, they'll keep me for days, questioning me, and I just can't afford the down time. Please, Bobby? Do it for me just this once? A fifteen-year old boy is missing and I've got to find him."

He pushed his notepad toward me. "Tell me where the body is." As I scribbled down the address, he was already taking an untraceable trac phone from his bottom drawer and looking up the number for Perry County's emergency line.

It was good to have friends.

I finished stripping down to my skivvies. Being half-naked in front of Bobby D. had long since ceased to be an embarrassment to either one of us. Besides, my closet-sized office was not big enough for a full-blown strip tease. Believe me, I'd tried.

"Where are you headed in such a hurry?" he asked, sniffing pointedly in my direction. "I strongly recommend a shower first."

"No time. I have to go see my client now," I said, somewhat grumpily. Damn it. The jeans were too tight. How long ago had I packed this damn bag? I tugged and pulled and wiggled until I was able to get the zipper shut, but I knew if I wore them more than a few hours my current lack of a decent sex life would become a completely moot point.

"And which of our clients, pray tell, deserves such speedy service and, yet, such poor hygiene?" Bobby asked as he watched me stuff my old clothes into a plastic garbage bag and tie the opening securely shut.

"Corndog Sally."

"So, exactly whose stink is that on your clothes?" Bobby asked, eyebrows raised.

"Her daughter's."

"Let me get this straight — you're rushing off to tell an old woman her daughter is dead," Bobby said. "But you look like you're going to kick her ass while you're at it. Why is that?"

Okay, Bobby was obese. That didn't mean he was stupid. And, god knows, he was often far more sensitive to other people's feelings than I was.

"She conned me," I explained as I sniffed myself thoroughly. Wild dogs would still follow me around the block, but it would have to do. "I think she knew all along that her daughter was dead. And there's a reason she came to me about it."

Bobby looked skeptical. "A reason?"

"Yeah. A big one. And I don't like being played like this."

Bobby stared at me with a look I'd never actually seen on him before. It seemed like... genuine concern.

"What is it?" I mumbled.

"If I hear you caused that old woman one moment of unnecessary pain," Bobby warned me. "I will personally kick your ass. I don't care what she's done to you. Her daughter is dead."

I was silent.

"Do you want me to come along?" he asked in a voice that was unexpectedly kind.

"No," I said. "I'll do it."

"Then do it kindly."

"Fine." My stomach hurt. "But I hate these kinds of visits."

# Chapter Five

I arrived at Corndog Sally's house on the outskirts of South Raleigh within seconds of an ambulance. My stomach dropped. I had been right about Sally being sick. Was I too late?

Worse, Alicia McCoy, Tonya's snooty sister, pulled up in a black Mercedes before I'd even climbed out of my car. She'd been following the ambulance.

"What are you doing here?" she asked rudely, her nose wrinkling in distaste at the smell that still lingered about me. What would she say if I told her that it was her sister's smell she was turning her nose up at? I had half a mind to, but Bobby's words of caution stopped me.

"That's between me and your mother," I said, brushing past her. "And I could ask the same thing of you."

"I'm here to take my mother to a hospice," she announced angrily. "I don't need you interfering."

"That didn't take you long," I observed. "Why don't you just have them drive her straight to the cemetery and toss her in a hole? It would save you time later."

I won't repeat what she said back to me, but I will say this for her: I didn't think she had *that* in her.

The ambulance guys were looking warily from one of us to the other. I had to act quickly or they'd start backing down the driveway with the stretcher, then make a run for it down the street.

"I think we just got off on the wrong foot," I said, beating her up the walkway. I stood rather foolishly at the front door and wondered what the hell I was supposed to do now, since I didn't have a key. "Let's start over: I need to talk to your mother alone for a few minutes. I found your sister and the news isn't good." I glanced at the ambulance. "It's a good thing you're here."

"You found her?" Alicia whispered. "She's dead?"

I nodded.

She put her head down and held her hands over her eyes and I could not tell if she was heartbroken or relieved. I'm not sure she could, either.

"Are you okay?" I asked her as kindly as I could.

"Could you be the one to tell my mother?" She held out her house keys and would not meet my gaze. "I don't think I can."

"Sure." And why not? At least my sympathy would be unpolluted by years of heartache and frustration.

I entered the small house and followed a hallway to a back bedroom. Sally was in bed, eyes closed, surrounded by sunny linens and a sunflower comforter, her face a startling dark brown against all that yellow.

"Sally?" I asked tentatively.

"Come in," she croaked. As I drew nearer, her eyes focused on me. "It's amazing what a difference a few days can make, isn't it?" she asked.

"I figured you were sick." I could not understand the conflicting feelings that warred inside me. "I figured out a lot of things."

She tried to sit upright. Her wig was on a stand on her dresser and her natural hair had come loose from the bobby pins that usually clamped it tightly against her scalp. It dangled about her head like gray wire mesh, giving her a wild, almost barbarian appearance. "Come closer," she demanded.

I inched forward cautiously. This was Corndog Sally, after all. She'd swung a pocketbook at bigger people than me — and connected. "What have you figured out?" she demanded.

"I've figured out that you're dying," I said quietly. "And that's why you need me to find Trey so badly."

She nodded. "Fair enough. I can't let go unless I know my grandson is safe. And I'm tired and I miss my husband Mac and I want to go to him. It's time for me to go, but I can't. Not yet. Can you understand that?"

"Yes." I took a step closer. "And I figured out you already knew Tonya was dead, didn't you? You knew that already."

She closed her eyes. She had known, but not quite believed, and now had to face a bitter reality. "I hired a private detective before you," she admitted. "He told me she was probably dead. Maybe he even knew for sure and didn't have the nerve to tell me. But you must understand that, in my heart, my daughter Tonya died a long time ago."

"Okay," I said. "But you've known who Trey's father was for a long time, too, haven't you? That was why you came to me. Because you knew I'd have to find the boy. For him."

"I wasn't sure you'd do it just for me."

That hurt my feelings. "You could have just asked me," I said. "I would have done it for you. You could have been upfront, Sally. You could have trusted me."

She peered at me through milky eyes. "Miss Jones, I did not get this far, I did not live this long, I did not survive the times that I survived by trusting white people. That's all I can say to explain. You will understand or you won't."

"But you could have trusted *me,*" I said stubbornly.

"I trust you now," she whispered fiercely, taking my hand. "Tell me you will keep looking for him."

"I have to tell his father," I explained. "I owe him that much."

She nodded. “Fair enough. Will my boy be taken care of?”

“Better than you could ever imagine,” I said. “I guess you don’t know his father.”

“Only his name,” she said. “Only his name and that he was a friend of yours. People tell me that he was your friend.”

“He’s a good man,” I said. “Trey will be more than well taken care of. He’ll have everything he could ever want in life, including his father’s love.”

“That’s if you can find him,” she reminded me gently.

“I will find Trey,” I promised her. “I will find him.”

“Are they waiting outside?” Sally asked.

“Yes. Alicia and an ambulance crew.”

“Have patience with her,” Sally told me. “That girl never did know how to relax. I’ve seen her grow old before her time because of it. But underneath it all, she’s not as strong as you and me.”

“I’ll try but I wouldn’t exactly call her likeable,” I muttered.

To my surprise, Sally laughed. “Me, either. But be kind to her. And come back to me soon with good news. I need to know before I go.”

“How will I find you?” I asked.

“Alicia can tell you. I don’t know where I’m going.”

“Don’t you care?”

Sally shook her head. “It doesn’t matter. Soon enough, I’ll be going home to Jesus.” She peered at my tee shirt. “Isn’t that Jesus on your tee shirt?”

“No, that’s Jon Bon Jovi,” I explained. “A rock star. Sort of.”

“Well, thank goodness,” Sally said, closing her eyes. “That boy is way too white to be Jesus.”

* * *

IT WAS GOING TO BE a long, long day. And I'd be damned if I would face *him* jammed into tight jeans and an embarrassing tee shirt while smelling like last week's corpse. I went home and stood in the shower for over ten minutes, trying to wash it all off — the smell, the sadness, the what-might-have-been. I couldn't do my job carting all that shit around.

When you don't actually want to do something, it's amazing how fast you get to where you have to go in order to do it. I arrived at the rambling old Victorian house outside the town limits of Pittsboro in record time. I stood on the edge of the lawn, just before sunset, wondering if they had made a real home together and if they were happy.

It was a bitter truth. He had been right about me. I had loved him as much as I could, but never as much as he had loved me, and I would never be able to, it just wasn't in me. But she had loved him that much and then some. He deserved more than I could give him, but I still wanted him, and it hurt that she had him instead. Yet how could I hold it against her? She was as fragile as an orchid, her life no larger than the walls of that house. He was all she had.

It didn't matter. I still wanted him. And part of me hated her for having him instead.

I noticed the gardener leaning on his rake, staring at me as if he could read my mind. "Hello, Hugo," I said.

"Miss Casey," he answered, doffing his straw hat in respect. "I have not seen you in a long time."

"It has been a long time," I agreed. "You look well."

"As do you," he said formally.

But he still watched me cautiously as I took a deep breath, walked up the ramp and rang the doorbell. He, too, was under her spell — what man would not feel the urge to protect her fragile happiness?

*Rest easy. I am not here to do harm, my friend,* I thought as I waited for someone to answer the doorbell.

"Yes?" Helen asked from the other side of the front door. Her voice was the same as always, tentative and a little fearful.

"It's me, Helen. Casey. I need to talk to him. I'm working on a case that involves him."

I had to give her credit. She did not hesitate. She opened the door wide, hiding behind it, as was her habit. She looked a little older, but no less beautiful. Blonde and frail, pale and delicate, a Southern flower wilting in the heat, someone who needed taking care of by a big strong man or through the kindness of strangers. While me? I was no Southern flower. I was as tough and stubborn as cat briar taking root on the side of a mountain. I needed no taking care of, by anyone, except maybe myself.

"Come on in," she said. "He's in the sunroom."

I had not seen her since he left me to be with her and her poise was disconcerting. She did not appear to feel apologetic toward me. I didn't blame her. He was not an easy man to love. She probably earned the right day after day.

Other women would have wanted to tag along to hear what I had to say after so many months of silence. But Helen had an odd quality of containment that went with her inability to face the world outside her house. She lived in the space immediately outside her body and she did not ever seem to want to be anywhere else except exactly where she was. In a way, I envied her.

"Do you want me to show you the way?" she asked.

I shook my head. "I can find it."

"Can I get you anything to eat or drink?"

*Well, wasn't she just the lady of the house?* The thought was a bit snide. Stop it, I told myself. It was not her fault. It was mine.

"No, but he may need a drink by the time I'm done."

Anyone else who knew me would have made a joke with a set-up line like that, but Helen just nodded and turned away, willing to wait until the news reached her.

We were so different. Maybe that's what hurt so much.

As I walked toward the sunroom, my footsteps echoed in the hallway, each slap of shoe on wood as loud as a rifle shot to my ears. I entered the sunroom, not knowing how I felt and only knowing I was, somehow, terrified.

He sat with his back to me, looking out through the glass walls at the sunset, staring past the horizon at something only he could see.

"Burly," I said clearly.

He wheeled around slowly, instantly recognizing my voice. He was backlit by the sunset and I could not see his face because of the glare.

"I have to talk to you about something," I explained, fighting to get my emotions under control. All I wanted was to sound normal, to appear normal, to not give him the satisfaction of looking like how I felt.

"Is everything okay?" he asked. His wheelchair was smaller than the last time I'd seen him, sleek and low to the ground. It threw me off and I did not answer. "It's been a long time since we've seen each other," he prompted me.

"Everything's okay," I said. "My grandfather's fine. I'm fine. Bobby's fine." I tried hard not to babble. I took an envelope from my back pocket and extracted the photo of Trey that Corndog Sally had given me. "Burly, I don't know any other way to say this, so I'm just going to say it. You have a son. His name is Trey." I placed the photo in his lap. "His mother was — "

"I know who his mother was," he interrupted. He took the photo and held it closer, staring at it. "There's only one person his mother could be." He stared at the photo, not challenging my pronouncement. He didn't even ask if I was sure. He didn't want to question the verdict, I realized. For him, a son was probably the greatest gift anyone could have given him at this point in his life.

"Burly?" I asked when he said nothing. And that was when I realized he was crying. He made no sound and he made no move to hide the tears. They flowed down his face and over his hands, staining the photograph of Trey.

"Burly?' I asked again. "Are you okay?"

He looked up at me. "How old is he?"

"Fifteen. He's a very good student, apparently, a really great basketball player and, by all accounts, a fine boy." I hesitated.

"What is it?" he asked. "Why didn't you bring him with you? You know me well enough to know that I would want to see him, to be a part of his life."

"He's missing," I said and I suddenly felt so close to tears myself that my voice cracked. "His mother is dead, something to do with drugs, and the boy is missing. Trey is missing."

He could not take it all in. "He's missing?" he asked.

I nodded. "I'm looking for him now."

"Looking for him where?" Burly said.

"I don't know yet." It was all I had to offer.

It had taken awhile for all my words to sink in. "Tonya is dead?" he asked.

"Yes," I said. "I saw her. It was ugly."

"Why didn't she tell me about him? Why didn't she come to me for help?"

I thought of her ravaged body, of what she had become, of the way drugs had robbed her of all youth and beauty. "I don't think she wanted you to see her that way. I think she wanted you to remember her like this."

I handed him the photo of him sitting on his Harley, legs outstretched, a younger, happier Tonya by his side.

He stared down at it and I wondered if he was remembering what it had been like, back before the accident, when he'd been able to use those long, lanky legs, before his life had shrunk to his wheelchair.

"I would have stayed with her," he said. "But she didn't want her parents knowing I was white."

"They kind of found out when Trey was born. I don't think it mattered to them then. They love him very much. At least his grandmother does. The grandfather died a few years ago. It's the grandmother who hired me to find him. That's how I found out about Tonya."

"You said he was a good student?" Burly asked me. "He's not into drugs or anything like that?"

I shook my head. "Apparently not. Whatever happened to his mother, whoever got to her, she kept it all from affecting him." As I said it, I realized how hard that would have been and I decided that maybe Tonya Blackburn had not been such a bad mother after all, that maybe she had been something of a miraculous one.

"Except that he's missing," Burly said, unable to take his eyes off the photo of the tall, confident boy, twirling a basketball on his fingertip, his face filled with the same cocky grin I had seen on Burly so many times.

"Yes, and I have no idea where or why. It may be that someone took him to keep him safe."

"Then how are you going to find him? Do you need money? What can I do to help?"

I shook my head at all the questions. "I'll find Trey," I found myself promising for the second time that day. "I will find him. If I need anything from you, I'll let you know."

Burly was still staring at the photo of his son, but then he looked up at me with his amazing dark eyes. It was a look I knew well, a look that told me he knew what I was feeling and what I was thinking and it was okay that I couldn't say any of it aloud. "I love you, Casey. You know that, right?"

"You don't have to say that," I told him. "I'd look for him anyway."

"I know you would," he answered. "And that's one reason why I love you."

* * *

THERE ARE PEOPLE WE NEED TO LEAVE BEHIND in our lives, people we cannot leave behind in our lives and, all too often, people who turn out to dominate both categories. I spent the better half of that night and the next day wondering if I would ever be able to leave Burly behind and if I was doomed to forever pursue hopeless cases simply because my pride drove me to try and solve them. I thought of all these things, and more, because I had no idea where to start when it came to fulfilling my promise to Corndog Sally and Burly that I would find Trey no matter what. How can you find a fifteen-year old who has disappeared off the face of the earth?

I surfed the Internet, I made phone calls to his former teachers, I googled, I hacked, I ate, I wanted to drink. None of it got me anywhere. I found out one thing and one thing only: that the Perry County authorities had finally discovered Tonya Blackburn's body, winning her two inside paragraphs in *The Perry County Herald* that could pretty much be summed up as "body found in rural trailer" and "cause of death unknown." Like so many others before her, Tonya Blackburn had left this world, not with a bang, but with a whimper.

By the evening of the next day, I was still at square one, my head ached from too much computer time and my mind was on the house in rural Chatham County where Burly was living with someone other than me. So, naturally, I did what I always do under such circumstances: I went to find a friend.

I did not come empty-handed. When Marcus answered his doorbell, clad in a silk kimono with a green mud mask covering his face (his usual evening wear when his partner was not around) I handed over a gallon-sized freezer bag stuffed with a fragrant green herb, the buds bursting with resin, the leaves jammed in so tightly that you could barely see the stems.

"You shouldn't have," Marcus said.

"I know."

"No, really, you *shouldn't* have." He took the freezer bag from me and held it up to the light. "You know the new policy. Random drug tests."

"That's catnip, you idiot." I brushed past him, expecting to see the crack-addicted kitten I had given him dangling from his drapes or mangling a mouse somewhere. Instead, his living room was as spotless as ever. "Where is the little dickens?"

"Catnip?" Marcus opened the bag and inhaling deeply. "*Fresh* catnip. Where did you find it?"

"Farmer's Market," I explained. "It costs more than pot. Make it last."

"Bless you," Marcus said. "Follow me. Theresa is in her room."

"Who is where?"

"The kitten is in here."

"You named your cat *Theresa?*" I asked incredulously, but the question died on my lips. I was struck dumb by the sight that greeted me. Marcus had transformed his home office and occasional guestroom into something out of Dr. Seuss. It looked like a carpet salesman on acid had locked himself in his home workshop for three weeks to make all of his LSD fantasies come true. The room was filled by a vast creation of wood, burlap, roping and carpet consisting of platforms, stairs, scratching posts and little tree houses, all joined by a series of balance beams and tiny walkways. "Oh my dear god," I said.

What else was there to say?

"Theresa!" Marcus called out. The tiny calico darted out from behind the sofa then scampered across the room until she was as far away from me as she could get. She stood behind the curtains, peering out at me suspiciously.

"I keep her happy time box behind the sofa," Marcus explained as he dragged a cardboard box out into view and poured half of my catnip offering into it. "She loves to roll around in it."

"You bought her that carpeted monstrosity and she's spending most of her time in a cardboard box?" I asked. "What exactly does that tell you?"

"That she's addicted? Wait until she smells the good stuff. She's going to go crazy over this."

Marcus was right. Theresa got a whiff of the fresh catnip all the way across the room, launched herself through the air, sailed over a coffee table and landed smack in the middle of the herbal mountain that filled the cardboard box. She then proceeded to roll back and forth with her legs held straight up in the air before burying her head in the stuff, all the while purring as loudly as a six-hundred pound tiger.

"I'll have what she's having," I said, staring fascinated at this display of feline ecstasy. Why had I not been born a cat? Happiness was so… simple. You just rolled in catnip all day long and no one ever nagged you to go into rehab.

"No," Marcus said. "This is what *you* want." He took a stack of papers from beside his computer and handed them to me.

"What's this?" I asked.

"Tonya Blackburn's Department of Corrections records and parole officer reports."

I stared at him, dumbfounded. "How did you know I'd want these?"

Marcus looked away, his dark eyes huge chocolate cookies in the green sea of his facial mud mask. "Burly called me."

"Burly called you?" I asked slowly.

"Well, we are friends," Marcus said, beating me to the defensive stage and claiming the high ground for himself before I could even start in that direction. "Perhaps he wanted to discuss the fact that he had a son with a friend."

"How much did he offer you?" I asked coldly.

"None of your business. He just said to pull everything I could that could possibly help you and to make sure you took the information and he'd pay me whatever it took."

"Charge him plenty," I ordered as I grabbed the papers from Marcus, irked that Burly had gone behind my back — but also mad at myself for being irked. It wasn't like I had gotten anywhere on my own, and it was his son, after all.

"I will," Marcus said — and I believed him. I'd lost count of the number of brothers and sisters he had in college. He was a walking directory of university and college tuition rates. At least he'd put Burly's money to good use.

"Get me a drink," I begged him as I sat down and started thumbing through Department of Correction records and Parole Officer reports on Tonya Blackburn. It was good stuff, far beyond anything I'd been able to hack on my own. Marcus must have been given a higher clearance level than the last time I had bribed him to go fishing in the official State of North Carolina database.

Marcus brought me something pink in the kind of expensive, long-stemmed cocktail glass that only a childless gay man could keep unbroken in his house for more than two weeks. The drink was tart and tasty and lethal. It went straight down like a shiny pink ribbon of peace, soothing my anxiety all the way to my chubby, tingly toes. “This is strong stuff,” I declared. “Keep them coming.”

Marcus kept them coming. I read and got drunk for a couple of hours, escaping in alcohol and work. Somewhere along the way, I fell asleep — or passed out, depending on your perspective. I woke the next morning with my skin stuck to the leather sofa like it had been super-glued on, a cashmere throw carefully tucked in around my shoulders and a stoned cat sleeping right on my crotch. Too bad it had stopped purring somewhere along the way. It would have been the biggest thrill I’d had down there in months.

I smelled fresh coffee down the hall and staggered into the kitchen.

“So where are you going to start?” Marcus asked as he handed me a cup of coffee and politely ignored the fact that I looked like Blanche Dubois on a bad day — compared to his Denzel Washington on the very best of days.

“Find where the mother has been and you will find out where the son has gone, Grasshopper,” I decreed as I sipped coffee that had been excreted by fetal Madagascar monkeys or some such nonsense. Man, did it taste good, monkey shit or not. Curiously, I had no hangover. I never did at Marcus’s apartment. It was as if he had the power to banish anything so tacky as a hangover from the utter swankness of his place.

“And where has the mother been?” he asked mildly as he spooned no-fat yogurt and fresh raspberries into a bowl. He pushed a box of Krispy Kreme doughnuts across the counter toward me. “Here. I got you these. Knock yourself out. I’ve got insulin, too, in case you need it.”

“Piedmont Technical College,” I told him. “That’s where she’s been. I can account for her whereabouts pretty much the entire time except for a little under a year when she was going there, and it was pretty recently. She seems to have been in and out of some women’s prison in the mountains on drug charges, and there's no way I can get in there. So I'm going to start with the college and see what happens."

"Did you find anything else?"

I shook my head. "It doesn't make much sense. Her prison records say she was a model prisoner. She was released early for good behavior. Her parole officer says she was clean and submitted to drug testing voluntarily. Her friend Everly swears she was doing great. But then I find her with a needle sticking out of her arm, and I've got a crack head who swears she was back to dealing, and…" I shrugged. "Somewhere in between those two versions of Tonya is the unknown person who took her son. The kid is with someone. I can feel it. He's alive and someone took him."

Marcus was staring at me from over his cup of coffee, saying nothing.

"What?" I asked.

"Be careful," he warned me.

"I'm always careful." I suddenly felt grumpy and didn't know why. "What? You afraid the registrar at Piedmont Tech is going to leap across the desk and hit me with a thirty-pound print-out?"

"I wasn't talking about that," Marcus said calmly.

"Then what were you talking about?" I demanded.

"When you let your personal feelings get in the way," he said, "you tend to make bad decisions. Very bad decisions. Do you want me to give you some examples?"

"No, I do not. Point well taken."

Marcus smiled. "I'll make you some eggs."

"No, thanks," I said. "I think I'm ready to move on." I wasn't talking about the case, but he knew that.

"You sure?" he asked.

I nodded. "I don't know how far I'll get. I just know I'm ready to get started."

# Chapter Six

I have looked for a lot of people in my lifetime. Mostly people who don't want to be found. So I know that it's remarkably easy to disappear, if that's what you really want. Anyone can try on a new identity, and people move around so much these days no one even notices when they go. Departing neighbors become like ghosts, leaving little more than wisps of themselves behind. All of which meant that chances were good my trip to Piedmont Tech to find out about Tonya Blackburn's time there could be a complete waste. But I had to try.

Chances were certain that the official people there — the registrars, professors, guidance counselors and staff — would be absolutely no help when it came to knowing more about Tonya Blackburn. I would not even waste my time trying. But I also knew people almost always hung out with other people just like them. That was the way of the world. Sometimes you met people who were exceptions, like me, but most people stuck to their own. Which meant, if I wanted to find out more about Tonya Blackburn's life, I needed to find the older students at Piedmont Tech. I was certain that someone still there had to have known her. The college was over two hours away from the trailer where I'd found her, and that was driving like a bat out of the hell the way I did. Tonya had driven a broken down old truck that hadn't passed an official inspection in a couple of years. There was no way she had commuted. And she'd attended during the time Trey was living with his grandparents, which meant she'd shared an apartment with someone or, more likely, a lot of someones, to keep it as cheap as possible.

If they were there, I would find them.

Piedmont Technical College was little more than a collection of unremarkable brick buildings and asphalt parking lots in the middle of ordinary former farm lands west of the Haw River. It had carved out a reputation for producing graduates in health services who actually knew what they were doing and actually wanted to work. A lot of the rest homes and hospitals in North Carolina hired as many Piedmont Tech graduates as they could each year to occupy the lower paying, but not quite lowest paying, jobs they had. It was a good place to go for two years if you needed a degree, especially one from this country, and you were ready to settle down and work hard when you got out.

Tonya Blackburn had been ready to settle down. I knew from the records Marcus had obtained for me that she had been training as a lab tech during the nine months she had spent at the school. I also knew she'd gotten good grades during her first stint there. I just didn't know why she had withdrawn before the end of her second attempt at completing the program or where she had gone to next.

I set up shop outside the one place I figured most students had to pass through sooner or later — an on-campus convenience store manned by a grumpy Indian woman who wore an orange sari and looked like she would rather be staring out over the Ganges River instead of the Haw. She recognized the photo I showed her of Tonya — Burley's money had inspired Marcus to print me out a plethora of official snapshots of her — but that was all she could tell me. Well, that and the fact that Tonya liked to drink Dr. Pepper with a pack of boiled peanuts almost every afternoon.

She couldn't tell me who Tonya had hung out with, or why she had left, and she didn't act like it mattered much to her.

I bought a supply of diet sodas, pork rinds and a consolation pack of Hostess Sno-Balls, then claimed a bench outside the store and settled in for a long afternoon's worth of work. I had my system down pretty well. I'd wait until a older student drew near, let them go into the store, then accost them as they were leaving and ready to rip into whatever pack of junk food they'd just bought. I'd show them the best photo I had of Tonya, recite her class schedule during her last semester and wait for them to insist they'd never seen her before in their lives.

Most of them were lying, of course. Or at least a good quarter of them were. They figured I was a determined bill collector or a process sever or someone who worked for The Man. Some of the ones from foreign countries, and there were quite a few, wouldn't even talk to me. They scurried away like I was with Immigration. But I knew that if I kept it up, and stayed right where I was, I'd flush out a friend of hers sooner or later, someone who'd be alerted by one of the dozens of people I had talked to first before they'd come marching over to find out what the hell I wanted with Tonya.

Sure enough, a little after three o'clock, a friend of Tonya's who was willing to go on record as such, came stomping up the brick path toward me. Even for me, she was a little intimidating — close to six feet tall, skin as black as coffee, muscles as prominent as most of the WBA. She was in her late thirties but she moved like a panther and I was pretty sure she was prepared to kick my ass if I so much as looked at her sideways. Her braids danced and swung as she marched up that path toward me.

"What the hell do you want with Tonya?" she demanded before I could say a word.

There was only one way to play it. "Tonya's dead," I said.

That stopped her in her tracks.

"I'm sorry," I added.

She sat on the bench and folded her hands in her lap. She didn't seem too surprised. "How?" she asked.

"Drugs."

"No way. You sure it was her?"

"I saw the body. And now her son is missing. I'm trying to find him."

"Her son?" The woman looked relieved. "We're talking about two different people. Tonya didn't have a son."

Now I was the one who was surprised. Tonya had bragged about Trey to a lot of people. He was the best thing she'd ever done. I knew she'd have told people here about him.

"I'm talking about her," I said, showing the woman Tonya's photo. She looked at it for a long time.

"That's Tonya all right, but I didn't know she had a son." She sounded hurt. "Why wouldn't she tell me about him?"

"I don't know. But it's probably important. His father wants to find him. I'm trying to find out where he may have gone."

"I didn't even know he existed," she said sadly. I held out my bag of pork rinds and she took a few absent-mindedly, her chin propped on one of her hands as she chewed thoughtfully. "I lived with her and I didn't even know. You think you know someone and then…" She shook her head and sighed. But then she told me a lot about Tonya that I didn't know. That she was a neat freak and thoughtful and paid her own way and never bogarted anyone else's groceries. That she was funny and watched a soap opera every day at four and wasn't gay but didn't seem to have a problem with women that were — but who would after spending time in a women's prison? Which she knew Tonya had. And she said that Tonya had a wicked sense of humor. "But she wasn't mean," she added. "She never made fun of other people for a laugh." She stared at me for a long time, as if she had just noticed me. "Are you sure it was drugs?" she asked.

"I don't know," I said honestly. Then, because she had been so honest with me, I told her all about how I had found Tonya and how the scene had somehow seemed staged. "I'm not sure I buy it," I admitted.

"It was that boyfriend of hers," the woman said suddenly. "You talk to him?"

"What boyfriend?" I asked. "What did he look like?"

"He was white," she said. "White and kind of tall and in good shape. I thought maybe he was a cop."

"He could walk?" I asked, visions of Burly betraying me, of him somehow knowing about Tonya and their son together flooding through me irrationally.

The woman stared at me like I was wearing a tank top in a snow storm. "Could he *walk?*" she repeated.

"Never mind. When did you see him?"

"Right before Tonya left school."

"Can you tell me about that?" I asked. "Why did she leave school? Did you know she was going to or did she just disappear?"

The woman shrugged. "A little bit of both." She stared at me again, trying to decide if she liked me or not. But I've learned that when people size me up like that, they usually come down on the side of liking me, because, up close, I look like them: like someone who's never caught a break in her life, like someone who is always barely one step ahead of the landlord and maybe even the law.

"Look," she said after a moment. "I'll be honest with you. We were good friends our first semester. We shared an apartment with four other women, and we all liked each other, but when we came back after the semester break…" she hesitated. "I think maybe Tonya started selling drugs and I wasn't the only one living there who thought that."

"You said there was no way she'd have died from drugs."

"I didn't say she was doing them, I said I thought she was selling them. Pills. I found a lot of them once, she left them in the bathroom in a bag, and she was getting a lot of people calling her day and night. I'd see her meeting people I didn't know for just a couple of minutes at a time. And she had a lot of cash on her, a lot of cash. So I figured it out pretty quick. I've been there. I grew up on the south side of Greensboro. I know what's going on. And I didn't like it. I was getting ready to call her on it and make her move out when she disappeared."

"Disappeared?"

"Pretty much. That boyfriend of hers started showing up more and more her second semester. I didn't like it. Tonya was different around him. Quiet."

"What was his name?"

She shook her head. "I don't know. Larry, Leonard. Something like that. He never stayed at the apartment. He'd come by, she'd leave with him. She'd come back a few days later, quieter than ever. Not saying much. She'd make up time she missed out of class and go from there, until the next time he showed up. I didn't like him, so I stayed away from him."

"And she was with him when she disappeared?"

"I don't think so," the woman said. "I had a couple of roommates, they graduated last year, who were there when she left for the last time. It was about a month before the end of the semester. They said two guys came to get her in a silver car, you know, like an official state car. They figured they were cops. Tonya packed up her things and left with them. Didn't leave a note or anything. Never called. I owed her money, too. But I never heard from her again."

"No one knew where she'd gone?" I asked.

The woman shook her head and her beads clacked to silence as she thought. "A rumor went around she'd been arrested. I figured it was probably true. I was one of the few people who knew she'd served time and that she had hated it. That was why I was surprised when it looked like she was back to dealing drugs. I just figured she'd violated her parole or something. That she'd been caught selling and that was it. She was going back in."

“She wasn’t on parole,” I said. “I’ve seen her official records. Tonya had competed her parole by the time she enrolled here.”

“Then I don’t know what to tell you,” the woman said. “One of my roommates said the men who came to get Tonya had on jackets with something about Silver Top Detention Center printed on them in the front and big initials on the back. I remember because we couldn’t believe those guys were dumb enough to walk around with jackets that had ‘STD’ on the back of them in big letters. I thought maybe they were parole officers or something.”

“Silver Top?” I knew the name from the records Marcus had given me. “That was where Tonya did most of her time. It’s in the mountains.”

The woman shrugged. “Maybe they sent her back there?”

It didn’t make sense. There were no records indicating Tonya had been sent back to jail anywhere. I sighed and I guess I sounded as frustrated as I felt. The woman shot me a look of sympathy before she stood up.

“I got a class in five minutes,” she said apologetically. “I’m sorry I couldn’t be of more help.”

“You helped,” I assured her. “Believe me, you helped.”

“Listen,” she said. “When you find her son, will you do me a favor?”

“Sure.”

“You tell him that his mother was a good woman and a smart woman, that she was working hard to make something out of her life. I always wondered why she was working so hard, why she studied so many hours, what was driving her, you know?”

I nodded.

“Now I know. She was doing it for him. Will you let him know that?”

“Yes,” I promised. “When I find him, I’ll let him know.”

I hoped it was a promise I could keep.

* * *

MARCUS WAS MORTALLY OFFENDED when I implied his search of official records had been lax.

"I do not make mistakes," he snapped, his voice rising like it always does when his pride has been wounded. "I practically wrote the code for the reporting system. If my data says Tonya Blackburn completed her parole two years ago, then the woman completed her parole two years ago."

"Her roommate says some guys who looked official came in without warning and dragged her away."

"Perhaps you should be poking around Guantanamo Bay?"

"Very funny. Are you sure you didn't miss something?"

"Look," he said archly. "I'm just going to pretend that you are unaware of my stellar reputation for thoroughness. And I am just going to explain that if Tonya Blackburn was taken into custody for any reason, there would be a record of it. Even if it was just for questioning and she was later released. Gone are the days of gunny sacks over people's heads and us black folk disappearing in the night." He hesitated. "At least in most parts of the state."

"Maybe those guys were renegades?" I suggested.

"Well, obviously they were renegades, Miss Casey," Marcus said, slathering on the sarcasm like cream cheese on a bagel. "I suggest you get your big old butt up to Silver Top Detention Center and find out what's going on."

"Oh, god, you're right," I said. "Why didn't I think of that?"

"Because you need to get laid properly. Your blood is congealing somewhere a lot further south than your brain." He hung up without waiting for my reaction. I wasn't done paying for doubting him, I knew.

My next call was to Bobby D. For someone who was as big as Jabba the Hut, the man was a master at blending in. He'd be the perfect cover when I went up to the mountains and poked around.

Plus he had a cooler head about this case than I did — when I'd told him about Burly being Trey's father, he'd just laughed at how smart Corndog Sally had been to hook me in the way she did. He said I had no right to feel betrayed, that I wasn't the one who had lost a daughter and was in danger of losing a grandson.

He was right, of course.

So I asked him to go with me to the mountains. When I explained where I was going and why, there was a long silence. I heard the sound of cellophane being torn off a Little Debbie snack cake — Bobby was addicted to them and ate them like other people ate pretzels.

"Well?" I asked, before his mouth became too full to answer. "You in?"

"You want me to pose as your father?" he asked dubiously. "Why not your boyfriend?"

"Because I have a finely-tuned gag reflex, that's why."

"I suppose you're right. No one would believe a man of my refinement would have a girlfriend like you."

"But a trashy daughter is so much easier to explain?" I asked dubiously.

"Certainly. I'll just say you went wrong in your teens. Every parent on the planet will believe that one. No further explanation needed." He was silent and I could practically hear the wheels turning in his head. He loved going undercover and inventing new histories for himself. God knows what he'd turn up posing as. Once he had actually tried to palm himself off as a former wrestler. Just the thought of Bobby D. in latex had made it hard for me to keep a straight face. But we needed to be grounded in reality to pull this one off. We'd be dealing with law enforcement, and they'd be tougher to fool. I'd have to rein in his fantasies.

Bobby was chewing as he considered the situation. It sounded like some small wet animal was crawling through the phone wires toward me. "I suppose I could swing a few nights. I've been hearing about a bed-and-breakfast up that way I want to check out."

"We're not staying at a bed-and-breakfast," I told him. "They're just an excuse for crappy bathrooms and nosey proprietors. You have to talk to all the other guests or everyone else thinks you're snooty. I'm not doing it."

"You think you have a choice? We're talking about Bartow County, darlin'. There are no hotels. There are no motels. We'll be lucky to find a place with indoor plumbing. It's this joint or camping."

The thought of sharing a tent with Bobby D. or, even more horrifying, a cramped trailer, gave me a whole new perspective on the downside of bed-and-breakfast living. "Fine. You make the reservations. I'll bring cream puffs from *Guglhuphf's* for the ride."

"Bring a couple dozen," he suggested. "It's a five-hour drive from Durham."

"Sure two dozen will be enough?" I asked sarcastically, but when his silence told me he was actually doing the math, I hung up and started to pack. I wasn't sure why I was headed up to the mountains. I only knew I had to keep moving or die.

* * *

WE PASSED THE TIME to the mountains quickly, fighting over who got the next cream puff while we tooled along in Bobby D.'s vintage Cadillac, and reviewed our cover story for who we were and why we were there.

Yes, I had wanted us to stick close to the truth — but he hadn't exactly gone out on a limb, so far as I was concerned. He was going to retain his own name, under the theory that no one knew who he was or would give a rat's ass if they did, although I suspected it was more because that was the name on the American Express Platinum card that his rich girlfriend had given him. He was going to be a highly successful lawyer on a trip to the mountains to bird watch and to console his dear daughter, whose husband had recently left her for a younger piece of trailer trash. My name was to be Debbie Little, in honor of his favorite junk food brand.

"What's wrong with that?" he demanded when he noticed me pouting.

"There was a time when I would have been the younger piece of trailer trash," I pointed out.

"Sorry, babe, but we're all getting older."

"Don't you think 'Debbie Little' is a little obvious, what with you pulling out Little Debbie cakes every five minutes and eating them like peanuts?"

"It'll help me remember your name," he said. "Frankly, I think it's genius."

For him, it probably was. "How desolate am I supposed to be?" I asked.

"Desolate enough to want to spend a lot of time alone."

"I like that part of the cover," I admitted. "I can ditch you at will."

"Absolutely. Besides," he added mysteriously, "I've got my own little project up my sleeve."

"You did not bring that thing along," I said. "Please tell me there is not a six-foot fiberglass hot dog in our trunk."

"You bet there is," Bobby said cheerfully. "At this very moment, you are riding with the biggest wiener in all of North Carolina."

"I'll say I am," I mumbled, but Bobby didn't hear me. He was too busy eating the last cream puff.

* * *

WE REACHED SILVER MOUNTAIN in late afternoon, just as the sun was setting behind the tops of trees that were just starting to display the vibrant yellows, reds and oranges that would soon bring thousands of tourists flocking down from the North to clog our mountain turnpikes and triple the prices on accommodations. It was a migration so reliable it put those Capistrano sparrows to shame. Thank god that chaos was still weeks away.

The road was steep and precariously narrow, especially for a land boat like Bobby's. But its engine could have powered a cruise ship, and Bobby steered it around the looping turns with practiced ease, taking turns licking the last of the cream filling off his fingers every time he hit a patch of straight-away.

We were heading for the Pampered Princess Lodge, which, from its Internet photos, looked to be a massive faux log cabin monstrosity jammed into the side of Silver Mountain. Fortunately, high season was a good two weeks away and Bobby had not only been able to book adjoining rooms there, he'd been able to book them for a week without mortgaging his condo. Burly was footing the tab and would reimburse us without question, which was a damn sight better than billing Corndog Sally for the digs, but I was not about to be beholden to Burly for more than I had to. I wanted to end this episode in our lives with him owing me, not vice versa.

By the time we reached the bed-and-breakfast, the sun had disappeared behind a distant peak, the air had cooled and a half dozen deer had gathered at the edge of the adjoining forest to watch us unpack the car. Those deer made me nervous. The lodge's website had promised that the *"deer would browse at you from only a few feet away,"* which, frankly, sounded vaguely menacing.

"Leave that thing in the trunk," I ordered Bobby when he started to hoist the giant hot dog on his back. "You'll freak out the deer and, frankly, they look angry enough as it is." In truth, the deer had not so much as twitched since we'd arrived, but Bobby was a city slicker and I was willing to do anything to keep that hot dog under wraps.

Fortunately, Bobby's idea of wildlife was the oversized ceramic rabbit he kept in his front yard, even though someone had shot its right ear off years ago, then planted a bullet right through the center of its mouth, leaving it with an expression of perpetual dismay. So he took me at my word that the deer were dangerously excitable and put the giant hot dog back in his trunk. "It would be hard to explain to the other guests anyway," he conceded.

"Plus then they'd all want one for their own," I pointed out.

He missed my sarcasm.

We surveyed the massive, sprawling log structure together. The Pampered Princess Lodge was only two stories high, but it spread across the rocky terrain in a series of different levels that made you think of fairy enclaves in science fiction worlds. Behind it, to the right, a wide path led to a meadow that stretched upward, then leveled off and disappeared into the dusk.

"I think there's a spot up there where I can run my experiments in private," Bobby said. "It might be best to remain discreet so no one can steal my idea."

"Whatever you say, Sherlock." I hoisted my backpack up on one shoulder and grabbed one of Bobby's four suitcases. Bobby never did anything lightly, most especially packing.

"Remember," he reminded me, "Your name is 'Debbie Little' and your husband left you for a younger girlfriend who is having his baby. And just to make you even more sympathetic, I'm thinking of shipping your husband out to Iraq in a month."

"Please do," I agreed. "I hate him for what he's done to me."

Whatever charm the bed-and-breakfast offered on the outside was killed by the interior. A Laura Ashley bomb had gone off, saturating the premises with floral patterns that clamored and fought for attention. It was like being trapped in a florist shop while on Ecstasy. I didn't know whether to run screaming for the car, rent a bee suit or join the Junior League right then and there.

As far as I could see, the entire lodge was filled with floral drapes, floral carpet, floral upholstery, a big honking floral dress on a big honking proprietress and, in a shocking departure from the theme, huge floral paintings. Not the good kind that remind you of head-sized hooha's, either, but giant daisies that looked like they ought to be in the lapel of a giant clown.

"Welcome, welcome, welcome!" cried a mountain of purple and pink flowers topped with a swirl of orange hair. "I'm Bunny Rogers and this is my humble abode. You must be Debbie." She turned her, well, florid, face on me and honed in like a heat-seeking bosom missile. "You poor thing." Her voice dropped so that only the entire first floor could hear instead of all twenty-four rooms. "Your father told me about your troubles. Men can be such *beasts.* Throwing us away for younger models like we were garbage. You can forget them here, honey. Here, you will be our princess and we will pamper your cares away."

I'd been planning to drink them away, but if she wanted to pamper me, who was I to argue?

"Cool," I said. "Where's the bar?"

Bunny looked confused. "No bar, dear. Although I suppose there is sort of a speakeasy down the road a few miles. It's a little dicey, if you know what I mean." Her face brightened. "We do offer complimentary blush chardonnay each evening for Happy Hour. Come five o'clock, this is the happiest house on Silver Mountain!" She meant her laugh as tinkling, but I suspect it sent any lingering deer leaping deep into the forest, convinced that a tribe of drunken hunters was heading their way.

"Allow me," Bobby said smoothly, intervening before I sunk to a level too trashy even for his cover story. "I am charmed to meet you." He bent over and actually kissed Bunny's plump little hand, a gesture that inspired a strange fluttering sound from her. I think it was an attempt at cooing, but it sounded more like the engine of a Plymouth Rambler trying to start.

As Bobby and Bunny flirted, I looked around for a floral vase to hurl in. I saw only a huge door leading down a short hallway. It was good enough for an emergency escape.

Bunny saw me looking. "I see you've noticed the delicious odors coming from our dining room," she cried, grabbing my elbow and propelling me down the hallway. "You must say hello to our other guests."

Oh, crap. Before I could stop her, I was thrust through a massive doorway and pinned in the eyes of perhaps a half dozen couples and several trios of old ladies. Mouths stopped chewing, forks froze, eyebrows rose as Bunny dragged me into the room as if I were a scullery maid who'd been caught boffing the stable boy on the mistress's dining room table.

"Hi," I said weakly, looking around the room at my audience. Average age: sixty-two. Favorite fabric: khaki. Favorite designer: L.L. Bean. Most popular hair color: Clairol 106B. Median attitude: annoyed at being interrupted while stuffing face, but intrigued by the possibility of fresh meat.

"We have two new guests for the week," Bunny announced grandly. "And this is their very first time at the Pampered Princess. As regulars, I hope you will make them feel welcome."

I smelled a ritual sacrifice coming and made a hasty escape, mumbling about freshening up and backing out of the room. But Bobby had my back. He waded goodnaturedly into the dining room, commandeered a table and was already busy making friends as I fled upstairs.

I changed my clothes and made a hasty retreat onto the front porch, where I promptly tripped over a mop someone had stupidly left in the middle of the doorway. As I went sprawling on my ass, the mop stood up, ambled over and began licking my face. Ugh. It was a dog. One of those yappy little dogs with so much hair you can't tell if it is coming or going. Plus this one's breath smelled like tuna. He'd been raiding a cat bowl somewhere, and if I knew my Bunny types, there were a dozen cat bowls to choose from.

"Get off me," I said and the dog retreated under a rocking chair, either mooning me or giving me the evil eye — it was impossible to tell which.

A Fed Ex truck had been lumbering up the crest and turned into the drive-way just in time to witness my fall from grace. The driver hopped out and helped me to my feet. "You okay?" he asked.

"Depends on how you define okay," I mumbled.

He laughed and headed into a side door to the left of the main entrance. When he came back out, holding a package under his arm, I was waiting in his passenger seat.

"Deliver me to the nearest bar," I begged.

"Overnight or standard two-day shipping?" he asked cheerfully. He was about fifty years old, portly, with thick grey hair and a brush mustache. Not your hunky Fed Ex man of sitcom fantasies, but at least he had a sense of humor.

"Whatever gets me there fastest," I said.

"Then hang on," he advised me as he ground the gears. The truck lurched into a wide circle and went barreling toward the winding mountain road. "I'll have you at the Dew Drop Inn within ten minutes. But don't get too excited. It's just a bar. The Princess is the only place to stay around these here parts. Like it nor not, you'll have to stay there. Though I understand the urge to escape. That Bunny has been crazy about flowers her whole life. Never saw her wear anything but flowers on her clothes from first grade on. If it gets to be too much for you, just give me a holler and I'll deliver you to the Dew Drop for a break."

"Have I ever told you that you're my hero?" I said as the truck rocked around a curve and I slid toward the open door. The driver reached out, snagged the edge of my shirt and dragged me back into place.

"Careful there," he said cheerfully. "You don't want to get swept away by the wind beneath my wings."

# Chapter Seven

"Whatcha got there, Noah?" a reed-thin old man with six teeth at most called out as the Fed Ex man gallantly delivered me right to a bar stool.

"Another refugee from the Pampered Princess," my savior said. "I think she's allergic to flowers." He picked up an outgoing package from the bartender, waved me a cheerful good-bye and headed out the door.

"Wow," I said. "He's efficient."

"That's Noah for you," the skinny old man said and cackled. He eyed me hopefully as his beer mug was empty.

"I'll take a shot of whatever you have that's closest to Jack Daniels," I told the bartender. "And you can give him another one on me."

The old man smiled his gummy thanks while I checked out the bartender. He was at least six feet six, with muscles that strained under his flannel shirt and a head of cascading wavy black hair just starting to turn gray. Imagine if Bigfoot had gone to bartender school and you'll get the picture.

"The closest I got to Jack Daniels is Jack Daniels," he said, setting down at least two fingers worth in front of me.

"Good enough for me." I downed it in two gulps and shuddered as the warmth flooded through me. Though all my clothes fit into a knapsack, I had brought way too much baggage up into the hills with me. I needed to lighten the load. I thought of Burly and Helen, living in domestic bliss. I thought of the promises I'd made to Corndog Sally that I'd find her grandson before she died. I thought of the sorry state of my love life. And I thought of how I was about to open up yet another wound to pick at with my next phone call.

"I'm going to step outside and use my cell phone," I explained to the bartender. "Need me to settle up first?"

"Naw." He stuck a toothpick in his mouth and parked a massive boot up on an empty wooden crate. "I'll just hunt you down and kill you if you skip out."

"I bet you just rake in the tips."

He grinned and pointed to the backdoor. "Reception's better out that way."

The mountains are iffy when it comes to cell phone service. Sometimes you can find a spot as clear as if you were standing next to the person you're talking to. At other times, the "No Signal" message will taunt you even as you kneel in the shadow of a transmitting tower, staring hopefully up at its girders.

The cellular gods were with me that night. I discovered a little clearing out back behind the bar, a few feet away from a towering pile of cordwood aging for the winter ahead. Evidently, the barman came out here for smokes on a regular basis. A tree stump had been leveled off for a stool and was encircled by a months-old ring of cigarette butts. I sat on the stump and stared up at the stars — there were millions dusted across the heavens, far more than you could ever see near the electric glow of an urban area. It took my breath away and it gave me courage. I took a deep breath and dialed.

"Yeah?" Bill Butler always just sort of growled into his cell phone when he answered. He had to carry one because he was a detective with the Raleigh Police Department and being off the grid was frowned upon. But he hated them and acted like you had personally pissed him off each time you called.

"It's me," I said. "Casey."

"Well, well, well," he answered in his Texas drawl. "And to what favor do I owe this honor?"

"Why can't I just call to say hello?" I protested.

He laughed. "Just tell me what you need, Moonbeam."

"I'm up in Bartow County, looking into the disappearance of a teenage boy. His mother was..." I hesitated. If Bill knew I'd had anything to do with Tonya Blackburn's death, even just finding her body, I'd probably get a lecture that didn't end until spring. "His mother was killed and now he's missing."

"And you think he's in Bartow County?" Bill said. "Because that's such a magnet for teenage run-aways?" His tone was beyond sarcastic. "You know, I'm not even a native of our great state, but even I could tell you that people run *away* from Bartow County, they don't run *to* it. It's what? The dirt-eating capital of the world? Soon to be the meth-running capital of the world? You are not even in Kansas anymore, Moonbeam. You are in hardcore Appalachia."

"I know," I said. "It sounds crazy, but I tracked the mother's movements before she died and supposedly she was sent to Silver Top Detention Center. Only no one can find any official record of that happening."

Unlike Marcus, Bill did not insist that this was impossible. He had not built the computer system, he used it, and had a very different perspective on it. "That's not good, Casey," Bill warned me. "For a lot of reasons. There are a lot of renegades with badges up there. I want you to watch your step."

"I will be careful. That's why I called. Can you find out about the sheriff here for me? Find out who he is? Maybe ask around and see if he's a stand-up guy?"

"In other words, you want to know if he's single?"

I laughed. "No. I want to know if he's honest. I might need his help with a case I'm working on. Trust me, I can find out if he's single on my own."

"You know, that's one thing I always admired about you, Casey. You've got a wild streak in you, but you draw the line at married men."

"What's that got to do with anything?" I asked.

"I am one now," Bill said.

"Oh." It caught me by surprise. I had been prepared to hear the voice of yet another good man I'd not been able to stick with, but I had not expected to learn that someone else had done what I could not do.

"Who?" I asked.

"It doesn't matter. She's a good woman. X-ray technician. Hot. Blonde."

"How old?" I asked sternly.

"Older than you."

"Really?" I admit, that made me feel a *little* bit better. "Congratulations?"

"That sounded like a question," Bill said.

"It was," I admitted. "I'm not good at this. I never thought of you as the marrying type." I hesitated. "I guess I kind of liked having the company."

"Well, I'm getting older and time makes me bolder," Bill said. "Don't make me sing it."

I laughed despite myself. "Call me back about the sheriff?"

"Will do," he promised. "I owe you."

"For what?" I said.

"Just for being you, Moonbeam. Just for being you."

Now I really needed a drink. I guess the bartender saw it in my face. Two more fingers of Jack waited for me at my seat.

"Thanks," I said. "You read my poor, rejected mind."

"Don't thank me." He nodded toward the end of the bar. "Thank him."

Maybe it was the three ounces of Jack I'd already slugged back. Maybe it was the thought of Burly and Helen together. Maybe it was learning that Bill Butler had gotten married and was forever out of my reach. Maybe it was the millions of stars that had soaked into my soul from above. Who knows? All I know is that when I looked at the stranger leaning against the far end of the bar, grinning at me, the world stopped revolving on its axis, the jukebox in the corner fell as mute as a tomb — and every cell in my body stood up and began to sing.

I smiled back at him and he unfolded into a string bean of a man plainly dressed in blue jeans and a freshly-ironed work shirt. Cleanliness really is next to godliness in a middle-aged man. He already had points in his favor. He stood up from his seat at the end of the bar and started walking slowly toward me.

It was the oddest thing. He was plain looking, at least from far away. Tall, not more than a few pounds of extra meat on his six foot frame, an ordinary nose on an ordinary face, brown hair cut a little shorter than I liked it and a smile that hovered around the edges of his mouth as he drew closer. But then he slid into the seat next to me and stared right into my eyes. No guile, no pretense, no nothing but poor curiosity. I felt my world shift beneath my feet. He had the bluest eyes I had ever seen — so dark they were nearly sapphire. His skin was tanned from being outdoors. He smelled like soap and not only did he have all of his teeth, they were as white as the stars above me had been. This is not to be underestimated in a mountain man. It is the icing on a very fine cake.

I've always had a thing for mountain men, but this one was not only the real thing, he was clean as a glacial stream. And I could tell from his eyes that he was also smarter than most.

The other men in the bar agreed: they evaporated away from me as he approached. Even the toothless old man managed to effortlessly make room and a stool magically opened up right beside me by the time he reached my seat. In fact, I realized, the entire room was tracking his approach. Even two men playing pool in a corner stopped to watch as he took a seat by me.

"Whoa," I thought. "I do believe I have just snagged the alpha male in town." Something deep inside me stirred to life. I reached for my drink.

"Thanks for the drink," I said, downing it in one long gulp. "I needed that."

"Bad news?" he asked and his voice was smoother than the Jack snaking its way down my throat and into my stomach and straight south to the parts of me that were gearing up to behave very irresponsibly indeed.

"In a way," I admitted. "I just found out my ex- got married."

"That's rough," he said sympathetically. "Been divorced long?"

"Oh, this was an ex-boyfriend, not an ex-husband. Though I've got one of those, too." That's right, Casey — make yourself sound good. Maybe I should tell him about that case of *chlamydia* while I was at it?

"I think you need another drink," he said sagely. "And you know what else? I think I need one, too."

He was barely done saying the words when the barman slid a highball glass of amber liquor his way.

"You must be a regular," I said.

He smiled like that was funny. "In a way," he admitted. "How about you? You are not from around here. I know everyone."

"I bet you do," I said and it came out sounding dirty. "I mean, it's not that big of a place."

"No, it is not." He cocked his head and looked at me carefully. "But you don't sound like you're even from North Carolina. I hear Alabama, or maybe Florida in your voice."

"You're good," I admitted, and the rubbery feel to my legs told me I better sip, and not gulp, the drink heading my way. "The Panhandle."

"A country girl," he said. "I could tell. You look strong."

I looked down at my body. "Is that a euphemism?" I asked. "Because I worked hard for these pounds."

"Not a euphemism," he said quickly. "I like a girl who doesn't disappear when she turns sideways."

"Do you? I'll drink to that." As I raised my glass, I realized that the whole room was still watching us. We clinked our glasses in a toast. "I guess you do know a lot of people here," I said. "People who like to know your business?"

He shrugged. "I'm a popular guy."

"What's your name?" I asked.

"Shep." He grinned. "Shep Gaines."

"You sound like an astronaut."

"Not even close." He had not taken those amazing eyes off me since he'd sat down next to me and if he kept it up, I was going to have to rip my clothes off right then and there and climb on top of him, whether the rest of the customers were minding his business for him or not.

"What's your name?" he asked, leaning so close I got another whiff of soap, which reminded me of the shower, which sent me off on a whole other fantasy.

"Debbie," I told him, almost forgetting my cover story and giving him my real name, which did not say a whole hell of a lot for my sobriety. But you know what? I'm human. I was down-trodden and tired. I was lonely. I was a little tipsy. I had gotten a few emotional kicks in the teeth that week and his eyes were just... amazing.

"I've got an idea," he said.

"Bring it on."

"Let's sit here and drink and be two completely new people. Let's tell each other only those things we'd want a stranger to know about us," he said. "We'll make ourselves sound irresistible. You go first. Tell me why I'm lucky I ran into you."

"It might take me a week to cover it all," I warned him.

"Bring it on," he said with a grin.

* * *

I CAN'T PRETEND TO UNDERSTAND why these things happen, or why the rules of time and space seem to bend when you discover someone you are connected to, and someone throws a couple bottles of hootch into the mix, and there are winding roads and DUI's to consider, and all of a sudden you realize there's a clean well-lighted place just a few steps away. All I can tell you is that three hours later, I found myself in a little cabin on the edge of a bluff a few hundred yards up the road from the Dew Drop Inn, with my clothes hitting the floor and his clothes hitting the chair, and a fire sputtering to life in a fireplace and a dog well-bred enough to stay sleeping by it while the humans wrestled and laughed and cried out on the bed a few feet away in the dark.

I didn't know if I had wandered into Twin Peaks or would wake up next to the reincarnation of Davy Crockett, but I do know that the man had the kind of body that had felled whole states full of trees in the olden days and could bring me to my knees. Repeatedly.

Within two minutes, I had forgotten all about lost love. Within an hour, I was laughing like I had not laughed in over a year. Within two more hours, I was so hungry I ate three bowls of

Fruit Loops by the fire and then shared my milk with his dog so I could get back to bed where my mountain man waited for me in the dark, grinning that crooked smile of his and matching me move for move. And by the end of four more hours, I was well and truly in lust, if not love, and planned to never return to the real world again. I had never encountered such a cheerfully carnal man before, nor one so considerate and skilled. His ordinary exterior concealed an extraordinary maleness and an appreciation for the female body that made me feel like a queen. No, I would not leave his realm. I would stay by his side and carve little doll faces out of apples for the tourists. I would wrap myself in nothing but cellophane and greet him each night at the door with a martini in hand before leading him to his nice hot supper. It would be so worth it if we could spend our nights like this one. Why, the days — and how we spent *them* — would hardly matter.

But then, inevitably, before I wanted it to, the sun was coming up over Silver Mountain and I woke to the sensation of soft nibbling at my ear. I raised my head groggily, realized the love licks came the well-bred collie that had shared my milk and cereal just hours before and guessed that even the most perfect dog has to take a pee sometimes. What the hell — I'd let my new furry friend out. His owner had earned the right to sleep in.

I stumbled from bed and stumbled to the door to let the dog out. Our presence surprised a deer bounding across the front yard. Both animals froze, looking at each other warily, then, as if some sort of tacit agreement had been silently reached, each dropped its eyes and wandered nonchalantly away as if they had never spotted one another in the first place.

Lassie, as I had taken to thinking of the dog in a burst of originality, took the longest pee ever witnessed by mankind — I swear to god, it must have had an auxiliary bladder stuffed under all that fur somewhere — before it sauntered happily back to the cabin steps. I gave it a few scratches behind the ears, and it sniffed my crotch in return and followed me back inside.

That was when I saw the badge.

I could have seen it the night before. I should have seen it the night before. It was right there, pinned just above the pocket of a dark blue uniform shirt hanging on the outside of the closet door, the metal twinkling away in the morning light that filtered through the cracks in the curtains. Five happy star points, as gold as Marcus's left front tooth.

I had just ravished the sheriff of Bartow County and vice versa. Over and over again, to be precise.

What the everloving hell had I done?

I pulled a chair up to the edge of the bed and sat on it naked, staring at the man sleeping soundly in front of me.

*What the hell had I just done?*

Without so much as a flicker of warning, his eyes flew open and he stared back at me, not moving a muscle, his voice as clear as if it were mid-day.

"Is there a rabbit boiling on the stove?" he asked. "Because you're making me just a little bit nervous sitting there like that."

He did not look unappreciative, mind you, of my nakedness, but I was not letting him off that easily.

"Why didn't you tell me you were the sheriff?" I demanded.

"You didn't ask," he said. "And not to piss you off or anything, but it wasn't like I could get much of a word in anyway."

I hit him with a pillow and he groaned and covered his face with the quilt. "I would have told you. What difference does it make?" He peeked out from under the covers. "Sheriffs are people, too, you know."

I had to laugh despite myself. "I hate you. You tricked me."

"I did not." He sat up indignantly, letting the quilt fall away from his amazing shoulders. "I didn't hide anything."

"But you weren't exactly forthcoming about it."

"You have a problem with sheriffs?" he asked.

"Of course not. I've slept with dozens of them."

"Have you now?" He stared at me, smile hovering. "Is that supposed to make me feel better?"

"Oh, shut up," I said. "And move over. I've earned a few more hours sleep."

He laughed and made room for me in his bed. "Get in here and I'll give you a proper frisking."

* * *

TALK ABOUT YOUR WALK OF SHAME: I arrived back at the Pampered Princess just in time to meet a dozen other guests coming out of the dining room. Somehow they just knew, although the state of my hair, the lack of make-up, the pair of panties sticking out of my back pocket and the fact that I was wearing the clothes I'd had on the night before may have given me away.

Half the men grinned at me, the other half looked frightened, and all the women gave me the bug eye, flaring their nostrils like they could smell the sex on me. Which, come to think of it…

Bobby D. played his part. "Debbie!" he cried, sailing out of the crowd with such fatherly affection he sent three women flying like bowling pins. "Have you been sobbing on a mountain top all night long?"

"I'm so sorry, daddy. I hope I didn't ruin your appetite."

The snickers running through the crowd told me that he'd not been shy about the homemade apple corn cakes and syrup.

"Where have you been, my child?" He grabbed me by my elbow and steered me toward the stairs with surprising agility. "Keep moving," he mumbled grimly, then marched me upstairs as if I really was his daughter and had just returned from boinking the local basketball team.

"Ouch," I complained once we were alone in my bedroom. "You didn't have to play it quite that hard."

"Yes, I did. Look in the mirror."

I parted the jungle of fake flowers that blocked my view and leaned closer to the dresser mirror. A trail of hickies led across the top of my right shoulder and up my neck. Good god, I hadn't had a hickie since seventh grade. "That little vampire," I complained. "I don't remember getting these."

"You were probably too busy getting those," Bobby pointed out.

I checked my left side. Three parallel scratches started at the base of my neck and disappeared under the left shoulder of my tee shirt.

"That man is a cougar," I declared.

"Don't sound so self-satisfied," Bobby D. advised me as he threw himself down on my bed and groaned. The mattress buckled in the middle like a coyote had dropped an anvil on it from a canyon wall a mile above. "I really was worried about you. Where the hell did you go all night? Or, more accurately, who the hell did you do all night?"

"It's a long story," I admitted. "Full of lurid details. But to make a long story short, I've been establishing a relationship with the local law enforcement — "

"Oh, no," Bobby interrupted. "Don't tell me you slept with another deputy? When are you going to learn?"

"The *sheriff,*" I said indignantly. "I slept with the sheriff."

Bobby threw himself back on the bed dramatically, his arms outstretched. "Just so you know, I will not accept any foundlings left on my doorstep in a basket in nine months hence."

"I wouldn't dream of it," I retorted. "I'm too afraid that you'd eat it."

"What do we do now?" he asked. "I like this place. The grub is fantastic. But you're going to get us run out, tarred and feathered, for your slutty behavior."

"They should be so lucky," I said, troweling foundation over my hickies. It looked like I'd had skin harvested from my ass and grafted onto my neck, but it would have to do.

My cell phone rang and I saw it was Bill Butler calling me back. I answered with a cheerfulness light years beyond my mood when we'd last spoke.

"Yes?" I asked, drawing it out.

"The sheriff's name is Shep Gaines and he's a stand-up guy."

I started to laugh.

"What's so funny?" Bill demanded.

"Nothing," I said happily. "Thanks for the update. Let's talk soon."

I hung up and started to laugh again. Stand-up guy indeed. The man stood up more than anyone I'd met yet in this lifetime.

"You seem way too happy," Bobby complained. "This does not bode well for the case."

I set my make-up down and glared at him. "First you complain I need to get properly laid and then, when I do, you complain because I have?"

"I'm only saying that when you get too happy, you sort of lose your edge and maybe aren't as driven as you should be."

"So the trick would be to only get laid occasionally, or to get laid badly?"

"The trick," Bobby intoned sleepily, and I realized the fat bastard was planning a post-breakfast nap on my bed, "is to not forget about the case and why we're here in the first place."

The remark stung. Because it was true. I'd not really thought of Tonya or her missing son since the night before. Bobby was right. I needed to get my ass in gear. But where to start? I couldn't flash photos of Tonya around the mountain and ask if she'd blown through town, perhaps as an escaped prisoner? This place was too small; the bad guys, whoever they might be, would be tipped off immediately. I needed a more subtle approach.

About the only thing I had to go on was the postcard I'd found among Trey Blackburn's packet of carefully saved mementos, the one Tonya had sent to her son from the mountains. Maybe it had been sent from around here? If so, it would tell me one thing: there was something fishy going on up at Silver Top Detention Center. I knew she'd been taken from Piedmont Technical by men wearing official STD jackets. And she'd gone with them reluctantly. But if she'd been taken into custody, there would not have been a postcard. Guards don't stop to let prisoners send postcards to their loved ones. No way. And I could think of no legitimate reason why she'd be hanging out with her former guards around this mountain.

Maybe it was just a postcard — but it could tell me a lot.

I fished Bobby's car keys out of his pants pocket. He had started to snore and barely stirred. Then I retrieved the postcard and examined it under the lamp. If it had been sent from somewhere around here, I could at least confirm Tonya had been staying nearby. There couldn't be that many places that sold postcards in this godforsaken place. I'd snoop around and see what I found.

I started with the rack on the check-in counter at the Pampered Princess. While the rack held an assortment of tacky postcards, most featuring vistas of wildflowers and autumn colors not seen since Chernobyl, it did not hold the postcard I sought.

I slid out the front door, evading the stares of the other guests. It was not going to be easy sneaking around. Every move I made from here on out would be watched and discussed *ad nauseum* over the cheap blush wine they served each Happy Hour. I hoped my tumble in the hay would turn out to be worth it.

I had a sudden and vivid flashback to the night before and decided it was.

There was a tourist trap half a mile up the road, but the only postcards it offered were emblazoned with religious slogans and paintings of a modern-looking Jesus beaming out at the buyer with benign confidence. Tonya had not bought her postcard there. I tried another shop without luck as well, stumbling into a den of calico and wicker so thoroughly poisoned by the stench of potpourri that I could barely breath. I tripped over a ceramic goose while making a desperate escape.

I went back down the mountain, knowing there weren't that many more places left to check. And if Tonya hadn't been on this mountain, then where the hell had she been?

I wasn't as confident as Bobby when it came to steering along the narrow mountain road so I proceeded at a cautious pace, which was probably why I saw what I had missed on the way up the mountain: the road to Silver Top Detention Center. On a whim, I turned in, figuring I would get a quick peek at the place. The single paved lane led down a few hundred feet before ending in a vast asphalt parking lot that bordered an enclave as out of place on Silver Mountain as a space station would have been in Middle Earth. The structure was massive, stretching out on either side of the parking lot in twin concrete fortresses, linked by a fenced walkway and central guardhouse. There were exercise areas on either side, but only a small corner of each faced the parking lot. The rest curved toward the back of the facility, facing the slope of the mountain. All I could see was what seemed like miles of yellowish concrete and barred windows no bigger than portholes. I tried to imagine who lived within this godforsaken place. It was hard to believe that human beings moved back and forth inside there each day, eating and sleeping, hoping and despairing, caught in the most manmade of hells while, just a few feet away, outside the chain-link fence topped with barbed wire that rimmed the perimeter, nature exploded in all its glory, stretching for miles and miles.

I saw a flutter of white at one of the window. I had been spotted. A prisoner was signaling to me, driven by the need to prove to someone, anyone, that they existed.

I wondered if it was a man or a woman. I could not tell which side of the prison housed which. I only knew it housed both — Silver Top represented equal opportunity hopelessness.

I waved back, wishing my unseen friend well, then returned to Bobby's car and fled. I had spent eighteen long months behind similar walls and I never wanted to go back. Just seeing the prison made me want to turn around and head home to Durham.

In fact, by the time I reached the small convenience store that marked the midpoint of Silver Mountain and was the only place to get gas for miles, I had about decided to forget the whole thing. What was the point of poking around a mountain trying to retrace Tonya's last steps? What made me think that might lead me to her missing son, Trey?

But as often happens during an investigation, I was sent a sign at the very moment my feet were ready to turn me around and take me back home: there, in a dusty black iron rack crammed between a display of wild honey and basic hardware, a row of postcards gleamed beneath an overhead light. They were definitely printed by the same company as the postcard I had in my back pocket. The colors, the size, the lettering, the sentiments, all plucked straight from the seventies. I glanced up to see if I was being watched. An old man sat on a stool behind the counter, a toothpick dangling from his mouth. He was dressed in overalls and his John Deere hat was pushed back on his head so he could see the overhead TV as it flickered images of a NASCAR race: cars zoomed in endless circles, incomprehensible to me, despite my Panhandle pedigree, but fascinating to him. There were no other customers in the store, which was crammed with every provision known to man. Clearly, this was where the locals and visiting hunters stopped when they'd forgotten something from the Food Lion or Home Depot at the base of the mountain, or where vacationers stopped to snap photos and congratulate themselves on discovering a genuine mountain store off the beaten path.

This was also where Tonya Blackburn had bought, written and mailed a postcard to her son six months ago. There, above a rack of mountain sunsets stored ten postcards deep, I saw the exact same scene I had in my back pocket. There was no doubt about it.

I grabbed a can of stand-ups from the shelf and a grape Nehi so I'd have an excuse to approach the counter.

"Don't see many women buying Vienna sausages," the old man said, stretching out the first vowel in "Vienna" so it sounded like a long "i".

"They probably don't like to be reminded of their short-comings," I said, but the old guy didn't get the joke.

"Most of them are too busy watching their calories, I expect," he said. *Was he actually staring at my ass, the old coot?*

"I have a craving for them," I lied. In truth, they were disgusting, but I figured I could feed them to the odious little dog at the Pampered Princess next time it annoyed me and, with any luck, it would die of gout right then and there.

"Maybe you're pregnant?" the old man drawled, then broke into a cackling laugh. I had an uneasy feeling that perhaps the entire town already knew I'd spent the night in a cabin letting the local sheriff frisk me.

"No chance of that," I assured him.

"Why not?" he asked as he wiped my bottle of grape soda down, something I had hoped would not be necessary, but perhaps he knew something I didn't know. "You one of them lesbians? We had a couple come by last season, wanted to go out hunting. Had shotguns bigger than a cannon."

"Yes, well," I explained, "there's a reason for that. It's the same reason men like to carry guns. It's called overcompensation."

"No one's getting compensated for hunting around here," he assured me. "People are lucky if they can bring back a four-pointer in high season. The times they are a'changing. The world is moving on without me."

I thought it was pretty poetic of the old dude to put it that way. It made me feel like I could risk asking him a few questions.

"Look," I explained. "I'm trying to find an old friend. She's disappeared. She wrote me from here." I showed him the postcard I had in my back pocket and he peered at it with milky eyes.

"Like to be," he agreed. "Them's one of mine. Bought a carton back in 1970 from a distributor who went out of business about the time those damn hippies made Nixon resign, so I was stuck with 'em. I sell maybe three a season and that's with me offering to mail them right from here."

"Do you remember anyone buying one this year?" I asked hopefully.

He stared at me a little more closely. "Who did you say you were?"

"I didn't," I admitted, trying for cheerful.

"That's right, you didn't." He bagged my purchases and handed them over. "That'll be a dollar and sixty-eight cents total. Vienna's are on special on account of the expiration date on 'em has passed."

I handed him a couple of bucks. "Would it make a difference if I told you my friend was black?" I asked.

*"Black?"* He sounded incredulous. "Why didn't you tell me that in the first place? Imagine, an actual Negro in these hills."

When he didn't go on, I realized he was being sarcastic. I'd sort of hoped we were at a high enough altitude to render such an attitude unpopular, but the mountains had changed on me, too.

"You have a nice day," he added as I headed for the door.

"You, too," I said through gritted teeth. God, but I hated being outsmarted. All I'd accomplished was to give myself away. The whole mountain would know I was looking for Tonya now. I was seriously off my game.

# Chapter Eight

I considered changing into a skirt before afternoon tea, since the brochure on my nightstand touted a ceremony so elaborate it implied Prince Charles himself might serve it, but the waistband was too tight so I nixed it. I was hungry, having missed my lunch, and planned to cram as many of those little tea sandwiches in my craw as I could in the shortest possible time. And why not? The other guests already thought I was a slut. I may as well be thought of as a pig, too.

Fortunately, the door between my room and Bobby's had been left unlocked and I was able to snag a Little Debbie zebra cake from the suitcase he'd devoted to snacks from home. It would hold me another fifteen minutes. I sat on the edge of my bed and contemplated my next move. I could pack it in and start off in another direction. I could try and shake Shep down for info on Silver Top Detention Center. Or I could keep poking around, talking to folks about the prison and, sooner or later, I'd run into someone who worked there and might have known Tonya Blackburn. There could be few other employers in Bartow County.

The only thing was, if you wanted to find off-duty prison guards, the best place to look was a bar — and the last time I'd walked into a bar, I had come mighty close to compromising my investigation in the course of assuming a number of highly compromising positions.

Plus my little escapade with Sheriff Shep was still getting me into trouble — when I headed downstairs in search of high tea, he was waiting for me. He was in full-blown sheriff's gear, too, his tailored tan slacks and matching shirt fitting him like they had been sewed on to his body. *Oh my god.* I wanted to rip his uniform into khaki shreds and claim him right then and there. It would be a Happy Hour the Pampered Princess would never forget.

Shep stood when he saw me coming and took off his hat.

I started to kiss him, but he gave me a look that froze me in my tracks. "Are you nuts?" he mumbled. "I can't be seen picking up tourists."

"I'm not a tourist," I mumbled back.

"I know that now," he said. "We need to talk."

"Fine." I turned my back on our nosy audience, which was threatening to explode out through the sitting room doorway and into the hall, where it would no doubt take ten cranes and a squadron of roustabouts to get them all upright again. "Do you want to handcuff me?" I asked hopefully.

He grinned. "Certainly. But not here. And not for the reasons you think."

I was reassured he could joke. I was reassured he still wanted me. I was ready to be a fool for love yet again.

"Miss Little," he announced loudly for the benefit of our audience. "I must speak with you at once." God, but he was a terrible actor — another point in his favor.

"It wasn't me, officer. I've been here the whole time," I said dramatically. "Just ask them." I pointed at a dozen guilty faces. As the other lodge guests attempted to duck back inside, they succeeded in merely jamming themselves more firmly in the doorway, looking panicked.

"Let's talk outside," Shep suggested pleasantly.

He was smiling, but I could tell it was costing him effort. My feelings of lust evaporated as my gut told me something was wrong. Fortunately, my brain told me to do something about it.

"I'll be right back," I said. "I need to get a sweater."

I didn't really want my sweater, but it had pockets and what I really needed would fit into one of them. I grabbed what I needed from my bedroom and raced back downstairs. Shep was still grinning pleasantly when I rejoined him, but his smile faded the moment we reached the front porch and were alone.

"Who are you really?" he asked as we headed up a path toward the meadow behind the inn. "Why are you here in my county?"

That old man in the country store had ratted me out.

What to do now? I could tell Shep the truth and — if he was part of whatever trouble Tonya Blackburn had been in — tip my hand. Or I could lie to him again and he'd know it soon enough and then he'd never, ever trust me again. I had a feeling that he'd not give me another chance to come clean.

I decided to do something very uncharacteristic. Praying that Bill Butler had been right and Shep Gaines really was a stand-up guy, I told him the truth. I told him my real name, and what I did for a living, and all about Corndog Sally, and Tonya's death, and how Trey was missing and I wanted to find him to bring him back to his family. I told him all I had to go on was a postcard sent from a store in his county and some witnesses who had seen men from Silver Top Detention Center put Tonya into a car a little over half a year ago. The only thing I left was out was that I'd discovered Tonya's body — I was too ashamed to admit I'd just left her there.

He let me talk and didn't say a word, but he didn't try to talk me out of my belief that she'd been taken back to Silver Top, off-the-record, either. In fact, he didn't even seem surprised.

"You're sure she was here?" was all he said when I was done.

I nodded. We'd found a boulder with a flat surface and were sitting side-by-side, staring into the adjoining forest. The sun had dropped lower in the sky and the air was cool. Winter was definitely coming.

"I can't figure it out exactly," I admitted. "All I know is that she served some time at Silver Top. But that was a couple years ago. Her official records don't show a stay there since. In fact, she's stayed out of jail completely. Her old roommates tell me she was selling drugs and had wads of cash on her, but her lifestyle was right on the edge of poverty. It doesn't make sense."

His silence told me that maybe it made sense to him.

"What is it?" I asked. He looked so grim, I felt a wave of fear. I had walked into something I did not understand.

"I can't tell you," he said. "I can't tell anyone yet."

"Look," I explained. "I just told you the truth. Do you understand me? I squandered the truth on you and I've got nothing else left. I need to find this boy. His father is someone important to me. He's in a wheelchair. He'll never have any other children. This kid is the only family he'll ever have."

"You really pull out the stops," Shep said, avoiding my eyes.

"I know it sounds like a line, but it's true. You can look it up. His name is Burly Nash. Google him. I'm telling the truth."

"*Google* him?" Shep looked away. "No thanks. I prefer to evaluate people the old-fashioned way. In person."

"Then do you trust *me?*" I asked.

"I do. And, just for the record, I always knew you weren't some downtrodden woman fleeing from an ex-husband. But I wasn't sure what you were and, let's face it, you weren't the only one throwing back shots at the bar. I get it now, though. It all makes sense."

"I had no idea you were the sheriff when I went home with you," I said. "I wasn't trying to use you."

He would not meet my eyes.

"What is it?" I asked.

"I need to use *you,*" he said. "Because I don't have any other way to play it."

"What do you mean?" I reached for his hand. It was smooth and dry and hard and strong. It was real and it calmed me.

He sighed and right there, in the middle of the sigh, I felt him reach a decision. "Something *is* wrong at Silver Top," he told me. "Something inside. I think the guards are running some sort of scam with the female prisoners, but I've got two problems."

"What's the first problem?"

"There's not a person in this county who isn't related to at least one of those guards. And I'm not sure enough about who is involved to take it further up the food chain yet. If I take it to the wrong person, before I get real evidence, I'm dead meat."

"What's the second problem?"

"I'm an elected official, you know that, right?"

"Sure," I said. "All sheriffs are."

"If I go public, and I'm wrong, my career is over. But if I do nothing, and it continues, what good am I as a sheriff? I need to find out more."

"More about what?"

"More about what they're doing in there. I don't know if they're trading sex for favors, drugs or what. But something is wrong."

"What makes you say that?"

"I drive inmates up there sometimes for processing," he said. "If I'm down in Harnett or Winston-Salem on business, they'll ask me to transport prisoners up on my way home. So I know more than a few of the faces."

"And what?" I asked. "You see them again and again?"

He nodded. "I've seen a couple go by again."

"Maybe they had to do another stretch? Or violated parole?"

He shook his head. "I mean that I've seen them go by in private cars driven by the guards. Private guards don't transport prisoners. And they're damn sure not supposed to date the prisoners, not before, not after, not during. Plus I've had more than a few strange reactions from women prisoners, even when I'm doing them a favor like giving them a ride down the mountain once they're released. You'd think they'd be grateful that I was helping them get back to their families. Instead, I get attitude and glares."

"That's not a lot to go on," I pointed out.

"I've had them ask me questions that made me wonder what they meant. One woman asked me last week if it was 'worth it.' I was taking her down to Winston-Salem to catch the bus home after she'd done a year for possession. You'd think she'd have been glad to be going home, but she just sat there shooting me glares the whole way. Wouldn't make small talk or even look me in the eye. As I was letting her off, she leaned in my window and said, 'I just want to know one thing — do you sleep at night? Can you live with yourself knowing you take advantage of people who have no way to fight back?' I tried to ask her more, but she was in no mood to stay and talk."

"Okay," I conceded. "That does sound bad. But what makes you think drugs are involved? Female prisoners and male guards equal sex every time."

"This county's being ripped apart by drugs, that's what. You can't tell at first, not by walking around and meeting people for the first time. But if you lived here even a month, you'd see the signs. You'd know the mountain is changing and not for the better."

"But hasn't this place always been, well, a place for people who don't fit in elsewhere? People who don't really think the law has anything to do with them?"

"A little, but it's not the same thing. Lots of people in Bartow County used to run moonshine in my daddy's time. I'd ride along with him in his truck and we would chase the same old families across the same old roads again and again, never once coming close to catching them." He paused. "Probably because he wasn't really trying. What else are people supposed to do? We've got no industry and the real tourist country is forty miles south. Most people around here have nothing more than some tumble down house or a little farm clinging to a rocky mountainside. These days, I think over half the families are running drugs, and everything that goes along with them, up to and including guns. And when I say drugs, I mean it all. We've got a pipeline to the Mississippi and meth's heading our way through it in rivers. Pills, too. The feds tried to shut down the oxycodone when the disability claims grew ridiculous and people were maiming themselves just to get a steady prescription. But enough crooked doctors set up shop here when they got run out of somewhere else to keep the whole mess going. And the ones who can't afford black market oxycodone? Well, they're switching to heroin, cheap black tar from Mexico, so now we've got that to worry about, too, especially in the schools. People know I haven't got the resources to shut the drug trade down and that the county is too poor and too underpopulated for any state agency to give a crap about us. I'm on my own here and it's breaking my heart. I've got nothing to fight these people with and I'm seeing things I never thought I'd see."

"Like what?" I asked reluctantly, wondering if I really wanted to know.

"Like the most beautiful homecoming queen this town has ever seen reduced to being a toothless hag at age twenty-six, with three starving kids, trying to sell blow jobs behind the Dew Drop Inn to score her next meth fix. Like fourteen-year-old boys in borrowed trucks flying off of bluffs and dying surrounded by hundreds of thousands of dollars worth of illegal drugs, drugs that disappear between the time I find their bodies and I can get someone to go pick up the pieces for their parents. Or having three old people die in their sleep within two months of each other, years before they should have, because some relative had an eye on their possessions or home. I've seen too many bruises, too many accidents, too many families ripped apart. This county is at war with itself and you will find drugs beating at the heart of that war. The worst part of it? It's people from here doing it. We're destroying our own mountain. We're destroying ourselves."

He was silent, staring up toward the top of Silver Mountain. I thought maybe he was going to cry.

"You sound overworked," I said softly. "No one can keep going like that forever."

He shook his head. "It's not that."

"What is it?"

"When I bring them down, and I will bring them down, I'm going to find out I went to school with them, that their daddy cuts my hair, or that I've sat there at the Dew Drop next to them for the past fifteen years, raising glasses of whiskey to their health. They're going to be my own people."

"But they're the ones destroying your people," I said.

"Yes, they are." He glanced down at me and I could feel his pain; it filled him and spilled out as vividly as the sunlight filtering through the pines.

"What do you want from me?" I asked. It's better to get right to the heart of it at times like this. Sometimes, too many words can just get in the way.

"I need you to go inside at Silver Top."

I froze. Willingly go back behind bars, where I would be at the mercy of the guards, where the noise and the smells would remind me of the miserable life I had once lived, the men I had once chosen, how little I had once thought of myself? Go back in where I would be trapped in a world where I found it hard to even breathe?

How could I tell Shep that? He didn't know about my record. With shame, I realized that I didn't want him to know, either. Shep was one of the good guys. He was a walking, talking Wyatt Earp of a man, on the side of the angels, clean and just and true, willing to fight for his people and his mountain. To tell him I had a record? To tell him that I'd been married to a drug dealer and had taken the fall for him, and done my time the hard way, a part of me believing I'd die behind those bars — believing that because there was a good chance I could have died, that I probably would have if part of me hadn't learned to fight back, if part of me hadn't shut down so I could survive.

I didn't want to go back there. I didn't want to lose part of myself again. But I couldn't tell him that.

It was unthinkable. I was on his side. I was one of the good guys, too. I had been for fifteen years and I needed him to see me that way. I had worked too hard putting my old life behind me to return to it now. Now was not the time to stop and look back. I had to leave the past behind sometime. I wanted that time to be now.

"What do I have to do?" I asked.

He told me. I listened. And I agreed.

* * *

I HAVE BEEN A FOOL FOR LOVE more than once in my lifetime. Who among us has not? But the older I get, the more determined I am to never again be a fool for mere lust. Thus it was that I decided at least one other person on this planet needed to know what I was doing for Shep Gaines and why.

The fact that this person was lugging a six-foot fiberglass hot dog up the hill as he huffed and puffed toward me did not fill me with confidence. But we can only choose our friends. We cannot control their passions.

"I was just coming down to get you," I said.

"I figured. I saw the sheriff drive away."

"I must be the talk of the town," I said. "Or at least the bed-and-breakfast."

"I'd say that was pretty accurate," Bobby admitted. He was breathing so hard I feared he might stroke out.

"Let me help you." I took one end of the giant hot dog and joined him in trudging up the hill. It was surprisingly light for its size. "Taking it out for a test run?" I asked.

Bobby nodded. "I've got these until we're ready for the real ones." He pulled a pack of three rubber hot dogs out of his pocket — eliciting a yip of joy from the inn's resident dog. It had been tailing Bobby with an intensity that suggested the little beast was convinced the giant hot dog was real and might result in the biggest score of his furry little life.

"I think he's seen these before," I said, dangling a rubber hot dog in front of the dog while he danced enthusiastically on his hind paws. "Let's throw the big one and yell fetch."

"Let's not," Bobby suggested.

"What are you getting ready to do?" I asked.

"Funny," he growled. "I was just about to ask you the same thing."

We reached the meadow and Bobby sat on a fallen log gratefully, his immense weight causing it to tilt at one end like a playground seesaw. He leaned the giant fiberglass hot dog by his side. "I know you are up to something and I don't appreciate being left out of the loop," he said. He sounded angry, which was rare.

"I'm not leaving you out," I protested. "I was going to tell you everything."

"Yeah?" Bobby sounded unconvinced. "Why don't you start with why the sheriff dropped by to see you today? It wasn't a social call. His uniform told me that. If you don't want me to watch your back, why did you bring me up here in the first place?"

He was right. So I told Bobby everything. He didn't like it one bit.

"This is a bad idea," he said. "If I recall, you don't speak very highly of your time behind bars. Can you even do three days in the joint? And you might be inside for weeks."

"I know. That's why I need you to pretend to be my lawyer. Come by every day. If something goes wrong, you'll have to get me out of there."

"How?" he asked.

"If anything goes wrong, call Bill Butler," I told him. "He'll know what to do."

"How do you know Butler will believe me?"

"Play him this." I handed him a micro-cassette recorder. "I've got the sheriff on tape suggesting I go inside for him and why."

"You taped last night's tryst or this afternoon's come to Jesus meeting?"

"This afternoon's. All of it."

"I guess trust is an issue for you?"

"I'm not stupid, Bobby. Hell, I'm still sore from sleeping with the guy. My judgment might be impaired and I know that."

He struggled to his feet. "You know what? That makes me feel better. Seems like a little blood is getting through to your brain after all. I am going to let you walk into the lion's den. I'll even drive you there myself."

"It doesn't work that way," I explained. "Shep is going to arrest me. Everyone knows we slept together, so our story is that I told him something in the throes of passion that made him check up on me and he found out there's a warrant for my arrest."

"I see. So he gets to look like a law enforcement genius instead of a dumb ass for sleeping with a woman on the run? I'm sensing this guy knows how to watch his own ass a whole lot better than he knows how to watch yours."

I ignored his comment. "They use Silver Top as the local jail on account of they don't have their own. He'll process me in."

"For how long?"

I shrugged. "A week at the most. Long enough for me to befriend some of the other prisoners and find out what's going on. I just need to get a lead and I can get out."

"You sure this Shep guy isn't behind whatever's going on there?" Bobby asked. He was kneeling now, shoving one of the rubber hot dogs down the barrel of the giant weiner.

"No, I'm not sure. That's where you come in. You can pull the plug on this at anytime."

He grunted like it was no big deal, but I could tell he was pleased that my life was in his hands.

"Help me with this thing," he said.

"How? Want me to see if they have a giant jar of mustard in the kitchen?"

"Just help me to my feet," Bobby grumbled.

I grabbed an upper arm as thick as a ham and heaved. Bobby was surprisingly agile and soon the giant fiberglass hot dog was perched on his shoulder, balanced just enough that he could walk. "Now watch this carefully," he said to me. "And you might want to stand back."

"Why?" I asked. "It doesn't work on gunpowder, does it?"

"Of course not. It's hydraulic. How could you shoot hot dogs into a crowd with gunpowder? They'd come out all charred."

"Like that would stop anyone," I said. It was true. The whole reason Bobby D. had been carting a giant hot dog around was that he was determined to single-handedly solve a problem that had plagued the Durham Bulls Triple A baseball team for years. Once a mainstay game promotion, their hydraulic hot dog-shaped wiener shooter — which had once rocketed real hot dogs into the stands — had been retired in favor of a less powerful gun that merely blasted rolled-up tee shirts into the crowd. Bobby missed the thrill of seeing free meat whiz over his head and, I suspect, the entertainment value of seeing a pack of well-fed humans fighting over a free hot dog like starving dogs. Personally, I thought the Durham Bulls had pulled the plug on using real hot dogs for sanitation reasons. By the time the winner had claimed the wiener, it was invariably a mangled, dusty nubbin of meat capable of causing a dozen different diseases just by looking at it. But Bobby insisted it had been a matter of safety, that the gun was simply too powerful, and that management feared they might put someone's eye out with an errant hot dog.

"How is your version going to be any different?" I asked.

"Haven't you been paying attention? I have discovered a massive breakthrough in promotional hot dog technology. Watch this." Bobby braced himself and pulled back on the trigger beneath the fiberglass barrel. I heard a zinging sound as the rubber wiener shot from the gun and sailed up into the air. "Watch for it!" Bobby cried. "Watch for it!"

As the rubber hot dog reached the pinnacle of its flight and started back toward earth, a tiny parachute bloomed above it, slowing its descent with a tidy jerk. It swayed gently as it sailed downward on the wind.

"Perfect," Bobby shouted triumphantly. "Look at that hang time! I knew it would work!"

Visions of fans shoving and fighting for a paratrooper hot dog danced in my head. All Bobby had really done was buy people more time to assault one another. "Are you sure you've thought this through?" I asked.

"Of course. You're just jealous you didn't think of it first."

And with that, the tiny dog that looked like nothing so much as a mop sans a handle launched itself into the air like a champion Frisbee-playing canine. It hurled its body through space, higher and higher, defying gravity with sheer determination. The little beast snagged the rubber hot dog perfectly, plucking it from the air neatly before hurtling back to the ground. It landed on all fours and was off like a shot, heading straight for the forest, Bobby's test hot dog still clamped in its mouth and the deflated parachute trailing in the dirt behind it.

"Holy shit!" I yelled. "Did you see that? That little fucker just out-jumped Michael Jordan!"

"Oh, shut up." Bobby poked one end of the hot dog gun toward me. "Help me get this thing back in the car. It's almost Happy Hour."

* * *

IT WAS HAPPY HOUR FOR SOME, but not for me. As planned, Shep arrived, lights whirling, right after five. I knocked back my glass of wine, hastily poured another, and knocked that back while the other guests ran to the windows. A few of the more savvy ones turned and stared at me.

Ask not for whom the bell tolls. It tolls for thee.

He had two deputies with him, a rather unnecessary touch, I felt, since they were clearly not in on the plan — not if the way they threw me against the wall and handcuffed my hands behind my back was any indication. That little maneuver pretty much killed the fantasy aspect of my arrest right off the bat.

The guests were scandalized and the proprietor, Bunny, turned white, her little hot dog-snitching pooch returning from the forest just in time to yap furiously as the deputies led me through a gauntlet of gaping faces and out onto the front porch toward the waiting squad cars. Shep had not even looked at me when he read me my rights, informing me that I was under arrest for suspicion of murder. It gave me a bad feeling from the start. He was supposed to have gone into a whole cover story about how my husband was missing and incriminating evidence had been found, but he said nothing more than that I was under arrest for suspicion of murder before he gave me the usual Miranda warning.

"I'll take her up to Silver Top," Shep told his men when we reached the cars.

"You sure?" one of the deputies asked, eyeing me dubiously. "She looks like a hellcat to me."

I hissed at the deputy and his hand inched toward his gun. What a pussy.

"I can handle her." Shep said and the other deputy smirked, making it obvious that he, too, had heard about our Dew Drop Inn encounter. Shep put his hand on top of my head and pushed me into the backseat — why, oh why, do cops always do that? And why did Shep have to do it with such zeal?

"Suspicion of murder?" I complained once we were alone. "You couldn't come up with anything with a little less kick?"

"Look," he said grimly. "I'm trying to protect you. You're not exactly going to be inside with a bunch of angels. You might need a reputation to proceed you."

"Then you should have arrested me for girlfriend bashing."

"You can joke at a time like this?" He looked glum.

"What is it?" I asked. "What's wrong?"

He shook his head. "I don't know yet. But something is. I got a call from Doris down at the bank. The feds are poking around in my bank accounts. I'm not supposed to know, but we went to high school together so she told me. I don't know what they're looking for, but it's a bad sign."

"What's bad about it?" I asked. "It probably means they're looking into what's going on at Silver Top, right?"

Shep shrugged. "But they didn't come to me about it. That can't be good."

"Well, at least you're not the one going inside today," I joked.

His eyes met mine in the mirror and he smiled. That smile lifted a lot of my anxiety. Going inside was starting to feel a little too real for my tastes.

"What am I getting into?" I asked. "How long can you stay with me once we get there?"

"I have to hand you over to the guards immediately. I transfer custody to them and then I'm gone. But I'll be back to interrogate you, of course, and you can let me know what you find out then."

"If I find out anything," I said.

"You will," he predicted. "I have faith in you."

An absurd degree of pride filled me and I felt vaguely ashamed I needed his validation. "I hope this is worth it," I told him. "Did I mention I was claustrophobic?"

He glanced at me in the mirror like he thought I was kidding, saw my face and knew I wasn't. But I had agreed and that was it. There would be no backing out now.

"I owe you one," was all he said.

"That you do," I agreed.

# Chapter Nine

The prison guards started my intake by stripping me of my individuality and more than a little of my dignity. I had to hand over my clothes, receiving a denim work shirt and high-waisted jeans in return. Great, the Appalachian nerd look. "This is going to do nothing for my figure," I complained. But the guard — who looked like a career Marine, so ramrod straight was he in both posture and personality — did not crack so much as a hint of a smile. The other guard looked equally humorless and equally paramilitary. In fact, both looked like they ought to be invading Paraquay instead of guarding liquor store robbers and domestic abusers. They were as white as genetics can get you, sported whitewall haircuts, wore spotless uniforms and didn't seem to have an ounce of extra fat between them. For a privately-run prison, Silver Top sure had high standards. There were no big-gutted prison guards with bowl haircuts here.

It didn't make me feel very optimistic. It only made my processing in seem very, very real. I was playacting, but those two? They were as serious as a heart attack.

After the guards finished my paperwork and took away everything I had that might remind me who I was, they turned me over to a businesslike black woman who gave me a full-body search — and I do mean full body, the kind involving rubber gloves. I gritted my teeth while she performed personal maneuvers that I usually required people to buy me a drink before even considering.

"Is this necessary?" I asked.

"Yes," the guard replied indifferently. She was neither mean nor friendly. She just seemed bored. "And you'll know why once you're inside."

"What's that supposed to mean?" I asked, illogically hoping she'd spill the beans on some illegal scheme right then and there so I could back out of this hare-brained plan and go home.

"It means you need to keep your head down, mind your own damn business and tell your lawyer to get you the fuck out of here as soon as you can."

She didn't have much personality, but I decided I liked her nonetheless. Her nameplate read *Officer Alldread.* I thought that was funny.

"Great name for a prison guard," I pointed out.

She grunted.

One day, I'd be sure to write her and thank her for her kindness, even if her version of kindness came at you colder then a pair of penguin balls.

"What happens now?" I asked, once I was dressed in my official "Ellie Mae Clampett rides the short bus" outfit. I was standing in an otherwise empty concrete-floored room while she ran a comb through my hair, collecting the contents onto a sheet of black construction paper. I didn't ask her what she was doing. That part I remembered. She was making sure I wasn't bringing a couple thousand little friends in with me.

"You gonna check for crabs, too?" I suggested.

She paused, comb in hand, and took a long time evaluating me. Then she shook her head and kept combing. "Didn't anyone ever tell you black roots look cheap?" she asked.

"I'll be sure to take care of them now that I have plenty of time on my hands."

"You better watch that mouth in here," she advised me. "You're not going to find too many women with a sense of humor in this place. If they had a sense of humor, they would not be in here. Know what I'm saying?"

"Not really," I admitted.

"What are you in for?" she asked. "Not that I give a rat's ass."

"They think I killed my husband," I said.

"Of course they do." She sounded more cheerful. "You and the three hundred and ninety eight other women in here."

"How many women does this place hold?" I asked. It was bigger than it looked from the outside.

"Four hundred in all," the guard told me. "Every single one of them a widow. What are the odds?" She smiled ominously. "You'll fit in just fine."

"That's what I'm afraid of," I told her.

"That means you're smarter than you look."

* * *

THE JEERS CAME FROM RIGHT AND LEFT as I walked to my cell. Man, some of the women had filthy minds and even filthier mouths. I am all for women's equality, mind you, but adopting the least attractive traits of the male sex was not my idea of progress.

I ignored them all, resolved to wash any and all vegetables that might have even gotten near one particular woman in Cell Block C with a very green-friendly sexual persuasion, and gritted my teeth as a new pair of guards walked me further and further down a gray linoleum hallway. Each step seemed to take me a little more out of my body, out of my life and into some unknown hell.

*What had I been thinking?*

"Here you go," one guard announced as we neared the end of a long row of double cells. My escorts were as buttoned down as their earlier counterparts. They ran a tight ship in here.

The second guard tapped the bars of a cell close to the end of the row and nodded. The lights were off inside. In the shadows, I could make out a metal bunk bed and the back of a woman huddled in the lower bunk, her face turned away from us toward the wall. "Home, sweet home," he said. "Your roommate for the duration will be Chatty Cathy."

"Why you got to call her that?" a voice yelled from next door. "It's not like there aren't enough people running their mouths in this place. You ought to be encouraging people to be quiet, not making fun of them for it."

"Yeah, yeah, yeah," the second guard said mechanically, making it clear he didn't give a crap. "We want your opinion, Peppa, we'll ask for it."

The unseen inmate's voice was scathing. "Like you'd ask me for anything seeing as how I'm never getting out of here."

"Now, now," the second guard said. "There's always the women's prison in Raleigh. You could get out of here… and go to there."

As the guards laughed, I caught an undercurrent of something more than simply bad-natured teasing. They were close to taunting her and I didn't like it.

One of the jerks swung the metal-barred door open for me with mock courtesy. Just the sound of metal scraping on metal terrified me with an intensity that took me back fifteen years, when I'd been deep inside a Florida prison, my husband's hollow promises still ringing in my ears as I did time for his crime. Worse, back then as now, I had done it willingly. A least for the first month, until his lack of visits revealed his betrayal. I finally realized that every woman in the place was there because of a man in one way or the other. I was no different than the rest of the fools.

I could not afford to be different here.

“Step inside,” one of the guards said, prodding me slightly.

I took a deep breath and, with one simple step forward, just like that, I went from freedom to imprisonment, from purgatory to hell.

“You’ve got a new roommate, Foster,” one of the guards announced into the darkness. “Try to get along with this one. We’re running out of options.”

Oh, great. They’d probably put me in with a bad-tempered killer. Things had gone from bad to worse. I wanted to ask what had happened to her last roommate but was afraid I’d just be inviting her to show me. I sat on my bunk, stared ahead and tried not to notice where I was.

The cell was clean enough, what there was of it, but I can’t say that a ten-foot square cell is a lot of room for anyone, much less two people. The floors were a smooth white concrete, the walls painted an anemic green. A machine designed to suck your soul from you could not have done a better job.

My cellmate was still huddled on the bottom bunk, her back turned to me. She had not so much as twitched when I stepped inside. All I could tell about her was that she was on the plump side and either terribly tired or terribly unhappy. I couldn’t even tell what color she was. Probably anemic green.

That green was getting to me.

So were the walls. They started to close in on me. Less than a minute in the damn cell and the walls started to close in on me.

I needed to think of something else.

“My name’s Debbie,” I said to the silent figure huddled in the bottom bunk. I got no response. Fine. Conversation was no requirement with me. Yet my mouth moved of its own accord, nervous and needing an outlet. “Nice we have our own sink and toilet.”

Still no reply.

I could take a hint. I'd just sit here in the dark and feel claustrophobic. Or better yet, I'd check out the only saving grace in my cell: a small barred window that looked out over a beautiful mountain vista. You could even slide the pane to one side to let in fresh air. Was it cruel or kind to give prisoners a taste of such freedom? I couldn't decide.

*"Pssst."*

At first I thought it was the pipes hissing, but then I heard it again: *"Pssst."* It was as forceful as a rattlesnake hissing.

*"Pssst* yourself," I said back.

"I'm your neighbor," said a voice from the other side of the wall. I recognized it. The woman who'd been sassing the guards.

"Howdy neighbor," I said brightly.

She did not laugh. Instead, a thick brown arm snaked around the edge of the wall dividing my cell from hers and poked its way into my cell. "Come here," she said. "Let me get a look at you."

I stared at the hand dangling there, trying to feel its way through my bars, and I didn't really think it was a look she wanted to get so much as a grope. "I don't think so," I said. "I'm not in a meeting-new-people mood."

"Yeah," she said unexpectedly, her voice softening. "I know what you mean. But the first week is the worst. You'll get used to it. I've been here six years and I've got eighty more to go." Her laugh was a booming sound and brought immediate catcalls to shut up from the rest of the residents on our row.

"My name's Peppa," the voice said. "What's yours?"

Some undercover investigator I was. I came this close to saying "Casey" before I caught myself. "Debbie," I said. "Debbie Little."

"Debbie Little?" My neighbor thought that was funny. As her laughter brought more catcalls our way, she settled down into a simmering giggle. "Like the Little Debbie snack cakes? Get it? I like the banana roll-ups myself."

"That's funny," I muttered. "I figured you for an oatmeal pie kind of girl."

"How could someone do that to their own kid?" she asked. "Giving you a name like that?"

"My father had a sense of humor," I said, needing the contact.

"I killed mine," Peppa announced abruptly.

Talk about your conservation stoppers. I wasn't sure what to say, so I kept quiet. It didn't stop Peppa.

"I'm not the only one on this row who killed their father," she said. "There's three of us. And six others who killed their husbands. Plus a few who jumped the gun and took care of their boyfriends. I'm sensing a trend, aren't you?"

Okay, I admit it. This time I laughed. And this time no one told us to shut up. The block got very quiet as women up and down the row stopped whatever they were doing to listen in.

"What are you in for?" Peppa asked, inevitably.

"I don't want to talk about it," I said. I don't know why, but I didn't want to lie anymore that day, not to these women shut away from everything behind bars. I'd lied about my name, that was enough for now.

"Fair enough." Her voice dropped. "I didn't get a good look at you. Sure you don't want to stand a little closer so I can take a better look?"

"I don't think so," I answered as cheerfully as I could.

"Oh, come on. There's not a lot to do around here," Peppa complained.

"I'm going to spend my time reading books and improving my mind," I said solemnly. Oops, there was that mouth the female guard named Alldread had warned me about: my own. And she was right. It got me into trouble.

"Yo," a voice shouted from across the row. "Shut the fuck up, college girl. No one cares what you're going to do."

"You don't have to be in college to read books," I pointed out. "Just ask Dr. Seuss. Or better yet, answer me this: Would you, could you in a cell? Would you, could you down in hell?" I couldn't help it. This place was already chipping away at my sense of self and I had to get some back quick.

Peppa's hand was waving wildly in a sort of "no, no, no" universal gesture, but it was too late. My mouth had gotten me into trouble in record time.

"What did you say to me?" the belligerent voice challenged from the shadows. "Shut your hole or I'll do it for you."

I was going to say something else witty, but Peppa was in danger of busting her wrist trying to signal me to be quiet, so I mumbled "What's with her?" to Peppa instead.

"Girl's got permanent PMS," Peppa told me. "Got processed in two years ago for shooting a cop and she's been in a bad mood ever since."

"Who is she?" I whispered.

"Doesn't matter," Peppa said in a burst of wisdom. "We call her Martha Ray on account of she has got one damn big mouth."

"People in here know who Martha Rae is?" I asked.

"What you talking about?" Peppa asked. "A Martha Ray is just someone with too big of a mouth for her own good."

Fine. So I was a little rusty with my prison lingo. I'd steer clear of anyone nicknamed for a semi-famous name from here on out, just in case.

"Who are these people?" I asked, suddenly curious as to who my block mates might be. Shep had arranged for me to be housed in the general population and I wondered how hardcore they might be. “Have I heard of any of them?” I couldn’t believe I was asking this, but apparently not even incarceration can quench the thirst for celebrity brownnosing.

“Turn to the right,” Peppa instructed. “Now look down. Do you know who you’re looking at?”

“I’m not looking at anyone. I’m staring at my feet and wishing I had some toenail polish.”

“I meant your roommate. She’s famous.”

I stared at the woman curled up in the bottom bunk. She looked like she was trying to melt away from the world. I was dubious.

Peppa felt it. “Seriously,” she explained. “That’s Risa Foster.”

“No shit.” The words escaped before I could stop them.

“Yup,” Peppa confirmed. “It’s her. They moved her up from Raleigh on account of all the bad ass lifers kept challenging her so they could grab a headline and she’s not the type to fight back.”

Not the type to fight back? That sounded a little off to me. Risa Foster was one of North Carolina’s most notorious murderers, male and female alike. Five years ago, she’d taken a shotgun, packed a knapsack with plenty of extra rounds and systematically killed every male in her family, seven of them in all, ranging in age from eighty-four down to twenty-two. She drove to four different houses and discharged her shotgun a total of fifteen different times to get the job done, her old man apparently calling for bonus rounds while her younger brother had his crotch blown off after he was dead. When she was done, she laid the shotguns out across the lawn of the last house, pulled up a lawn chair, sat down and waited for the cops to come and haul her away.

She never said a word about why she did it. And neither did any of the other women in her family, up to and including her grandmother all the way down to Risa’s three-year-old daughter, who was often photographed in the weeks that followed staring at her mother with a solemn look, thumb tucked firmly in her mouth. Risa Foster remained as silent as the other females in her family, and now she was paying the price — she'd opted out of a jury trial and the judge who heard her case sent her away for over nine hundred years, with no chance of parole. That she was not on death row was a testament to the fact that the judge had been a woman, and to whatever that judge had heard in a closed-door session the final day of the trial. It was this never-released secret testimony that had caused her to opt out of a lethal injection for Risa Foster.

I sat, staring at my roommate's immobile back, her body as still as in death, and I wondered which punishment would have been kinder.

"I think she's asleep," I said to Peppa. "I'm going to take a nap myself so as not to disturb her."

"She's not asleep," Peppa said. "She just never talks."

I'd give her some peace and quiet anyway. I climbed up to the top bunk and stared at a ceiling the color of washed out celery. I wondered what the hell I had gotten myself into.

* * *

SO FAR AS I COULD TELL, and it was a long, long night with little sleep, my roommate only moved once during those lonely hours. She got up deep in the night and took down a photograph that was pinned to the wall and got back in bed with it. I didn't dare look, but I was pretty sure she was curled up in the shadows of her lower bunk, staring at it through the night.

Me? I had nothing to stare at but the ceiling and nothing to contemplate but my own sorry fate. And the more I stared at the ceiling above me, the closer it seemed to inch, like one of those scary torture rooms in the horror movies of my childhood, ingeniously-designed chambers where the walls and ceiling would slowly close in on a person until they were crushed to death.

That's where I was for many long hours, trapped in a death chamber, my chest growing heavier and heavier with the irrational fear I'd somehow forget how to breathe, an obsessive terror exceeded only by the thought that my cellmate might rise up in the night and kill me, having stayed silent out of rage, not grief. That's the trouble with quiet people. You never know what the hell they are thinking — and that worried me.

Thus I alternated between claustrophobia and mortal fear my first night back in prison, at least until I discovered the one thing that could take my mind off my predicament: sex.

Yes, the irony of it was not lost on me. Here I was, locked in a building with almost four hundred other women, unable to touch a man, not even with the ability to get up and see one, thinking of nothing but Shep's lean body in the firelight and the way his shoulders had looked when he brought me a glass of water early, early in the morning, the light of the sky barely visible above the strip of horizon outside his window, or the length of his fingers wrapped around my hand and the feel of his mouth against mine. Like some pornographic movie, our hours together played over and over in my mind, the only memory I had with the power to take me away from the grim reality of my present state. I could smell him, almost feel his skin, hear his voice, imagine his warmth. And as I relived our time together, I realized how much I would have to hold onto that memory in order to survive. I slowed down then, going over every move we made again and again, trying to recall our night through the haze of shared whisky and pure mindless joy, equipping myself for the long nights ahead.

I didn't think even that would be enough — and it scared me.

* * *

I SHOULD HAVE BEEN EXHAUSTED when the lights finally came on with a cruel wash of institutional glare early in the morning. But I wasn't. I felt strong again with the daylight. I had officially survived one night. I could do this, I told myself. I had

Shep in my head and the memory of his hands on my body. And I only needed to get through a few more days.

I rose at once, washing my face and brushing my teeth hurriedly in my tiny sink, determined to stay out of my cellmate's way. She did not move a muscle, not even when a guard came to get me, telling me I had a choice: I could clean tables in the kitchen, and wash dishes later, or I could work in the laundry scrubbing other people's underwear.

I chose the kitchen, where the stains would be more recognizable. As the guard — another tall man in outstanding physical condition with a military-style haircut — walked me over to the kitchen area, I tried to sneak a peek at Peppa, my unseen neighbor of the night before. Her cell was already empty.

In fact, many of the cells were empty, the doors unlocked and left open. There was a fair amount of freedom on this wing, I realized, as I noticed prisoners making their way to and from their jobs, occasionally smiling at each other and, just as often, bristling and stopping to block someone else's path until a guard intervened and moved people along. For a woman's prison, there was a lot of testosterone floating around.

Not all the women had the freedom to walk the compound unescorted. Some had their hands chained, a few even their feet, and stepped glumly between guards as they headed toward the dining room. I took one look at their faces, where hatred for the world was etched as permanently as if in granite, and decided I didn't want to know why they were chained.

It took ten minutes for the guard to walk me to the kitchen area. It was a good opportunity for me to get the lay of the land. The prison was busy with activity despite the earliness of the morning and I immediately noticed a difference in the way the guards treated some of the women. It didn't seem to be based on looks at all — which made me doubt the sex-for-favors theory — but some other factor I couldn't pinpoint. I watched more closely until I thought I had it: the prisoners in for short stretches were receiving better treatment.

Reaching the kitchen just before the breakfast rush confirmed my theory. I was introduced to a large black woman whose face was so flat she looked like she'd been hit with a frying pan, which was not outside the realm of possibility, I suppose. Her name was Pam and the kitchen was her castle. I wasn't even Cinderella. She ordered me to wipe down the tables before the crowd arrived. They didn't need wiping down, she was just showing me who was boss, but I grabbed a rag and went to work. It gave me a chance to watch the way the guards handled the traffic right outside the dining room doors, waving some women away without letting them go inside, while beckoning others to grab a tray and go on in.

There was a method to their madness. I was sure of it. The lifers were treated indifferently, almost as if they were invisible. And it was not hard to spot them. Not only did they wear the forest green shirts of lifers – versus blue shirts for those with hope – their whole demeanor seemed different. They had settled in and given up the charade of caring about the outside world. They seemed almost content, ambling along, stepping against the wall when told, letting others pass. There was a stillness about them, as if they welcomed knowing this confined world was all they would ever know again. The other prisoners, the short-termers, were less settled. They jostled and daydreamed and gossiped and postured and joked. But, most of all, they feared. You could smell it on them: *Please get me through this, God, and I'll never do anything to land me in here again. Just get me* through *this first.*

These were the women who received special attention from the guards. It took me about twenty minutes to be absolutely sure about it. And I saw it then only because I was looking for it. The guards would cock a head, or extend a baton, or stop another prisoner from walking up in order to move a short-termer ahead instead. It was all done very subtly, without fanfare, but done nonetheless, inevitably sending a short-termer to the front of the breakfast line before the coffee was gone.

"What are you looking at, Little Debbie?" a familiar voice said behind me as I was retrieving a tray that an enormous white woman with a bad mullet had left on the table in violation of rules.

"You must be Peppa." I took a look at my would-be suitor and talkative neighbor of the night before. She was a big woman, nearly six feet tall, with dark brown skin, lots of tiny braids swinging on either side of a round face with high cheekbones that hinted at more than a drop of Cherokee blood. Her face was so sprinkled with acne scars she looked as if she had been seasoned and I knew without asking where her name, Peppa, had come from.

"That's me. They call me Peppa because I'm hot stuff." She wore a white apron stained with ketchup and was trying to untie it. Sweat covered her face and arms. Free from the constraints of her apron she twirled it expertly over her head and launched it into a hamper of dirty linens near the kitchen door. Man, she was almost as muscled as Mike Tyson. I had found a friend.

"You're a little pale for my taste," Peppa said, grabbing my arms and holding them out like she was trying to find the biggest drumstick on the chicken. "But you got some meat on your bones and I do like me a dirty white girl with bleached hair and black roots."

Uh oh. Maybe I'd found too good of a friend. "You the cook?" I asked her, just to change the subject.

"One of them," she said. "I'll get you back there with us soon as I can." She nodded toward the dining room filled with long rows of steel tables now jammed with several hundred noisy, clamoring, arguing, laughing, shrieking, just-this-side-of-being-out-of-control women. "It's safer in the kitchen."

I looked out over the crowd and started to say I could take care of myself, but who the fuck would I be kidding? "Thanks," I mumbled instead.

"Who were you looking for?" Peppa asked. "You been standing there with your mouth open staring at those women for ten minutes. Keep it up and you'll be down in the laundry before you know it. Or out cold on the floor."

"Sorry," I said, starting to shine a stainless steel counter with my rag. "I thought I had a friend in here. Tonya Blackburn. I was hoping to see her."

"Yeah," Peppa agreed, smiling broadly. "A friendly face sure don't hurt in here. But you won't see Tonya in this crowd. She was one of the lucky ones. She left and she didn't come back."

I doubted Peppa would still consider her lucky if she knew why Tonya was never coming back.

"Tonya wrote to a couple of them," Peppa explained as she nodded toward a table of chatting women who seemed happier than the other short-termers — which meant, in prison body language, that they felt safer. They weren't worried about someone else coming up from behind and braining them. They were protected and I thought I knew who was doing the protecting — the guards.

"What did she write to them?" I asked. "Do you know?"

"Said she was back in school and doing real good. I remember because I didn't believe a word of it. Everybody always writes and says how good they are doing. Everybody always ends up back here anyway."

"Those were Tonya's friends?" I asked a little dubiously. The group of women seemed to have nothing in common. Some were white, others were black, one was Asian. A few were skinny, most were slightly plump from all the starchy prison food, and their hair color ran the gamut from white to screaming red. They were sitting at a prime table well out of the way of the food line, but near the big steel containers of ice tea and lukewarm coffee — they didn't serve the coffee hot for obvious reasons. "Nice table. Is it reserved for prom queens?"

Peppa laughed and reached for a coffee cup. "The guards? They have their favorites and then they have their *favorites.* You're looking at them."

I tried to figure out what they might have in common. “Favorites for what?” I asked. “Sex?”

Peppa shook her head. “I know women have offered, but I don’t know anyone who’s been taken up on that offer yet. At least not anyone I believe.” She looked over at a pair of guards leaning against one wall. They were scanning the crowd, their hands resting lightly a few inches away from their guns. “Do they look like they fool around to you? I mean, look at those two. They‘re acting like a plastic knife fight’s about to break out. They act that way every meal, too. Can’t relax for a second. They are not the type to relax enough to unzip their pants, trust me. Uptight bad asses, one and all. You ask me, they’re too busy swinging their dicks at each other to let us get near them.”

“Really?” I asked. I had to admit they looked all business, all the time. Definitely not on the prowl.

“Who knows with men?” Peppa said, rolling her eyes. “And who really cares? Back to the salt mines for me. But don’t bus no more tables for the girls, L.D. They’re baiting you, hoping you’ll take something off their trays so they can come back and say they wanted it and pick a fight.”

“I’m never gonna get the hang of this,” I admitted.

Peppa patted me on the shoulder. “I’ll look after you.” She eyed me with the astuteness of a used car salesmen. “You got some muscle behind that meat, don’t you? You and me need to go a few rounds.”

“They have boxing in here?” I asked timidly.

She started laughing like I had said something truly funny. “Oh, that’s a good one, Little Debbie. That’s a real good one. I like some sass in my women.”

I smiled weakly as Peppa walked away — but then I saw her shoot a glare at another woman who had started to move toward me and let me tell you, however friendly Peppa had been to me, it was a look that stopped the other woman dead in her tracks.

I decided to be glad Peppa was my friend.

"Hey, L.D.," Peppa whispered unexpectedly in my left ear. I jumped a good two feet. She had returned to my side with the stealth of a ghost. "You get a good look at your roommate yet?"

I shook my head.

"That's her." Peppa pointed to a table near the front door. A woman sat alone at the head of it, the seats cleared on either side of her. "Don't look much like a mass murderer, does she?"

Curious, I moved a little closer, polishing table tops, steering clear of dirty trays, trying to get a look at the woman I pretty much slept on top of. I could not believe what I saw. To say she didn't look like a mass murderer was the understatement of the century. The notorious Risa Foster looked like a younger version of Mrs. Santa Claus. Her jolly round face crinkled around kindly eyes and her rosy cheeks bobbed up and down as she ate. Her dark hair was peppered with gray, and cut short so that it feathered around her face and stuck up a bit on the top in a jaunty rooster-like comb. A milkmaid would have envied the creamy pinkness of her skin and the adorable freckles sprinkled across her nose.

Uh oh. She caught me looking. She stared at me, fork halfway to her mouth. I froze, not knowing what to do, before finally giving her a half-assed grin while I sort of wiggled my fingers.

Clearly, I was rusty on my bad ass moves. I'd have been less obvious with "Please don't kill me!" tattooed on my forehead.

But Risa Foster pretended not to have seen me and just kept eating, her jolly face and kindly eyes shining brightly beneath the harsh florescent lights.

* * *

I WORKED MY ASS OFF ALL MORNING LONG, and for the next few mornings as well, washing dishes, unpacking huge cans of soggy peaches and flaccid green beans, sweeping linoleum floors and scrubbing steel counters. Half the work I did was unnecessary, but the women who ruled over the kitchen wanted me to know they were in charge and I wanted them to know I wasn't going to argue. I consoled myself with the fact that the calories I was burning might make up for the anti-Atkins diet I was facing. I swear, breakfast was always grits with toast and fried potatoes while lunch usually turned out to be anemic spaghetti with a side of mashed potatoes. Now that's good nutrition for you.

Lunches and dinners were as chaotic on the surface as the breakfasts, yet also as carefully choreographed as a dance, with the same groups of women forming, the same challenges being made, the same demands for power and acquiescence and solitude. My cellmate, Risa Foster, dined alone and, always, the two chairs on either side of her remained empty. Whatever her secret was, no one bothered her and she had no problem whatsoever being granted plenty of personal space.

I, on the other hand, fought all day long to keep a one-foot radius around me clear. It wasn't overt, and maybe sometimes I imagined it, but I was being tested again and again. Women stepped too close to me, bumped into me, knocked me against walls, forced me to step back and make room for them to pass by. It seemed that the most precious commodity in this place, at least from what I had seen so far, was personal space and they were going to make me fight to keep mine.

I fought. I challenged no one on the surface, I kept my head down, but I am proud to say that I did not give an inch willingly. To show any sign of weakness would have been like standing in the middle of the Amazon River and daring the piranhas to eat you. I was not about to invite trouble and, well, my big ass and ample bust had to be good for something. Turns out both parts were good for swinging and bumping people away from the rest of my body. Finally, it seemed as if I wasn't being tested nearly so often. Word had gotten out that this was not my first visit to the coop and someone, I suspected Peppa, had started a rumor that I had sawed my cheating husband into pieces with a steak knife, fed most of him to his hunting dogs and flushed the rest down the toilet. I know because some sad-faced Latina woman had asked me, in broken English, if the hunting dogs had eaten all trace of my *ano* husband's bones or was it was necessary to bury the big ones? Yikes. I hoped for her husband's sake that she was not getting out anytime soon.

"You doing okay," Peppa said to me one afternoon after the lunch rush had subsided and I had finished rinsing several hundred plates smeared with sauce that looked like dried blood. We'd swapped bits of our lives in the darkness over the past couple of nights and were close to becoming friends.

"I'm hanging in there," I answered.

"I wasn't asking you a question," she said impatiently. "I'm telling you that you're doing good. You're holding your own and keeping your head down. How long you got to be here?"

"Couple months, I guess. Until my trial. Can't even begin to afford the bail." It was a believable lie.

Peppa nodded. "You're going to make it. I can always tell within a couple of hours who can hang and who's going down. You're gonna be okay."

I felt unaccountably relieved. But I still didn't want to be alone. Or, more truthfully, didn't want to be caught alone, not by the notorious big-mouthed Martha Ray, whom I had not seen since she'd yelled at me to shut up in the darkness my first night, nor by the amorous Peppa, for that matter, or my enigmatic cellmate. So when my free time rolled around each afternoon, I headed to the library and offered to shelve books. The librarian, a skinny little old lady who could easily have been jumped and trussed by any of the prisoners, looked at me suspiciously at first, decided I was serious and waved me toward several rolling carts of books waiting to be re-shelved. It was not a bad-sized library, at least for a prison library. Many of the hardback books looked fairly new. The titles weren't going to win any Nobel prizes, however. The stacks seemed heavy on crime fiction, which I re-shelved in the *How To* section just to be a smart ass. Then I hid two copies of *Our Bodies, Ourselves* under a radiator in case Peppa wandered in. I didn't want her to get any ideas.

I found I liked it in the library. It was quiet, unlike the rest of the prison. It smelled of dust and books instead of slightly old vegetable soup and cheap lemon disinfectant, and the women sitting at its tables, poring over their books, looked like they were trying to escape the chaos around them, not contribute to it. I could have stayed in there forever.

Best of all, plenty of the short-termers hung out there, no doubt for the same reasons I did, so I was able to wander through the rows of shelves, eavesdropping on inmate conversations. I heard all the usual disasters, complaints, betrayals and disappointments that marked the lives of women in general. In fact, the inmates clung to all the things wrong on the outside of the prison with a desperation that made me think that, rotten or not, having a bunch of losers waiting for you when you got out was still way better than having no one at all. But I learned little that would help me figure out what had happened to Tonya Blackburn until the afternoon I noticed that two of the women Peppa had said were in Tonya's group of friends were whispering together at a table near the hallway door. I grabbed a couple of books and hid in the row behind them, listening. Not a lot of it made sense.

"Tell her not to do it," one of them, a blonde, was whispering to her dark-haired companion.

"How can she *not* do it?" the other answered. "She's got no one waiting on the outside to help her and how's she going to pay the rent?"

"If she starts, they'll never let her stop," the blonde said angrily. "It'll be like she's still in here. They'll own her. She'll never be free."

"She'll never get out in the first place if she doesn't do what they say," the brunette argued back. "They can write anything they want on her reports. Who's going to believe her over a bunch of guards? She doesn't have a choice."

The blonde shook her head. "They're bluffing. They can't draw attention to themselves. If she says no, they'll just let her go and find someone else. Tonya was right — we're fools to believe their threats. They only have power because we're afraid."

"Of course we're afraid," the brunette whispered angrily. "They can keep us in here forever. And who cares what Tonya said? Have we heard from her? No. She doesn't give a crap. For all we know, she's living with them."

The blonde rolled her eyes. "Like they'd touch her. You know what Tonya said — black for their jack and white for their night."

"Of course they'd touch her. You think racists don't sleep with black women? Please. If I didn't know you weren't really a blonde, I'd say you were dumber than dog shit."

Well. As a bottled blonde myself, I resented the insinuation. But I had no time to contemplate what they might have been talking about as I had to get my ass to the common room for my daily five-minute phone call and I was not about to waste it. I waited for these five minutes every day and clung to them like a lifeline. When my turn came, I called Shep, needing to hear his voice. He answered like he'd been out jogging.

"I'm busting out at midnight," I said when he answered. "Have the car waiting by the back gate."

"That's not funny. These calls are likely taped."

"Like they have time to listen to any of them," I said. "By the time they figure out I was calling you from here, it'll all be over anyway."

"What do you mean? Have you found out anything?"

I was just about to tell him what I'd learned when I heard the dead spot that indicated he was receiving another call. He told me to hold on, then came back on my line a few seconds later. "Gotta go," he said. "I've got a call from the Raleigh Police Department on the other line. The guy's been calling all afternoon. Some guy named Butler. Know him?"

In a heartbeat, dread flooded every cell in my body. I could barely breathe. It could not be good that Bill Butler was calling Shep. I thought of my being at Tonya Blackburn's trailer and of the detectives in Perry County wanting to question me and me blowing them off and I suddenly wished very badly that I had not left that part of my story out when I confessed all to Shep.

"Casey?" he said. "You know him? Bill Butler?"

"I do," I admitted. "And listen, he may tell you this, but — "

I would get no further. I was shoved from behind. I stumbled and fell, hitting my head on the wall. When I turned around, a doughy white woman with splotchy skin, tiny eyes and frizzy brown hair was glaring at me. "You're a big talker, aren't you?" she said belligerently. "Seems like all I do is hear you mouthing off and I got to tell you, I'm a little sick and tired of it."

I recognized the voice. I recognized the tone. The elusive Martha Ray had surfaced at last after a couple of days simmering over my big mouth. And she was no prize. She was about the size of a refrigerator, her bad haircut went perfectly with her bad mood and her mouthful of intermittent teeth told me that she liked being in fights.

This was not good.

"Look," I said. "I've got no beef with you. Whatever position you're in, whatever power you have, you are welcome to it." She had the green shirt of a lifer on. "I'm just passing through. I'm not here to make trouble."

"Too late," she announced. I knew I was in deep shit then. She had no audience and she still wanted to kick my ass. "You've already pissed me off."

She took a step toward me — ready to deck me — just as an unlikely angel in the form of the small black woman guard who'd searched me my first day stepped into the community room and pointed at me with her baton.

"Little — you're coming with me," the guard said. "Your lawyer's here. You got fifteen minutes. Make it quick." She glanced at Martha Ray. "Is this your phone time, Petunia? Because if it's not, and you're not out of this room in five seconds, you'll be seeing nothing but the back of a door for a week."

Martha Ray scurried from the room but not without a backward glance to confirm that I was indeed laughing at her.

Hey, I couldn't help it. Her real name was *Petunia,* for godsakes.

# Chapter Ten

I had never been so glad to see Bobby D. in my entire life, even if he was channeling the ghost of Clarence Darrow. He wore an immense three-piece suit the color of vanilla ice cream and had a straw hat perched on the top of his tomato-shaped head. I gawked as I entered the prison room reserved for private meetings and took a seat across the table from him. "Anyone ever tell you it's tacky to wear white after Labor Day?" I asked.

"It's winter white. This is my card." He slid a business card across the table at me. It had more curlicues than a Geri-Curl commercial. His full legal name was emblazoned across it in a typeface last seen on P.T. Barnum's gravestone. An underscored "Esquire" followed his name and, just in case that wasn't clear enough, the words *Purveyor of Fine Law* were printed underneath that.

"Purveyor? Bobby, you do realize this is the 21$^{st}$ Century, right? We've landed a man on the moon and invented computers."

He ignored my comment. "The best lawyers are those who practice law in the classic sense," he said grandly. I noticed his voice had grown deeper and he was over-enunciating. Hoo, boy, was I in trouble. Did Bobby actually think he was a lawyer on some level? I'd need a real one quick if he kept this up.

"Where did you buy that suit?" I whispered. "They have a tall man's shop in these mountains?"

"I had to drive down to Winston-Salem for something. I stopped by Sears while I was there. Sorry I'm late. They had to take out the waistband a little."

*Sears?* I stared at the suit dubiously. Could this be leftover from the disco era? Had it been hanging in a backroom for thirty-five years, just waiting for Bobby to stumble in and buy it? I noticed Bobby's gold jewelry nestled at the base of his neck and began to giggle.

"What?" he demanded indignantly.

"You look like a cross between John Travolta and Marlon Brando right before he went belly up."

Bobby ignored me and looked at his watch. "It took me two days to get permission to even see you and we now have ten minutes left."

I collected myself. "Okay, listen — I've got bad news."

"What a coincidence," he said. "So do I. You go first."

"Shep got a call from Bill Butler while I was on the phone with him. I've got a bad feeling about it."

"You should have a bad feeling about it. That was my bad news, too. You're officially a 'person of interest' in Tonya Blackburn's murder."

"'A person of interest?'" I asked. "As in, the police think you're guilty as hell, but if they say that, the department and any newspapers that report it might get sued?"

"Exactly. Someone saw your car leaving her trailer and got your license plate and you, my friend, are the Perry County Sheriff Department's number one suspect. Numero Uno. The Big Cheese. The Grande Fromage. At the very top of Perry County's Most Wanted List."

"She'd been dead for days when I found her," I said. "You smelled me. It's ridiculous to think I had anything to do with it."

"Not really," Bobby pointed. "That was one obscurely-located trailer, yet you knew how to find it. You show up, you obviously go through the trailer — or someone did — then you leave and don't report the body? It looks like someone returning to the scene of the crime to make sure they didn't leave any evidence behind, even to me, much less the cops."

Great, so now Bobby was going to act like a lawyer, not simply look like one. Too bad he wasn't acting like a lawyer on my side. I wanted to brain him. "You know that I did not have anything to do with her death. You saw me afterward. I was green."

He held up a hand and his gold ring twinkled at me. I fought a sudden urge to kiss that ring — if Shep started doubting me, he could keep me here. Bobby was my lifeline. Bobby represented freedom. Bobby was my only ticket out.

"I know you're innocent, babe. I was just presenting their side." He looked at me carefully. "You don't look so good. You're kind of pale. You okay?"

"No," I hissed. "I'm not okay. If Bill Butler convinces Shep I was involved in the murder, who knows what will happen? What if Shep says, 'Say, buddy, what a coincidence? She's in prison already. *Let's just keep her there.*'" I broke out in a sweat just saying it. My lungs felt like a vise had clamped down on them.

"Whoa there, Nellie," Bobby said. "Bend over and breathe deeply. Stick your head between your legs. That's it. Breathe in. Breathe out. And listen up." He took deep breaths, encouraging me to keep going. I tried to get my panic under control as he brought me up to speed. "First of all, from what I know, Butler wasn't calling your sheriff boyfriend to rat on you. He was trying to find you, so he could tell you himself that the Perry County cops were looking for you. He may not even have told Shep about it at all."

"What if he did?" I asked miserably.

"Then I'd say, at least for the next few days, until his johnson recovers from your little tumble in the hay, Gaines is more likely to believe your side of the story. So you've got a couple of days at a minimum. We'll figure something out."

It was nonsense, but I needed to cling to it. "I did find a few things out," I told Bobby. "The guards are definitely favoring short-termers, and there's something that goes on when they get out of here, when the women get released. They're working for the guards in some way."

"Call girl ring!" Bobby guessed with enthusiasm. "It's genius. The guards bring in extra cash, the girls make a living and everybody wins."

"No," I said crossly. "Good lord, Bobby. Not everybody wins in a call girl ring, okay? And it's not sex they're selling when they get out, at least I don't think so. It's something else. I need more time. But not too much more time," I hastened to add. "What does Shep have planned?"

"What do you mean?"

"I mean, when is he getting me out of here?"

"He didn't say," Bobby said apologetically.

"What do you mean he didn't say? Aren't you supposed to stay in touch with him at all times?"

"I can't get him on the phone. He's been unavailable for days."

"He's ducking your calls?" I asked, panic washing over me again.

"Not necessarily," Bobby assured me. "He is the sheriff of this county. He may be busy." He patted me on the back. "Keep breathing. And here. I brought you something." He handed me two pieces of paper – color Xeroxes. I looked at them more closely. Tears welled up in my eyes.

Bobby was appalled. "Geeze, Casey. We have to get you out of this place. I've never seen you cry before."

"How did you know?" I asked as I stared at copies of my two most precious possessions in the world — a photograph of my long-dead parents standing in a soybean field, the Florida sun setting behind them, and another of my grandfather sitting on his front porch, tilted back in a rocking chair, enjoying the sleep of the righteous after a hard day's work. He had a big smile on his face, as if he were dreaming of the very best day of his life.

I remembered taking the photo like it was yesterday. I was fourteen, and he was all I had in the world. I'd been worrying for two years that taking care of me was a burden, that I'd ruined his life by entering it so abruptly and with so many needs. But when I'd seen him sleeping like that, with a smile on his face, I'd known we were going to be okay, that even with all the hard scrabble and the endless days of work, my grandfather was happy.

"You're getting the copies wet," Bobby complained. "I had to drive all the way to Winston-Salem to find a Kinko's. I didn't want to risk giving you the originals, in case anything happened to them in here."

"That's why you drove to Winston-Salem?" I asked as the tears came harder. "You're too good of a friend to me, Bobby," I said. "I don't deserve you."

"Stop it." He kicked me under the table.

"Ouch," I complained. "What did you do that for?"

"You're freaking me out," he said. "Stop with the tears. And if you're like this next time I come, I'm pulling the plug on this operation. You can't see it, but I sure as hell can. Whatever is happening to you in here, it's not good. I want the old Casey back."

"I'm fine," I insisted, wiping my eyes with the back of my hand as I stared at the photographs. "Thank you for this."

"Don't mention it," he said with a magnanimous wave of his hand, as if he always drove hours each way to help out a friend.

* * *

I SLIPPED THE PHOTOGRAPHS inside my shirt, where I could feel them against my heart. Two things hit me as the female guard, Alldread, escorted me back to the dining hall. One, I was a mess and could not take many more days inside. Two, I might have been wrong when I insisted to Bobby that whatever was going on, it had nothing to do with sex between the guards and the inmates. I say this because, just as we rounded one of the corners near the kitchen, a red-haired inmate hurried out of a bathroom, her head down and face grim, followed closely by a red-faced guard tucking his shirt into his pants. Very subtle, buddy. Twirling the condom over your head like a lasso would have been less obvious. Assuming he'd used one, of course. I took a closer look: he was as meticulously clean and as relentlessly in shape as all of the other guards I'd seen so far. Close-cropped hair, not an ounce of extra fat — and something on his forearm I'd seen on a couple of other guards. I stepped back against the wall to let another group of inmates pass and was able to get a few feet closer to him. It was a plain black tattoo, about two inches wide. I recognized the shape: it was the silhouette of a ploughshare linked to a sword, both depicted above an anvil. Weird. Or Biblical. Or both.

"Keep moving," the guard escorting me hissed in my ear. She guided me around the male guard. From the rigid set of her jaw, I guessed she'd seen the male guards and inmates come tumbling out of the bathrooms before — and she did not approve.

I knew better than to say anything. "I know the way now," I mumbled as we drew closer to the dining room.

"Rules," she said. "Sometimes we randomly escort prisoners. Helps us know what they're up to."

"What?" I asked, not believing her. Then I shut the hell up. It wasn't the rules, I realized. The guard was helping me out, just in case Martha Ray, a.k.a., Petunia, was lurking nearby, hoping to throw her weight and bad mullet around a little bit more that day.

"Thanks," I mumbled as we neared the kitchen door.

She shrugged and walked off without a word. I was on my own again.

I kept my head down. I scrubbed and fetched and kept my mouth shut while the dinner hour swirled about me, the sound level as excruciating as ever. I was willing to bet that a monkey house during a hurricane was quieter than that damn dining room. The chattering was immense. It came in waves, pounding against my head, which had started to throb. Everywhere I looked, the dining room was crammed full of noisy or angry or shouting women, hollering at friends three tables over, arguing with their table mates, shrieking with laughter a little too loudly, betraying their closeness to desperation. The noise seemed to build in a crescendo, break and cascade into my brain, then begin to build again. Every movement made in the dining hall emerged in hyper-relief, as if I was moving in slow motion. If I hadn't known better, I'd swear I had been drugged. But I knew better: it wasn't drugs. It was me. No matter how hard I tried, deep inside, I was starting to panic. I should never have tried this. I had been behind bars long enough. It would only get worse. I needed to get out of there fast.

I wasn't the only one suffering from the noise. I spotted my silent roommate, Risa Foster, as always eating alone at the head of a table, ignoring the chattering women sitting a few seats down on each side. I had no idea who she was, really. We'd spent three nights together, locked in a cell, and she'd never said so much as "boo!" to me. Which was just as well. I'd have crapped my drawers if she had. Seven dead men and a lawn full of rifles proved nothing if not that she was a woman of action.

The other women at her table had grown careless and were sitting much closer than usual. Worse, they were taking turns screaming witless jokes in response to pointless stories before collapsing in forced giggles that sounded like nothing so much as witches being boiled in their own cauldron. I saw Risa grow rigid, paralyzed by their shrill voices. They were encroaching on the space she kept around her. Her hand inched toward her fork.

I could foresee it all: Risa grabbing the fork, Risa standing up abruptly and lunging forward, Risa bringing the fork down at just the right angle to drive the plastic tines right through a hand, puncturing the flesh and pinning the hand right to the table top, the guards springing into action a heartbeat too late, Risa being hauled off to solitary, her lonely life made even lonelier.

I had to stop it. I rushed up the row between the crowded tables, reaching my cellmate just as she lifted the fork to strike. I pinned her hand to the table as I nearly enfolded her in my body and hissed into her ear. “Don’t do it. They’re not worth it. There’s a guard less than a foot behind you.”

She froze, shocked that I had dared touch her and even more shocked that I had dared to interfere. But she did not move and after a moment of silence, I felt her fingers release the fork she held.

“Look, they’re leaving,” I pointed out as the two women pushed back from the table, the metal legs of their chairs scraping angrily against the floor. “Just take a deep breath and wait it out. They’re not worth weeks in solitary.”

Those stupid bitches took forever to take their trays and get the hell away from what surely would have been agony for at least one of them. I don’t think my cellmate so much as breathed during that time.

“Why did you try to do that?” I asked. We were breathing in unison, as synchronized as lovers curled up in a bed might be.

“They made me mad,” she said, but her posture softened.

When the women were out of stabbing distance, I released her and walked away, knowing better than to wait for any sort of thanks. I could only hope she didn’t bring the fork to bed with her later. I had no desire to end up being a surrogate shish-ka-bob.

“What was that all about?” Peppa asked me, having witnessed the odd interlude. There was nothing Peppa did not see, I realized. Like the Great Oz, she knew all and saw all.

"You don't want to know," I told her. And I meant it.

You'd think that would be enough excitement for one night, but, having saved some worthless inmate from a stabbing, a cynical Universe rewarded me poorly. It happened right after dinner, when Peppa asked me to bring her a carton of canned peaches from the storage room. She was whipping up some peach cobbler, and if I played my cards right, I'd get to be the taste tester.

It was the best news I'd had all day. I hurried off to a concrete storage room filled with wire shelves stacked high with cartons of industrial-sized canned fruits and vegetables. The room was dark. When I finally found the light switch, it only turned on one row of lights, creating a thinly-lit strip of visibility that mostly made the shadows on either side seem even more menacing. As I walked down the aisle, peering at labels, I heard a scratching sound in the darkness on the other side of the wire shelves. I stopped and held my breath. Nothing. The room seemed eerily silent after all the noise of the dining hall. I started down the row and I heard it again. A scraping of feet across concrete. I stopped. The sound stopped. I waited, breathing deeply, trying to get my panic under control. The air in the room was stagnant, dry and hot, filled with dust and cardboard particles that swirled in the florescent light. I felt it coming on, a massive sneeze, the dust motes inching further and further up my nose. I could not hold it in any longer and bent over, hands on my knees, sneezing so hard it propelled me forward just as a stack of cartons piled high on a shelf above me crashed down. They missed my skull by inches, glancing off the back of my shoulders, sending me flying to the ground as sixty pounds of metal cans and sharp-edged cardboard boxes tumbled to the floor behind me, the sound as loud as an explosion

Footsteps echoed down the aisle hidden by the shelf in front of me. A door slammed as I lay in the darkness, afraid to move, my fingers searching the concrete floor for wet spots, my mind imagining my brains splashed across the floor, a five-pound can of creamed corn embedded in my skull. I had missed being flattened by inches and I'd have a hell of a bruise on my shoulders as proof.

A door opened at the far end of my aisle. Noise filled the room as people and voices grew closer. Figures bent over me as fingers fluttered through my hair and then gently ran over my face. “Talk to me, Little Debbie,” Peppa said softly. “Tell me you are not lying there dead.”

“I’m not lying there dead,” I repeated obediently. “Though not for lack of someone trying.”

I was lifted to my feet. Peppa used her rag to dust me off and to probe for injuries. “What happened?” she asked as the other women with her inched away. With me still mobile, they smelled more trouble coming and they wanted no part of it.

“Someone tried to kill me,” I whispered back. “That’s what happened. Probably Martha Ray.”

“Girl, you do work fast,” Peppa admitted, shaking her head. “I was in here three months before someone tried to kill me."

# Chapter Eleven

That night, the true darkness came. I lay in bed, the ceiling hovering what seemed like inches above me, and knew I had to get out the next day. I could hear my cellmate breathing evenly beneath me. She had once again fallen asleep in her lower bunk, the photo of her little girl in her hands, without a word to me. Risa Foster had crawled into a place so far inside her head that nothing could touch her, not the lack of freedom, not the walls, not even another human being. I envied her the ability, but I knew it came only because she had no hope and no expectation of ever getting out.

Me? I had to get out now. I should never have tried to go back inside.

I took out the Xeroxed photos of my family Bobby had given me and tried to remember what it was like to stand in the middle of a fifty-acre soybean field with nothing but skies above and rows of green stretching over the horizon, a verdant land so vast you could run for days and never hit concrete.

But I couldn't feel it. I could see it. I could wish for it, but the way it had felt eluded me.

Deep in the night, I gave up trying to sleep and wandered over to the bars that separated my cell from the block hall. I had noticed that night was the only time they bothered to keep the doors locked, an attempt to keep the women from finding private places for their private encounters.

It was deeply quiet. I stood at the bars of my window, drinking in the stillness. The air had shifted almost imperceptibly inside the prison and I knew that outside its stone walls, the temperature and barometer were falling. Snow, I thought, smelling the bite of it on the air. The mountains could be like that, I knew, one day bathed in sunshine, the next shrouded by snow clouds.

I froze, unmoving, as the outline of a guard unfolded from the shadows outside my cell. He looked like all the others, although his hair was a little thinner than most. He was lean and muscled, his face unreadable as he drew closer to the bars of my cage and peered in at me. A familiar tattoo peeked out from beneath one of his shirt cuffs: the tip of a ploughshare and sword.

"Can't sleep?" he asked, his voice a soft drawl.

"No," I said. "I can't."

He stared at my blue shirt. "At least you won't be in here for long."

"I hope not."

"You've been in before?" he asked. It was barely a question.

"Once. A long time ago."

"And you're ready to get out again?" he guessed. "I can see it in your eyes."

"It's worse, having been in before. I know what it's going to feel like when the days start to turn into weeks."

He stared at me quietly, as if sizing up the nature of my soul. He had odd eyes. Even in the murky lighting of the night hallway, I could see that they were a light greenish-gold, flecked with deeper spots of brown. They disconcerted me, but I forced myself to stare back at him. I would not be cowed.

"You seem like a smart woman," he whispered.

That whisper scared me.

"Not smart enough," I said. "I'm in here, aren't I?"

He did not smile. "I can make it easier on you. And give you a way to make it easier on yourself once you get out."

I was quiet for a moment, gauging how best to take a step closer to the truth. "I'm not big on giving it up to men I don't know," I finally said.

His laugh was more like a bark. "I'm not interested in sex."

"Than what?" I asked. "What do you want me to do?"

He sensed something in my tone and backed off. "Just think about it," he said, taking a step back into the darkness. "Think about what you'd be prepared to do to get out of here early and what you want for yourself once you get out of here. Think about it, and I'll be back." He turned on his heels and moved down the hall until he reached the end. He leaned against the wall, not a care in the world, whistling tunelessly.

I felt as if the devil himself had come to me in the night and brushed me with his tail.

"Don't go there, my friend," a familiar voice whispered from the other side of my cell wall.

"Peppa?" I asked. "You heard all that?"

"I heard all that."

I stepped back so the guard would not see us talking and lowered my voice. "Did you understand what he was talking about?" I asked.

I sensed her knowledge in her silence. She knew exactly what he'd been talking about. She just wasn't sure she wanted to tell me.

"You knew Tonya Blackburn well when she was inside here, didn't you?" I guessed. "You know what's going on."

"You're not in here for trying to kill your husband," Peppa said. "If you had tried to kill him, he'd be dead. Who are you and what are you doing in here?"

I hesitated, knowing I was taking a chance. But I also knew I had no other choice. "Come closer," I said. "Act like, well, you know." We huddled at the edge of the bars, as close as we could get, given the metal and concrete between us. "Don't even go there," I whispered when her hand fluttered closer to my breasts in the darkness.

"Can't hurt to try," she whispered back.

"I'm putting my life in your hands," I said softly. "And that's going to have to be enough."

Her hand grew instantly still. "Tell me," she whispered back.

I told her who I was and why I was inside. She listened without comment.

"Do you really think one woman can stop what's happening?" she asked when I was done.

"I don't know. But I know I can try."

"The guards are using the girls as distribution points," she said. "They're running drugs through them when the women get out. If they try to stop or say no, the guards say they've got a deal going with the parole officers. They'll claim they broke parole and the girls will end up back in here. Or they threaten their families."

I was silent for a moment. It all fit. "Where do they get the drugs?"

"That I don't know. But I know they got plenty. Meth, mostly, but coke and Oxy and heroin, too. You know how all the guards look alike?"

"I'd noticed," I said.

"A lot of them got that tattoo, the one curved kind of funny?"

"It's a ploughshare," I explained. "Like a farmer uses, only it's linked to a sword, like they want to turn one into the other."

"Whatever. If they've got the tattoo and they've got short hair and they look muscled enough to kick your ass, they're in on it, okay? They're some kind of group. I think they bring in the drugs from somewhere else, and then they force the women who get out of here to sell the drugs for them across the state. The guards send them off with the drugs, then the women come back and meet with them, or they go find them, and the women give them the money they got from selling the drugs, get more drugs, and go back home again. In exchange, the women get a cut of the money and they get out of here early, thanks to good behavior notations in their files."

"And that's what Tonya was involved in?" I asked.

"Yes," Peppa said. "I knew her pretty well."

"Why didn't you tell me that to begin with?"

"I didn't know you," she explained.

"Tonya had a son," I told Peppa. "He's missing. That's why I'm here. I'm trying to find him. Tonya was killed and her son is missing. I think these guards might be behind it."

"I thought she must be dead," Peppa said. "She always put money into my canteen account, you know? I got no one on the outside and she knew it. But the money stopped coming a couple weeks ago."

"That's when she was murdered," I explained. "I'm sorry."

"Tonya never said she had a son. Not even to me and we talked a lot, like this, in the middle of the night. She was just a couple of cells down and she had trouble sleeping, too."

"Maybe she was trying to protect him," I suggested.

"That makes sense. If you try to back out of their arrangement, they threaten your family. Tonya might have had to sell their drugs for the money, but she was smart enough to hide her son from them so they couldn't hurt him."

"Who do the guards represent? What do they want?"

"I don't know," Peppa said. "My guess is they want to blow something up. White men sure do like their explosions."

I was silent, trying to piece it together.

"Yo, Debbie," Peppa called out softly.

"Yeah?" I said.

"What's your real name?"

"Casey."

"Casey? I like it." She waved a hand in my direction and it fluttered like a bird finding its way through the dark. "Casey — don't tell anyone else what you just told me," she said. "It's not safe. You shouldn't even have let me know who you really are."

* * *

THE NEXT MORNING, I rose early, anxious to leave the confines of my cell. I needed to think about what to do next. I had learned from Peppa that it was possible to slip outside the back door of the kitchen and stand, unnoticed, in a small, enclosed area behind the main building. It didn't offer much in the way of ambience. It was basically a concrete stoop surrounded by a patch of ragged grass bordered by a gravel driveway that ended at a door to the storage room. The driveway began at a locked gate a few dozen feet away. Each time a truck delivered cartons of canned goods and other supplies, the gate had to be unlocked, even though it only opened onto the internal roadway that snaked through the prison complex. It was a gate within a gate within two more gates. Kind of like the outer circles of hell, minus most of the sulfur.

Still, the air was fresh and the sky stretched overhead, giving me a good look at the clouds I had glimpsed the night before. They blanketed the sky in heavy gray waves and the air smelled like steel, a sure sign snow was coming. I breathed in deeply, savoring fresh oxygen untainted by sweat or cheap perfume.

"Hey L.D., better wrap it up." Peppa stood in the doorway, a stirring spoon in her hand, and looked up at the sky with me. "Gonna snow for sure. But not until later. I know my mountain.

She's waiting for the afternoon." She waved the spoon at me. "Get on in. One of the guards is looking for you. You got a visitor."

"This early?" I asked. It wasn't even time for breakfast and, around these parts, that meant the rooster was still dreaming of the hen house.

"It's gotta be law enforcement," Peppa explained. "They don't bend the rules for anyone else."

It had to be Shep. It had been days since we spoke. My stomach started to bubble and I was sorry I'd had a third cup of coffee. I was walking into a lot of unknowns here: had Bill Butler told him I was a suspect in Tonya Blackburn's murder? Had Shep believed him? Was there any vestige left of the bond we'd had earlier or had I imagined it all? And then I asked myself the most important question — could Shep get me out of here? I hated that my mind had seized on the tiniest seed of doubt about him. I had no reason to doubt him. But I had no reason to trust him, either. Not really. I didn't know him at all.

"Why so worried?" Peppa asked as we stepped back into the noisy confines of the kitchen: clanging pots, steam hissing, women laughing, hot grits bubbling. "You look like someone just ran over your dog."

"I got a bad feeling," I explained.

"I was born with one," Peppa answered. "And there's only one way to deal with it — go see what you're up against."

Peppa pretended like she didn't care about anyone but herself, but I noticed she came to the edge of the dining room and watched as I followed a guard out the door. I don't know why, but knowing she was keeping watch made me feel better. If I never returned, at least one person would wonder where I had gone.

Shep was waiting for me in full uniform. He rose when I entered the meeting room. I hoped it was a good sign. But he said nothing until the guard had left and locked the door behind him.

"What is it?" I asked. I felt like I might throw up. "Why are you looking at me that way?"

He glanced toward the windows where the guard lingered outside.

"He can't hear you," I said.

"Don't be naive," Shep whispered. He placed his hands on the table, inches from mine. I longed to touch his fingers, just to establish contact. I'd settle for anything to bridge the chasm that seemed to divide us.

"What's happened?" I asked quietly. "What did Bill Butler say?"

Shep looked up at me but said nothing.

"I had nothing to do with Tonya Blackburn's death," I whispered furiously. "How can you even think that?"

Shep looked startled. "I don't think that," he said. "That's not why I'm here. Butler told me Perry County was trying to bring you in because they're hoping you can give them something to go on. They've got no leads."

"But if they find out I'm here," I said. "They could take me into custody."

"You're in under a different name, remember?" Shep spoke as if distracted. This was not what he had come to discuss. "They don't know you're here."

"Oh, yeah." I was losing it. I was silent for a moment. I took a deep breath. "Please get me out of here, Shep. I can't stay any longer. I found out what I need to know. You have to get me out of here today."

His amazing blue eyes slid away from mine and I knew I was in trouble. Deep, deep trouble. "I can't," he said. "I've been suspended from duty. If you look closely, you'll see I'm not wearing my badge. I only got in here because word isn't out yet and the guys at the gate know me. I wore my best uniform hoping to distract them. It worked, but I need to get out quick before someone makes a call and lets them know."

"What happened?" My heart started beating like a tom-tom. If Shep had no power, than who in the everlovin' hell was going to get me out of here?

"I don't know," he said. "The feds pulled me in for questioning yesterday. That's when they took my badge. Officially, I'm on paid leave. Unofficially, I'm in deep shit."

"About the inmate and guard thing?"

Shep nodded. "They know there's something going on, and they think I'm behind it."

"You?" I asked. "Why?"

"I think I'm being set up," Shep explained. "Someone found out I was looking into it and is setting me up. If I go down for this, they won't have to."

"Did you tell them the truth?" I asked. "Did you tell them about me?"

"I told them I wasn't involved," he said. "But they didn't believe me. I couldn't tell them about you."

"Why not?" I demanded.

"Because you're my only hope, Casey. If you don't find out who really is behind this, they're not going to let up. I'll go down for it. You're my only hope."

"But you're *my* only hope," I pointed out.

"Then we're both in trouble," he said. He leaned in closer as he spoke. I caught a whiff of soap and aftershave. It made my heart ache.

"I did find something out," I said. "Give them this." I told him all I knew about the arrangement between the guards and short-term inmates, about the drugs being brought in from out of state and distributed by newly released inmates, about all the guards involved being linked by the ploughshare and sword tattoo. "Does that help?" I asked when I was done.

"Maybe," he said. "If it's true. But, Casey, that's basically the word of one inmate, someone you barely know. Do you know what that woman is in here for? What she did to her father?"

"I don't want to know," I said quickly. "And I believe Peppa. Yes, she's locked up in here for life. Yes, she's hard on the outside. But she's not hard on the inside. She's not. And in this place? With the life she's had? That's a miracle in itself. She was telling me the truth, Shep."

I wasn't even sure he'd heard me.

"What is it?" I asked, brushing my fingers against the side of his hand. It was so warm, I wanted to cry.

"I'm from here," he explained. "This is *my* mountain. The feds think this ring is local, that the roots run deep here. They're not going to believe I'm not involved. I wouldn't believe it either."

"They have to believe you," I whispered furiously.

"No, they don't," he said. "And, trust me, they may not."

I sat in a silent panic as the whole mess played out in my mind like a bad movie: Shep going down for the conspiracy charges, the guards turning on him, testifying against him in exchange for reduced sentences, knowing full well that the real culprits were going free. And me? Me being transferred to someone else's supervision within the system where it would take weeks, maybe months, to establish my real identity and to prove the charges against me involved a man who doesn't even exist.

I couldn't last another day in here, much less a month.

I had to get in touch with Bobby. Bobby was all I had. If Shep couldn't help me, Bobby D. was all I had.

*Bobby.* Bobby had the tape I'd made of my conversation with Shep. That tape did more than prove my innocence. It did more than prove I was in prison undercover — that tape proved Shep was innocent as well. He had talked about his own investigation. It was clear he wasn't involved. Sure, someone might argue that the tape had been staged, but it might be enough to dislodge some stubborn fed's opinion, at least. It might be enough to get Shep off the hook for long enough to get me out of here.

"I taped our conversation," I said, too loudly. We both looked toward the window. The guard was leaning against a wall, eyes closed, as if he were asleep.

"Which conversation?"

"The one on the mountain. I trust you remember? *When I agreed to go undercover for you.*"

"You taped us without my knowledge?" He sounded pissed.

"Yes," I said defensively. "And it might save your ass. Take the tape to the feds. Let them listen to it. It'll convince them you aren't involved. And it will get me the hell out of here."

Shep's mouth curved in the oddest way, as he could not decide whether to smile or bite someone.

"What?" I mumbled. "Don't look at me that way."

"I love you, Casey," he said, taking one of my hands. "I love every inch of your suspicious little mind."

"My *mind?"* I complained.

"And every inch of your suspicious little body, too," he assured me.

Cool. I could live with that.

"I have to call Bobby," I told him. "He won't give the tape to you until I tell him to. And he'll want to make a copy of it first."

"Call him," he said. He nodded toward the window. "I'll get the guard to let you make a call."

"If I know Bobby, he's still at breakfast. He'll be in a good mood. How long until I get out of here?"

Shep frowned.

"How long?" I asked again.

"Look, I'm not a sheriff right now. I'm a suspect. Even if I can get someone to listen to the tape, they'll still have to verify everything I say, then check out that you're who you say you are. They'll need to verify that you're a licensed private investigator, but that's just a phone call and shouldn't take long." He noticed my expression. "What? I'm not going to like this, am I?"

"I'm not exactly a licensed private investigator," I mumbled reluctantly.

"Why not? A dead dog could get a P.I. license in this state."

"Not if it has a record. And I do have a record. In Florida. It happened over fifteen years ago."

"For what?" he asked grimly.

"Felony drug charges. I did a year and a half. I'm in the system."

"You're in more than that." He looked angry. "Why didn't you tell me?"

"I was a different person back then, it was a different life. I left it all behind a long time ago. It has nothing to do with this."

Shep shook his head. "Casey, I'll be lucky if I can get you out of here in a month. Forget any national databases, they're going to do a state-by-state search to make sure you have no outstanding warrants, and they'll do god knows what else to slow it down. No one is going to give a crap about expediting it now that they know you have a record. You are now officially at the mercy of the paper pushers. You should have told me."

"A month?" I repeated, horrified. I jerked my hand away from his. "I can't do four weeks in here. It was a mistake to try four days. I need to get out now."

He read the panic in my face. "Just call Bobby," he said softly. "Tell him I need that tape. Once I'm cleared, I'll do everything I can for you."

"How do I know I can believe you?" I asked bitterly. I wasn't angry at Shep. I was angry at myself, for what I had done so long ago, and all for such an unworthy person as my worthless ex-husband. I wondered if I would ever really be able to leave it all behind. Because the world sure didn't want me to.

"You don't have a choice," Shep pointed out. "You have to trust me. But I promise you this, Casey. And I want you to listen to me very, very carefully." He leaned toward me until his mouth was barely an inch from my ear. I could feel his warm breath against my skin and it made me not only shiver, it made me want to cry with an overpowering longing to be in a safe place with him, a place like his cabin on a sunlit morning.

"I will move heaven, if I have to," Shep whispered in my ear. "Or I will move hell. I will move this mountain itself to get you out of here. You have my word."

* * *

SHEP HAD BEEN RIGHT — the guard agreed to take me to the common room for a quick phone call. The rest of the women were still at breakfast and the room seemed eerily quiet, as if any conversation I attempted on the phone might echo to every corner of the cavernous room. I headed for the bank of telephones against one wall. The guard watched me closely from the doorway, even though Shep had stuck around to divert his attention while I talked to Bobby.

I said a pray and dialed. The reception was so terrible on Bobby's end I could barely understand him when he answered.

"Bobby," I whispered frantically, "Can you hear me? Can you hear me?"

There was big gulp on the other end then his voice came through as clearly as if he were standing right next to me. "Of course I can hear you. I was just finishing my corn cakes. They're quite excellent. Bunny puts a little…"

"It can wait," I interrupted. "I need your help *now.*"

"Anything, babe."

"Give Shep the tape I made on the mountain."

"No," he said.

"What?" I asked, the panic returning.

"I'm not giving him my only copy of the tape."

"Fine," I hissed. "Make a copy, then give him the original. It might be sent to a lab, so it's got to be the original. Please, I'm begging you."

"Just give me an hour to make a copy and it's his. I'll even drop it by his office on a silver platter. Dare I ask why I'm doing this?"

"No," I said. "And here's why: I'm going to tell you about it in person. Because I have to get out of here. *Today.* What can you do? There has to be something you can do."

"I'm not a real lawyer, Case," he started to say. "I'm not up to speed on how to — "

"I don't care how you do it." I glanced over my shoulder. The guard looked impatient and was only half listening to whatever Shep was telling him. "Bobby, this is the most serious thing I have ever said to you: you have to get me out of here. By any means possible."

There was a silence on the other end, then I heard laughter. The bastard was actually laughing at me.

"How dare you?" I said before he cut me off.

"Relax. I'm laughing because I've got an idea. Oh, it's a sweet one. I hope I have enough time." There was a brief silence and I wanted to scream with impatience. Hope. He was giving me hope and I needed to grab onto it now.

"What is it?" I practically yelled.

"It's better you don't know."

"Don't know what?" I asked. The panic was coming back, it was inching its way toward my brain. Was I insane? Did I not know, better than anyone, what harebrained schemes Bobby could come up with? What was I agreeing to?

"What time is exercise time?" he asked me. "When you're out in the yard?"

"From four to five. Unless something happens, like you come to visit waving some piece of paper that says I can get the fuck out of here. Which is what you really need to figure out how to do."

"Be in the exercise yard this afternoon," he told me, a curious confidence in his voice. "Dress warmly."

"Dress warmly?" I asked incredulously. "You think they hand out mukluks around here or something?"

"Dress as warmly as you can," he corrected himself. "Find an empty spot in the yard, near the fence. Scan the perimeter."

"Scan the perimeter? What the fuck does that mean?" I asked. "Scan the perimeter of what?"

"The mountain," Bobby said. "Check the edge of the trees on the perimeter of the prison grounds. I'll be hard to spot, probably in camouflage."

Bobby in camouflage? Not so hard to miss, actually. "Okay," I said dubiously. What choice did I have? "I'll scan the perimeter for Commander Kurtz minus the jungle natives. What then?"

"It's best you not know."

"How can it possibly be best that I don't know?" This time I did scream into the phone, which was a mistake. The guard was moving toward me.

"I've got to go," I whispered. "Just give Shep the tape. And get me out of here. Please. I'm begging you as my friend, Bobby. Please get me out of here."

"Be outside at four," he said. "I'll take care of the rest."

Oh, sweet Jesus god, what was I getting myself into? I hung up the phone and leaned against the wall.

"Life sucks and then you die," the guard said cheerfully. He took my arm and guided me toward the door. "Your favor is up. Time to get back to work."

I looked around, needing to see Shep, but he had disappeared. I thought I knew why. Word would start to get out any moment inside the prison that he was no longer acting sheriff.

Oh, god, I thought, as I trudged back toward the kitchen. My fate was in Bobby D.'s big fat, chocolate-stained, sausage-fingered, catcher's mitt hands now. Would he come through?

* * *

THE DAY CRAWLED BY. I sought refuge in the kitchen, scrubbing pots so furiously that Peppa stopped to stare at me.

"What?" I asked. "Prefer them dirty? I can always just leave this two inch crust of black shit on them to flavor the next pot of beans."

"What happened this morning?" she asked. "Who was here to see you?"

"I can't tell you," I said, realizing I sounded like a total bitch and that none of it was Peppa's fault. "I mean, I could tell you — but it's better for you that you don't know."

"Let me take a wild guess: you could tell me, but then you'd have to kill me?"

"Something like that."

"You hear about the sheriff?" she asked, watching me closely.

"What sheriff?"

"The Bartow County sheriff," she said. "Tall, tan white dude. Not as much of a jerk as some of them."

I shrugged as if unconcerned, but my heart was hammering in my chest. "What about him?"

"Feds got him. Say that he might be behind that thing I told you about. I never would have thought it. He was okay. For a sheriff."

Her gaze was making me uncomfortable. "So?" I asked.

"So, does that make much sense to you?" she said. "You think he's part of it. The leader or something?"

"How should I know?"

"Thought you might be working with him. He's the one who checked you into this place, right?"

"I work alone," I said glumly.

"Sure you do," Peppa said. "We all do."

I didn't say anything back and she just shrugged. "Well," she told me, "you just keep on working on those pots, L.D., ya' hear?"

"Thanks, I will," I mumbled, ashamed of myself for making it obvious that I did not trust her.

I avoided everyone after that, taking to my cell once work detail was done. I climbed up on my bed and lay there, feeling the minutes tick by, as silent and withdrawn as my roommate, Risa, who lay in her characteristic stupor on the bottom bunk, staring into the shadows.

Minutes inched by, who knew how many, before I heard Risa call out softly. "You okay?" she asked.

"Not really."

"You'll get used to it," she said.

"That's what I'm afraid of."

She fell back into silence and I spent the next hour going over every possible scenario Bobby might have in mind, plotting how I would react and what I might do. Was he really going to try and break me out of here? There was a double chain-link fence surrounding the exercise yard at the back of the prison, topped with coils of barbed wire. He was out of his mind if he thought I could hoist my caboose up a pair of twelve-foot fences.

I had visions of him ramming through the fences in his land boat, like a shark cutting through a bay, heading for its prey.

Then getting caught in one, like a shark in a net.

Oh, god. I had to be prepared for anything.

Just before four, I rose and pawed though my meager possessions. There wasn't much to choose from. I put on two tee shirts followed by both of the work shirts I'd been issued then hid the copies of my family photographs in the pocket of my inner work shirt. My roommate watched me don four shirts and three pairs of socks, all without comment. When I was done, I looked like I'd gained ten pounds, but you could not tell I was wearing four shirts. I had little else that would be of use. One pair of underwear would just have to do and well, I didn't actually own anything else at the moment. At least not within two hundred miles.

"Here," Risa said, rolling to her feet. She went to her shelf and dug through a neatly folded pile of clothes. "Take these." She held out a pair of gloves.

"I can't take those. You might need them."

She shrugged. "The cold doesn't bother me. We don't get to be outside long enough. Looks like it bothers you more." She stared at my shirts.

"Thanks," I mumbled, avoiding her eyes. Did she know what I was up to?

Oh, for god sakes, of course she knew what I was up to. I'd jumped out of my bunk and put on multiple layers of clothing then started pacing the cell like an animal in the zoo all while mumbling to myself. The only thing more obvious would be if I had a pick ax slung over my shoulder and held a sign saying, "Follow me to the secret exit tunnel."

But Risa didn't seem like she was going to turn me in. In fact, she was helping me.

"Thanks, I might need them," I said as I took the gloves.

But she'd turned her back on me and was silently staring at the wall again.

I thought she'd go back to sleep, but she followed me to the exercise yard at four. She was my shadow, darting in and out of corners, always there.

There weren't many of us outside on that gray winter day. Maybe a dozen of us, standing near the doorway that led outside to a red clay surfaced exercise yard no larger than a quarter of a football field. The sky overheard was pewter and the clouds so heavy with snow they looked pregnant. But the flakes had not started yet.

Women began to filter out into the yard, some in pairs holding hands, others with their arms wrapped around their torsos, needing the glimpse of the mountain — and the world beyond — badly enough to brave the cold.

No one gave me a second glance, but I knew my roommate was watching.

Was she just waiting for the right time to call the guards? Panic nibbled at the edges of my consciousness. Risa could get a lot of privileges for turning in someone planning to escape. She might even get time taken off her sentence.

Stop it, I told myself. Just stop it. What was time taken off of a nine hundred-year sentence with no chance of parole? That was ridiculous. She meant me no harm.

And, yet, there she was, on the edges of the yard, huddled by herself against the wire fence, pretending not to notice anything other than the sky.

But I knew her attention was on me.

"Concentrate," I willed myself. I could not afford to screw this up. Whatever harebrained scheme Bobby had cooked up, this was my only chance to get out before I was trapped in here for months. I had to be on my game.

"Well, if it isn't College Girl herself." I recognized the voice even before I turned and saw the mountain of aggression known as Martha Ray coming to get me.

"Get lost or I'll tell the entire world your real name is Petunia," I warned her.

I couldn't help it. Whenever I saw her, my mouth took on a life of its own. It was like being told not to put beans in my ears. All I wanted was to put beans in my ears. The more people told me to shut up around her, the more I just had to sass her.

She didn't like it, either. As a woman of far fewer words than me, she raised an arm and balled her massive hand into a fist. I can't be sure, but I think she may even have been growling.

"Don't make me mad."

It was a quiet statement uttered by a gentle voice, yet Martha Ray froze when she heard it.

My cellmate, Risa Foster, had somehow appeared at my side. "Don't make me mad, Martha Ray," Risa repeated. And though there was no malice in Risa's voice, Martha stepped back, dropped her hand and walked away without a peep.

"Wow," I said. "That's power. Thank you." I wanted to say more but Risa was already gone. I don't know how she did it.

After that, I avoided everyone, kept my mouth shut and surveyed the perimeter as Bobby had instructed, trying to separate the trees from the shadows, trying to spot anything moving in the darkness of the forest that surrounded the prison grounds. Pines grew down the slope in a canopy of deep green, but rhododendron bushes and other shrubs created a ground-level barrier my eyes could not penetrate. It was hopeless. I would not be able to see anyone coming. I'd just have to keep watch for movement along the edges, or anything unusual or out of place.

Like say, a giant fiberglass hot dog poking out from between two large stands of mountain laurel. Because that's exactly what I was looking at. I didn't know whether to laugh or to cry. An enormous hot dog tip was bouncing and jostling in the bushes with what looked like a grizzly shoving its way through the underbrush behind it. Then I saw a flash of yellow – painted mustard, I knew — and the tan of the fiberglass bun.

It was genius, I thought, whatever else he had in mind — because who would ever believe they were seeing what they were seeing if they saw any of this? They'd think they were hallucinating for sure.

Wait. Maybe I *was* hallucinating?

But, no it was real. The giant hot dog wavered, then steadied, as if Bobby had braced against a fallen log. My god, what was he winging toward me? A gun? Money to bribe the guards?

The sky had darkened. The first few flakes of fat white snow began a gentle fall from the heavens, spiraling lazily to the ground as I heard the sharp pop of the pneumatic gun going off. A dark object soared upward from the bushes, higher and higher. I spotted it at its arc and began to pray as it neared the top of the outer fence. As it cleared the barbed wire, I crossed my fingers and willed its trajectory to continue upward. But it only climbed a few more precious inches before the object began to fall back toward earth.

Oh, no, it wasn't going to clear the inner fence. It wasn't fair, I thought wildly, it wasn't fair. I was a good person. Bobby was doing his best. It wasn't fair that we should fail.

A second later, a tiny parachute popped and bloomed above the object, just as a gust of wind sent the snowflakes dancing in tiny tornadoes. The parachute jerked abruptly upward, cleared the barbed wire of the inner fence by two inches at most, then began its descent on my side. I raced toward it, but the wind gusts grew fiercer, the parachute filled and the object sailed away from me to my right. It was heading straight for my cellmate, Risa Foster.

She looked up, startled, as the object fell at her feet. I froze, not knowing what to do. She bent over and examined the object. She picked it up and fiddled with it, I could not quite see what she was doing with her hands. But when she straightened up, the tiny parachute and all of its strings fell to the ground. She planted one foot in front of her, cocked her arm behind her head like a third baseman for the Yankees and let fly, sending the object soaring a good forty feet across the exercise yard. It fell in the red clay a few yards away. I dashed forward, clawing at the dirt, extracting industrial wire clippers from the muck. Bobby D. had managed to send half a pound of metal flying over both fences with his stupid hot dog gun. And Risa had helped get it to me.

I had no time to waste. Bobby was waving at me, the hot dog gun leaning crazily against a pine tree. I dashed for the first fence, staying low, although I knew the guards were unlikely to be paying much attention, not on such a quiet day, with the skies heavy with snow and the small number of prisoners in the exercise yard. But there were still two towers with sightlines to where I now crouched next to a large metal trashcan, willing myself to be invisible. I frantically clipped thick metal with my tool, twisting each wire away from a hole that opened larger and larger as I cut and pried my way to freedom. My arms ached from the effort and it was taking longer than I thought. Someone would surely notice and not every inmate had as little to gain as Risa. Then there was Martha Ray, who'd turn me in for nothing in return.

But I had misjudged many things about Risa. When I heard shouting, I glanced behind me, expecting to see guards rushing toward me. Instead, I saw Risa hanging off Martha Ray's back, punching at the larger inmate's face as the other women crowded around, screaming for Martha Ray to fight back.

Risa was creating a diversion. God love her. My angel.

I clipped faster, pulling the wire up with strength I didn't know I had. When I had a hole big enough to crawl through, I twisted my way through the opening, not caring when the sharp metal ends tore at my shirt and pants. I crawled across the six feet of the open ground between the two fences on my belly. When I reached the second fence, I stopped for a moment to look around.

Snow was coming down furiously now, as if God himself had taken a knife and ripped an opening in the sky's belly, releasing a giant pillow full of feathers on the world. The shouts behind me grew fainter as I focused on what I had to do. I scrambled to my knees and cut and cut, twisting and pulling, yanking the heavy wires with my hands. I was inches from freedom and there wasn't a force on this planet that could stop me now. It was as if every fiber in my being, every cell in my body, was intent on flight. I would go fast and far. I would run, I would escape, I would flee confinement.

One more twist of the wire and I could wiggle through. I rolled out onto free land and kept rolling as the slope took me away and I tumbled down toward Bobby D.

He dashed out of the woods, a mountain of a man dressed in hunter's camouflage. He was breathing heavily as he pulled me to my feet.

"Keep moving," he said. "My car is by the highway. We've got a quarter mile of forest to get through first."

"Are you okay?" I gasped, brushing snow from my shoulders and eyes. "How did you get up the side of the mountain?"

"I don't know," he said, his chest heaving. "I just did. But if anything happens to me, you keep going."

"What?" I asked incredulously as we started hacking through the forest underbrush. "Are you out of your mind? If you have a heart attack, I'm not leaving you here. Forget about it."

“Then I won’t have a heart attack,” he promised, stumbling over a log and crashing into me. I tripped and he nearly fell directly on top of me. Mercifully, a bramble bush diverted his fall and spared me from being pancaked by his bulk.

“My god,” he gasped. “Did I kill you?”

No.” I scrambled to my feet, leapt over another log and darted through an opening in the underbrush. “You saved my ass, Bobby D. You saved my undeserving ass.”

“Just go,” he gasped, trying to stand up. “Don’t wait for me. I don’t think I can make it. Just go.”

“No way.” I dashed back to him. “No one even knows I’m gone. We’ve got time.”

But even as the words left my mouth, the sirens went off — their wail screaming over the open field and into the forest like the cries of banshees on the warpath. “Oh, god,” I said. “Oh, god.”

“Keep going,” Bobby shouted. He struggled to his feet. “Head down the mountain. I’ll try to keep up. The keys are under the right front tire. Don’t wait for me. Just take off. I’ll think of something.”

I knew the road was only a quarter mile away, but it was a quarter mile blocked by twisted vines, thick rhododendron and sharp-edged pines. I could hear Bobby gasping for breath behind me as the sirens from the prison wailed in the distance. Then I heard something that made me panic even more.

“Listen,” I said, holding out a hand. Bobby grabbed onto the trunk of a sapling and leaned against it, groaning, his huge chest heaving in and out. “Do you hear that?”

“Hear what?” he asked. Sweat trickled down his brow despite the snow raining down on us.

“They’ve already got the search dogs after us.” I could hear the hounds baying below. That was bad news. They’d had the dogs ready, housed at the prison, and were going to start searching from the road. They knew we had few avenues of escape and would have to make for the road sooner or later. “They’re coming in from the road side.”

“That means they’ve found my car,” Bobby gasped.

I brushed the snowflakes from my eyes and searched the forest floor, seeking another path. I saw brambles, bushes, decades of decaying leaves and pine needles. But no path.

“Over there.” Bobby pointed left. ”The trees thin out. See?”

I headed to the left, Bobby tumbling and cursing behind me. A few dozen yards down the slope, the thick growth gave way to the banks of a mountain stream that snaked through the forest less than two feet wide, cascading over rocks, winding through the shrubs, steaming in the cold air.

“This way,” I shouted. “It has to lead somewhere.”

“Yeah — to people,” Bobby pointed out.

“We can’t get through the other way,” I said. “We don’t have a choice. There’s too much undergrowth.” My face was already scratched from brambles and my calves ached from leaping over mounds of fallen logs and vines. I could not imagine how Bobby felt. His only option was to crash through obstacles and he had to be a few synapses away from a heart attack.

“Go without me,” he gasped behind me. “I could have made it back to the car, but we both know there’s no way I can make it if we head into the interior.” He was leaning on a pine tree now, heaving and choking from the effort of scrambling up slopes after decades of inactivity.

I crawled back to him over the forest floor, grabbing onto thick kudzu and ivy to hoist myself up the incline.

“What are you taking about?” I asked. “Let’s just keep going.”

“No way.” He tightened his grip on the pine tree. “I’m done. We both know it.”

The piercing bay of hounds in pursuit of quarry split the air. The sound was terrifying and the dogs seemed only yards away.

"Oh, god," I said, unable to see a thing through the waning light and the thickly falling snow.

"Get out of here," Bobby commanded me. "They're getting closer. Go on. You know what to do. Here — take this."

He pulled his cell phone from one of the many pockets hanging off his camouflage vest and tossed it to me. I caught it and stuffed it in my jeans.

"Take this, too," He threw me a pocketknife, followed by a hailstorm of snack cakes wrapped in plastic. "You might not have anything else to eat."

"Thank you, Bobby," I called out as I grabbed the pocket-knife. The Little Debbie cakes would have to stay. I was leaving Little Debbie — and Debbie Little — behind forever. Nothing was going to stop me now, be it starvation or snow or a dozen of the smartest hunting dogs on this planet.

As if sensing my determination, the pack let out an unearthly group howl that cut through the forest in a primal challenge. They had found our scent.

"The stream," Bobby shouted. "Lose your scent there."

Of course. I'd watched enough late-night prison movies to know that trick. But it was damn cold and the stream was wet.

The howling convinced me. I gathered my courage and leapt, clearing the banks of the stream and landing on its slippery, moss-covered far bank. I fell, grabbed the roots of a tree, couldn't keep hold and slipped into the stream.

The sensation was the oddest I have ever felt.

As snow swirled about me and I shivered from the cold, I could feel the wet slowly seeping through my tennis shoes — but it was like blood leaking inward instead of out. The water was *warm.* The stream should have been life-threatening cold, but the water was as warm as blood.

Of course. Silver Mountain was dotted with natural hot springs, one of the very few reasons tourists visited each year.

The stream might save my life.

I headed up it, away from Bobby and the eerie cacophony of triumphant howls beneath me. I headed upstream as fast as my sturdy legs could trundle my thirty-something ass, panting and splashing and heaving myself forward with the help of every root and vine I could grab. I have never moved so fast, I have never been so motivated, I have never wanted to flee as much as I did in those moments.

As I climbed, I heard Bobby's shouts of terror waft up through the snow-choked air. The dogs were closing in. He sounded as if he were in agony. I couldn't help it — I had to stop and look back. I found a thick hardwood and hoisted myself up on a branch so I could peer down the mountain.

And there I saw my dearest friend, sacrificing himself for me.

Bobby clung precariously to a bending pine as the pack of hounds surrounded him, baying furiously, their tails wagging in triumph as they crowded closer and closer to their prey. Bobby was emptying his pockets, throwing them the remaining Little Debbie cakes he had stashed in every crevice. The snacks sailed over the heads of the uninterested hounds, yet Bobby kept offering what bribes he had, even tearing a pack open with his teeth and poking it toward the dogs in abject terror. They were too disciplined to take the bait. I heard a whistle and knew the dog handlers would be on them in minutes.

Abandoning my friend, my true and forever friend, I dropped into the center of the stream and fled once again, turning as far from the prison as I could go, all the while praying the stream would take me somewhere.

# Chapter Twelve

More than eighteen million acres of forest land stretch across North Carolina, much of it in the mountains and most of that inhabited by wild boars, an occasional black bear, a few mountain cougars making some sort of miraculous comeback that I was in no position to appreciate, plus hundreds of songbird species, every one of them currently huddled beneath snow-covered branches, where they would stay toasty and warm. Unlike me. Right now, I was the only creature stupid enough to be tramping around those millions of acres and I had no fucking idea where I was.

When I could climb no more — and barely breathe — I pulled myself out of the stream onto a rock and tried to get my bearings. The snow was falling thick and fast and my feet were wet almost to the knees. I wouldn't last an hour if I tried to hike through the woods in wet shoes and socks in this weather. I needed a miracle.

And I got one.

At first the sound seemed almost like a hallucination: banjo music. Cascading, running, bouncing, unstoppable banjo music.

Just a few bars at a time at first, but then more as the wind shifted and brought the full tune to me. I didn't know the name, but I recognized it: my father used to hum it when I was a child. It was an old song, something from the Thirties maybe, or even earlier. But I knew that tune, and I knew that I had heard my father hum it, and I took that as a sign.

I sat there, unmoving, blocking anything else out but the music. I ignored the cold and the snow and the bite of the wind against my face. I followed the music. It couldn't be all that far away. The mountain and the trees would block most sound being carried over a distance.

I envisioned where I must be in relation to the prison. The stream had taken me west, I was sure, and at this point, that meant it would take me a day or more to cut inland and get to the other side of the mountain, where the narrow highway wound back around in its twisting journey. I figured the music had to be on my side of the mountain, off the same stretch of highway that led to the prison. I couldn't be more than a half mile or so higher than Silver Top, but I thought maybe, just maybe, most of the search crews would be looking for me below the prison, figuring I'd be heading down off the mountain.

It felt safer following the music. I'd keep following the banjo and start praying that I was more than a big rat following the sounds of a Pied Piper to my death. I had no other choice.

I kept going.

* * *

THE MOUNTAIN GAVE ME A GIFT — the snow had banished the usual forest sounds, bringing a contemplative peace to the wooded acres. I was surrounded by a churchlike atmosphere of solemn hush. The stream added to the illusion that I was safe by turning warmer with each few yards of progress I made. I must be nearing the area of hot springs that Silver Mountain was most noted for — and I was pretty sure hot springs meant people, or at least tourist cabins, preferably deserted and stocked with lots of coffee and something a little more substantial to eat than all those Little Debbie cakes I'd left behind.

Poor Bobby. Trying to feed those dogs his Little Debbie cakes. I could not shake the image from my mind.

Bobby. I had Bobby's cell phone in my pocket. Maybe I could call someone for help, at least someone who could tell me where to head from here. But who? It wasn't like I had a lot of friends. Most of them were associated with law enforcement in some way and I couldn't put them in the position of protecting me. They'd lose their jobs. You can stretch a lot of rules, but helping someone escape from prison was not something likely to be overlooked by anyone's Internal Affairs Department. That meant my friend Marcus was out, and Bill Butler, too, plus approximately 90% of the men I'd dated over the past ten years. The remaining 10% were probably in prison themselves. Bobby D. was no doubt in custody by now, being browbeaten instead of me. Who knew where Shep was — or if I could trust him? — and Burly certainly couldn't be of help to me in this.

Then I realized that there was one person in this world I could absolutely call on, someone who had done time himself, for a cause he believed in, someone who knew the mountains like the back of his long, work-worn hands, someone who would understand what I was up against and tell me what to do without needing to rub it in that he was coming to my rescue in the first place.

What the fuck was his phone number?

Oh, god. My brain was starting to go numb from too much fear, too much cold, too much everything. I found a rock and perched on it, my ankles warmed by the hot springs, and sat very still, envisioning my landline phone in my mind, pretending I was about to dial him. I didn't call him often, but for some reason, I had always remembered his phone number easily. There was something about it that always stuck in my memory. What the hell was it?

Birth dates: that was it. His number was my birth date, preceded by… a two, which I had once thought stood for the two of us together, before life and circumstance had divided us.

I took a deep breath and dialed, praying he would be home.

He answered on the third ring.

"Ramsey?" I said. "I'm in trouble."

"Casey? Are you okay?" He always got right to it. "Where the hell are you?"

"I don't know. Somewhere in the mountains and it's snowing hard and my feet are wet and I don't have a coat and, oh yeah, I just escaped from prison and there are maybe a dozen prison guards and cops after me and at least as many tracking dogs."

The silence on the other end seemed to last forever, but at last he said, "You're not kidding, are you?"

"No," I said miserably. "I'm not. I went undercover and it went bad and Bobby busted me out today and he almost had a heart attack in the process and they got him and now I don't know where the fuck I am, and I can't go back there, but I think I'm pretty close to freezing to death. The only thing I do have is gloves."

He started to laugh. I could not believe my ears. That bastard was laughing at me.

"Ramsey Lee, you tell me right now what is so damn funny about my predicament. I thought, of all people, you'd understand."

"I do," he assured me. "It's just that I always wondered what it would take for you to lean on me a little. Now I know: it takes frostbite, starvation, a prison break and eminent arrest. Less than I thought, actually."

"Did I mention I'm using Bobby's cell phone and I figure I have ten minutes of airtime left on it, at most, if I can even keep finding a signal."

"Okay," he said, all business again. "What can you tell me about where you are right now?"

I described where the prison was, and finding the stream, and the warm water, and my theory it was connected to an area of hot springs. "Oh yeah, I hear banjo music," I added, half joking.

"Banjo music?" Ramsey said. "That helps. Look, don't waste your air time. I'll call you back in ten minutes. I'm going to poke around the Internet. Let me see what I can pull up."

It was, hands down, the longest ten minutes of my life. While I waited for him to call me back, I passed the time on that icy boulder dangling my feet in the warm springs to keep from freezing and trying to count up all the men I had slept with. Hey, I needed something to keep from going crazy. It's amazing how much you can forget about your own life — and how okay it is that you are able to forget once you make the mistake of remembering. I was up to the year after I got out of prison, when I was trying to make up for lost time, which meant the per annum man count had peaked a little, when Ramsey called me back.

"You're in luck," he said. "I think you are probably about a mile northwest of the prison, which isn't bad considering what you were up against. And that means you are within hiking distance of Happy Times Family Campground."

"So happy times are here again?" I interrupted.

"If you shut up and listen, they might be." Truthfully, one of the things I had always liked about him was that he never put up with my shit. "They're hosting an old timey music festival this weekend," he explained. "They always do this time of year, right before peak season for the leaves."

"So I'm not crazy? I did hear banjo music."

"No, you are crazy, Casey, but not because you heard banjo music. In fact, I want you to follow the music."

"Over the river and through the woods?"

What can I say? I'm sarcastic by nature.

"Not over the river," Ramsey explained. "Whatever you do, stay on the east side of the springs. Otherwise, you'll be screwed and it will take us longer to find you than it took the feds to find Eric Rudolph. And you know how that went down."

"The east side of the stream?" I asked tentatively.

He didn't like the sound of that. "Aren't you a country girl?" he demanded.

"Look, buster, I was a country girl in Florida, where it's flat. Got it? None of this crap about mountains and clouds hiding the sky and all that shit."

"Then I want you to do this. Stand up by the side of the stream, stare at the top of the mountain and raise your right hand.

I felt like a fool, but I wasn't one, so I did exactly what he said.

"Now, just to be clear about this: what direction is the water going in?" Ramsey asked.

I glanced to my left. "Downhill."

"Okay, good, then you are definitely facing uphill."

"I see you have a lot of confidence in me."

"You should see that I'm serious about getting you home."

"You're right and I thank you. What next?"

"Look to your right. That is the direction you want to go in. You want to try and stay as parallel as you can to your current longitude."

"Are you sure it's not current *latitude?"* I asked. "I tend to get the two confused."

"You're definitely scaring me now," he said.

"I was just kidding. I've got it. I am to go no higher up the mountain."

"Correct. If you stay where you are and keep going east, you should hit the campground in about an hour, even if the woods are deep and filled with snow."

"You sound like Robert Frost," I said.

"Thank you. I have been called worse. Now, you are not going to like what I tell you next — take off your pants."

"I didn't know you still cared."

"It's to keep your ass from freezing," he explained. "And I mean that literally."

"My jeans are only wet up to the knees."

"Doesn't matter. Unless you have a knife to cut the wet parts off with, you had better take them off completely."

I thought of the contraption Bobby had tossed me as the dogs closed in. "I do have a knife," I said. "Bobby gave me his."

"Good. Cut the jeans off a couple inches above the wet part. Have you got anything else you're wearing you could sacrifice?"

I thought. I had two tee shirts on underneath my work shirts. "I have an extra tee shirt I could cut up."

"Take the tee shirt, cut it in strips and wrap the dry cloth around your feet. Wear that instead of socks."

"You want me to go barefoot?" I asked incredulously.

"No, I want to spare you from crippling blisters and sores. After you wrap your feet in clean cloth, find some dry leaves in the underbough of the thickest bush you can find. Look for rhododendron. Make sure the leaves are green and still alive. They should be waxy and shiny on one side. Pick enough to wrap around your feet. The goal is to encase them like you're wrapping fish in banana leaves to bake in the sand."

"Because I've done that so very often."

"Just do it," he ordered. "Then put your shoes back on. The leaves provide a temporary moisture barrier. But it won't last long. If you can't find the campground within two hours, stop where you are, find another bush to crawl under, cover yourself with dry leaves, take off your shoes, and pray they dry a little overnight."

"I'm going to find the campground," I said. "For one thing, the music is getting louder. For another, I am not spending a snowy night in the mountains under a damn bush."

"Actually, you are," Ramsey said.

"Why?"

"They're not likely to interrupt the music festival and announce a prisoner is on the loose," Ramsey explained. "They need tourism on Silver Mountain and that's going to look bad and you're minimum security anyway." He paused. "You *were* minimum security, right?"

"Yes," I assured him. "Well, medium security, actually. I don't think they consider anyone minimum, given it's in the middle of absolutely fucking nowhere and anyone else stupid enough to try to escape would find themselves in my predicament."

"Look on the bright side," Ramsey suggested, "You're unlikely to run into any other escaped convicts who might overpower you and take your clothes."

"Good point," I conceded. "What's next?"

"When you find the music festival, stay out of sight. Even if the sheriff doesn't send someone to alert the organizers, people will start to hear in on their radios, or CB's, or some asshole friend will hear it down on the mountain and decide to call and tell them. Blame it on a cell phone world."

"I'm kind of digging the cell phone world right now," I confessed.

"Grab dry clothes, steal food, not a lot from any one person, try to liberate a couple of blankets and find a warm, dry place to spend the night. Need help with that?"

"No," I assured him. "I have it covered. Warm. Dry."

"Good. It's going to take me at least six hours to get there, so we're talking first light. There's no point in trying to find each other if it's still dark. I've got to borrow a couple of guitars from a friend, so it looks like I have a reason to be on the mountain, but after that I'm heading your way."

"You're coming to rescue me," I said. I gave a long, fake sigh. "My hero."

"I'm going to remind you that you said that," he threatened me. "You need to wait until first light and then follow the access road out of the campground to the highway. Every map I pulled up, including the US Forestry Service map, shows only one road into those areas, so I'm trusting we won't go wrong there."

"Two lanes, black top, dotted line. I've got it."

"Once you find the highway, I want you to walk up it, without being seen, to the first straightaway beyond the campground entrance. Pick a spot in the middle of the straightaway, fade back into the bushes, keep dry and wait for me. I'm going to honk three times as I pass the campground entrance, just to let you know it's me coming."

"Are you driving the blue truck?" I asked, fond memories of its spacious bed flooding through me.

"I am indeed."

"I'll recognize it," I said happily. "And Ramsey, I'll never forget this."

"Just don't let anyone see you," he warned me. "You cannot tell by looking who is going to decide to be a good citizen and turn you in. Trust no one."

"The truth is out there," I countered.

"Trust no one. And keep those feet dry."

He hung up and I missed his reassuring voice within seconds. He was enjoying it, I knew. He was enjoying the challenge, the battle against the elements, but, most of all, he was enjoying helping me. Ramsey Lee was a chivalrous man by nature, a sort of old-fashioned man in many ways, and perhaps an odd man out by the standards of the modern world. He'd spent time in jail for so-called eco-terrorism crimes, and perhaps he had taken his hatred of the developers carving up his beloved state a little too far. He was rumored to have a fondness for explosives. But if he had ever hurt anyone, I didn't know about it, and if he had destroyed property, I didn't know about that, either, because he rarely said much about anything. Unless he was trying to get you safely off a mountain, of course. Then he was a regular chatterbox.

It took me awhile to hack the jeans into Daisy Dukes. It took even longer to find a dry bush, wrap my feet and line the shoes with dry, waxy leaves. When I was done, I had to admit — my calves were cold, but my feet were toasty and, my god, all I really cared about were my feet. Who know how much a pair of feet mattered? When I was ready, I stood by the stream as Ramsey had taught me, just to be sure, getting my bearings. As I raised my right hand to get my bearings, the snow stopped as if by magic. Way cool. I raised my hand again, wondering if the snow would start back up. Nothing happened, so I staved off a daydream about being a wizard and concentrated on what direction I was heading in, going through Ramsey's mental checklist in my mind. I felt a little foolish. I knew my way east and west, after all, and up and down a mountain, too, but I didn't want pride or, worse, panic to bring me down now. I had to be methodical. I headed off to my right, staying on as even a keel as I could.

As I made my way through the forest, it fell once again into an almost rapturous silence. Even the wind seemed to die away in silent respect for the glory of the night world. It was dark, but not really — though I could see not the moon above, the snow reflected light from somewhere and my eyes had long since adjusted to the nuances of the night. Without dogs on my ass and with less fear driving me, I could move more easily through the forest, side-stepping bramble bushes, rocks that could twist an ankle or logs that might trip me and catapult me face down in the snow. As I moved through the night, I imagined I was a panther, one that had to get home to its cave. This line of thought led me to wondering whether panthers lived in caves, and that led me to wondering if there were caves around here, and that sparked an entire fantasy involving a dry, cozy corner in a hidden cave, complete with me leaning against the walls and stretching my bare toes in front of a fire while my clothes dried merrily on nearby rocks.

It was a daydream that took me over a mile of rocky terrain. All the while the music grew louder. It was the perfect beacon in the snowy woods. Each note, each lingering reverberation, twisted its way past trees and over shrubs and through the snow to my grateful ears, calling me closer. An entire band had replaced the banjo. I could hear fiddles now, and an upright bass, even a piano, I thought, and maybe a washtub or two. The songs took me back to my youth, to concerts at a fire station miles down the road, to a checkered cloth spread over prickly grass and my mother's good cooking laid out in a picnic so bounteous I had no idea that we were dirt poor. My parents had been so young then, way younger than I was now, and I had darted between the picnic and the band, chasing fireflies, wiggling in time to the music, stomping my feet and never once suspecting for an instant that, like all lives, mine might take winding and twisting turns, some too painful to recall, including detours that would one day bring me to the point of fleeing through the woods from law enforcement, prison bars and lost friends not all that far behind. I knew that no one's life ever ended up being exactly as they imagined it would as a child — but did anyone's ever even come close?

As I got nearer to the campground, I heard people's voices wafting uphill. Either I had hiked further above the campground without realizing it, or Ramsey, as infallible as he was, had been slightly off with his maps. But that was good. Uphill gave me the advantage. I moved through the dark, following the sounds. Soon, the unbelievably enticing smell of cooking food wafted up to me. My stomach growled. Lunch seemed like a lifetime ago. My feet moved faster.

The oddest thing happened when I was fifty yards from the campground itself. I'd grown weary of pushing through brambles and ivy and the thick branches of mountain laurel just to take a few steps. I'd decided to screw it and chance using one of the campground's hiking paths the rest of the way. I was inching down it as silently as I could, on the alert for people, when I heard a snorting and shuffling that send a shiver down my spine. I froze — and came nose to snout with an immense black boar trotting up the path as jauntily as if it were a fine spring day. The wild pig froze when it saw me and stared at me through beady black eyes that glittered in the moonlight that had taken over the clearing night sky. Only a lazy snowflake or two still fluttered to the ground.

I stared at him. He stared at me. I noticed the graceful curves of the tusks on either side of his hard, mean mouth and thought of how he could slash open my belly and pretty much eviscerate me with a single jerk of his head. He probably was thinking the same thing about me. But then he simply snorted and shuffled off to his left, picking his hoofs up precisely as he danced off across the carpet of snowy leaves that covered the forest floor.

It was a sign. I knew it with all of my being.

I had met a kindred spirit.

That pig wasn't even supposed to be here. They weren't native to North Carolina. Every wild pig in the mountains was a descendant of a pack of domesticated boars that had escaped from the holding pen of a visiting German baron's estate in 1926. The baron had been a less-than-good sport. He'd imported the boars from his native land and had planned to hold a bogus wild game hunt for his rich friends. But the very day before the hunt was to take place, one hundred and twenty-four intrepid porcine prisoners dug and gnawed their way to freedom, breaching their fence and disappearing into the wilderness where they promptly adapted and happily reproduced for decades. Their progeny now populated the mountains for hundreds of miles around me.

In other words, I had met a true freedom fighter.

The thought filled me with hope: if those fat, domesticated boars, whose sole destiny had been to become Black Forest ham, had transformed themselves into sleek, feared fighting machines of the mountains then, by god, my fat ass could survive a night on Silver Top and I, too, could live free.

* * *

THE CLOSER I GOT to the campground, the louder the music became, with the sounds of a stand-up bass, guitar and a couple of fiddles now filling in around the more insistent chords of the banjo. I was nearing the edge of the campground and felt too exposed, so I took a detour to the right and ended up in a patch of woods behind a main stage. A hardy audience had gathered in front of the small covered stage to watch the musicians defy the October cold. I knew it was my chance. If I planned to lay in some supplies, I needed to move quickly.

I circled the campground, using the woods as cover, reaching the entrance and a field that had been converted into a parking lot for revelers. Many people had driven campers that had been pulled further into the campground itself, but there were still a couple dozen cars and trucks lined up in the darkness, probably people driving up for the day. I went down each row of vehicles, checking for unlocked doors. My, but people had lost all sense of trust. There I was, in the middle of nowhere, and just about everyone had locked their damn car doors. I finally found an old white truck with an unlocked passenger side door, climbed inside the cab and started searching for something to keep warm. There was a thick flannel shirt, more of a coat really, with a zipper up the front. It was a hideous green-and-red plaid but freezing beggars can't be choosers. I slipped it on over my other clothes gratefully. Most of all, I needed socks and shoes and a pair of britches that covered more than my ass. But I wouldn't find those in the truck. I kept moving and had better luck. By the time I was done pilfering, I'd scored a dry pair of jeans too small in the ass and too big in the waist, a length of rope I could use as a belt, tennis shoes a couple sizes too big and, most glorious of all, thick brown woolen socks that could have kept a hunter warm for a month.

It was a huge improvement. Yes, I looked like a backwoods Nirvana fan. But it protected me from freezing and freed me to stave off starvation.

That proved more problematic. The festival attendees had arranged their campers and tents in circular groupings, like pioneers of old circling the wagons. Clotheslines were tied vehicle to vehicle, chairs had been set out around bonfire areas and the more experienced among the festival-goers had assembled outdoor dining areas with metal tables and chairs alongside of the campground's picnic tables. The camper doors were shut against the cold, of course, but I knew that the occupants had very likely left them unlocked.

The trouble was that each grouping seemed to have at least one person at home. There was always one camper with a light twinkling merrily out of its windows and the shadow of someone moving back and forth inside as they prepared dinner.

My god, the smells that wafted forth on the wind to torture my hollow belly. I am an experienced country girl. I know chicken fried steak when I smell it. I can predict the diameter of a biscuit simply from how it smells while baking and I can smell the difference between a cherry and blackberry cobbler at fifty paces.

Right now, I was surrounded by frying chicken, sweet potato casserole, green beans with molasses and a pot of chili with extra onions. Plus something else with an odor so delicious I was going to end up as damp as I'd been before, thanks to drool, if I didn't do something quick.

A door slammed shut behind me and I scurried over to another grouping of campers just in time to hear a stout woman with wiry hair call out to her neighbor, "Betsy, do you have any butter? It's got to be real butter or Jimmy won't eat it. I left mine in Rocky Mount."

Good old Betsy had switched to margarine, so the woman set off, leaving the clearing in search of real butter she could borrow. God bless dairy, I thought as I did something I am still ashamed of doing. There is something so low and common about stealing food, about being so desperate you have to snatch and grab what you can find, then sit huddled in terror, afraid you will be discovered before you can cram a few morsels down your craw.

Fortunately for me, I hit the mother lode. Inside the camper, the air was thick with the smell of baking biscuits. A wrought iron skillet sputtered and simmered on the stove top, filled to the brim with cream gravy flecked with bits of spicy pork sausage.

Oh my god, biscuits with sausage gravy. I thought I might faint from joy.

I had no time to waste. I was taking a ridiculous chance as it was. I grabbed a coffee cup from a cabinet above the stove, stole an empty sauce pan from the drainer by the sink and quickly ladled a pan full of gravy before plucking three browning biscuits from the oven and slipping back out the front door, easing it shut behind me. I was out of the clearing and into the woods within two minutes. Sure, the wiry-haired woman would think her friend Betsy had slurped up her gravy and stolen her precious biscuits and it would probably cause a rift between them that would last until both were well into their nineties.

I could live with that.

I was dry, I had a whole pot of gravy plus biscuits to dip in it and I didn't have to share it with a damn soul. It was the best meal I have ever eaten in my life, even though I had nothing better than a boulder for a dining room table.

I admit it: I ate all three biscuits, each one nearly as large as my hand, and I licked the pot clean when I was done. I was celebrating being free, being full and being alive.

Revived by the meal, my senses became as sharp as they had ever been. I waited an hour before I returned to the camp, searching for more supplies. I learned something unexpected on that second foraging trip: old people really do have sex, they just need the powerful engine of a motorized vehicle beneath them before they feel inspired enough to attempt it. A lot of trailers were a'rockin, so I didn't go a'knocking, steering clear of a whole lot of shenanigans before I finally managed to snitch three blankets from three different campers, always from beds that had a plentiful supply in hopes no one would notice.

It turned out to be a wise precaution. I found myself a cozy spot on the edge of a ridge overlooking the back of the campground and wrapped up Indian-style in two blankets while I sat on the third. I leaned against a tree trunk in the darkness, enjoying my stomach being full and feeling as happy as I had ever felt in my life. That was when I saw a sheriff's car pull into the campground entrance. One of the deputies who had arrested me at the Pampered Princess Lodge a long week ago climbed out and began questioning people in the crowd that gathered. He was showing them something in his hand, and I was pretty sure it was a mug shot of me because, you know, that photo was too hideous not to share. But no one looked at whatever he was showing for long and the crowd quickly went back to their whiskey, spouses, other people's spouses and their old-timey music.

The deputy left and my heart slowed to a more normal rate helped, in part, by the impromptu concerts emanating from different bonfires. The sweet mountain melodies soothed me. But I had learned a lesson I could not afford to forget: they were, indeed, bothering to look for me.

# Chapter Thirteen

The night wore on and, in an odd way, I was happy. I was alone on the mountainside, hidden in the darkness, surrounded by hundreds of unseen creatures and a merry band of humans below. My belly was full and my feet were dry, and the comforters wrapped around me cozy and warm. There was nothing I could do about anything, nothing but rest — rest and think of my vow to Corndog Sally to bring her grandson to her before she died. Then I thought of how I could fulfill my debt to her daughter, Tonya, the debt I owed for witnessing the terrible aftermath of her death and then simply walking away.

Had the stay inside Silver Top been worth it if it brought me closer to finding the boy? It had been a soul-snatching, spirit-numbing experience for me, yes, and perhaps I had lost a man I cared for more than I wanted to admit in the bargain. But I had learned a lot, and once this was all over, I would have a place to look for Trey Blackburn: if I could find out where the guards lived, the ones with the plowshare and sword tattoos on their wrists, I could track down the men behind what had happened to Tonya Blackburn.

I fell asleep before midnight, the sweet, high tune of a mountain lullaby sending me off into dreams.

I woke before first light. My joints were stiff and protested when I left the cocoon of my blankets to creep down the mountainside. I skirted the still-sleeping encampment. Snores floated out from camper windows and bottles of beer littered many of the clearings. I probably didn't need to be worried about being seen, these people were still half drunk and likely to be sleeping it off until noon, but I didn't want to take any chances, especially not with Ramsey on his way to help me. He had a record and he didn't need any more trouble with the law. He'd go down for serious time if he were convicted again.

I was hungry in that greedy way the human body can get — the more food you give it, the more it wants. But I had no time for any of that: first light, Ramsey had told me. Wait for first light, and head up the mountain from the campground entrance until I found the first straightaway and wait for his signal. I did as I was told, ducking behind a strand of trees when a rattly old truck that sounded like it had pleurisy came chugging up the mountain, cab piled high with cordwood. After that, no vehicles passed and I grew cold from waiting. I had no way of telling the time, and I dared not turn my cell phone on. I'd need every minute of juice left should Ramsey fail to show up.

But I had no reason to doubt Ramsey and I was pretty sure I never would. I reached the first straightaway after the campground entrance in about ten minutes of hard walking and thanked the fading stars above that it had not been far. I waited in the darkness of the forest beside the road, trying not to think about all those encounters with black bears that tourists reported each year from the scenic overlooks along the North Carolina mountain roads. Surely they'd started hibernating by now?

With that unlikely thought in mind and my ears in overdrive for every crackle of brush and every rustle of leaves, I waited and placed my faith in my friend. It felt like over an hour, but it was more likely about twenty minutes before I heard three beeps, followed by the low grind of a pickup truck climbing the mountain. I peeked out and spotted bright blue rounding the curve. It had to be Ramsey. He was moving slowly, scanning the brush with the eyes of a true mountain man, able to see through the forests and into the dells, probably counting the stripes on the skunks sleeping there. He spotted the straightaway and slowed to a crawl, rolling down his window to call out my name. "Casey!" he said in a low voice that somehow seemed both loud and discreet at the same time. "Casey!"

I ran from the trees and hugged him through the window, breathing in his tobacco smell and the piney tang of his hair. Ramsey was one of those men who seems old the day he is born, springing forth strong and enduring, with hair that never quite seems to turn gray but can't be called a color either. He was like a human beech tree, silvery and supple and strong. I wrapped my arms around him and wanted to weep.

"Easy, girl," he said. "Get in the cab. I brought you sausage-and-egg biscuits."

That was all I needed to know. I jumped in next to him, ripped open the bag from Hardee's and started stuffing my face.

"You eat last night?" he asked, sounding concerned.

I looked up and had the decency to feel a little embarrassed. "It was too much of a risk," I lied. "Although I've got to say, whatever they were cooking at that music festival smelled good. It tortured me all night."

"Have at it, then," he said with his lazy grin. It was a smile that could pretty much cause me to melt — which was good, because the next thing he did was order me to slouch down so no one could spot me. I don't let a whole lot of people get away with telling me what to do.

"They're looking for me," I mumbled through a mouthful.

"I know. I heard a report on the radio on the way up. According to the announcer, you're armed and dangerous."

"No shit," I said. "Really?" I felt inexplicably pleased.

"They're saying you're part of some Mafia drug ring."

"What?" I almost shouted I was so startled.

"That's what they said on the radio."

Damn. I was in trouble now. You could be a homegrown boy, like Ramsey, and do just about anything and people would find a way to justify it. But if you were a Yankee who'd drifted down to rape, pillage or steal? Man, get a parking ticket and the populace would turn against you. No one would give me sanctuary now.

"I can't believe they said that. It's so unfair."

"Here." Ramsey handed me a Dr. Pepper nearly as big around as my head. "Drink something before you choke." He rolled his eyes as I slurped my way to happiness. "Lord, girl, no one could ever accuse you of being a picky eater."

"Nope," I said, more concerned about who had floated the story about the drug ring and why they wanted to find me so bad. Well, aside from the fact that I'd escaped from their stupid prison. "They say anything about Bobby D.?" I asked.

Ramsey shook his head. "Nope. Look here, you have got to sit lower and I'm putting this on top of you." He threw a blanket over me and pushed my head down until I hovered just a few inches from his lap.

"Seems like old times," I said cheerfully.

"Don't go getting any ideas," he warned me. "I'm about to pull a five-point turn on a two-lane highway and I don't need any distractions."

"We're going back down the mountain?" I asked.

"Yup," he said. "We need gas and we need to get the hell out of here. I'm not going to end up in West Virginia. I got me enough problems as it is without transporting an escaped prisoner across state lines."

He was serious about getting the hell out of there. Within a minute, we were barreling down the highway again.

"There's only one gas station," I said. "And it's not exactly a safe spot. The owner is nosy as hell. With a big mouth, to boot."

"We've got no choice," Ramsey said. "We need gas. It was closed when I was on the way in, but they'll be open now. I passed a lot of hunters on my way up the mountain. They opened a special two-week black bear hunting season on account of overpopulation." I could tell from his tone of voice that he was about to launch into one of his anti-development tirades and, sure enough, he was just getting started.

"We take their land and we build a bunch of unneeded houses on it and then we complain when the bears don't respect some fucking deed filed with the clerk of courts," he said. "Pretty soon, the bears are getting hit by cars, and they're crawling all over these damn woods looking for some room to breath that's just not there anymore until, finally, it's kinder to cull them through hunting, although I do think picking off a few humans might be a hell of a lot more effective."

*Bears were crawling all over the woods? Hunters with guns were heading in?* I was very glad I'd gotten out of the forest before the amateurs had started firing away.

"I owe you one," I told Ramsey. "I owe you a big one."

"Say nothing of it," he assured me. "The thought of you trapped inside a prison makes me a little bit sick. I've been there. I know what it's like."

I was silent. A flash of being inside Silver Top had washed over me at his words. I guess I shivered.

"It's okay," Ramsey said. "You're out of there. Just hang on and I'll get you home."

I have loved many a man in my life but at that moment I knew that I would always love Ramsey Lee.

* * *

MY LOVE FOR RAMSEY lasted six minutes, which was how long it took us to reach what seemed to be the only country store and gas station in all of Bartow County, the one with the nosy owner where Tonya had sent her son a postcard. Ramsey had called it correctly: though it was not yet six o'clock in the morning, the place was bustling. Trucks and cars pulled up to the pumps, disgorging hunters who dashed inside to take a final pee before they went commando. Meanwhile, their companions gassed up their vehicles, bought beef jerky and purchased beer over coffee at a ratio I pegged at about twelve to one, although it was difficult conducting surveillance crouched down in the cab of Ramsey's truck while he, in a rather paranoid fashion, attempted to block me from anyone's view.

"This is pointless," I complained. "All I can see is your ass. Literally."

"Too bad," he answered. "And just for the record, this is a bad idea. Sitting here is asking for trouble."

"I have no other options," I said. "Sooner or later, one of the guards has to show up here and we can follow him home."

"Sooner or later one of the deputies has to show up here and we could both end up back in the slammer."

"Well, when you put it that way," I mumbled. "I guess this means you're not going to help me?" I'd told Ramsey the whole story about what I was doing on the mountain, about Tonya's death and my attempts to find her son. He seemed most interested in the fact that Burley was Trey's father. Of all my ex-boyfriends, Ramsey said he disliked Burley the least, which was practically a compliment coming from Ramsey. He even said he'd consider helping me once I was done telling him the whole story. Hope had flared in me like a gasoline fire at his words: I still might find the boy. But now it appeared he was backing out. I didn't blame him. It was a lot to ask.

"Relax. I'm going to help you," he told me. "I'm still sitting here, aren't I? Oh shit." Ramsey sat up straighter. I tried to join him and he pushed my head beneath the dash. "Stay down."

"Is it the cops?"

"Yes," he said. "And I think it also might be the guys you're looking for. They seem mighty friendly with each other, for the record. You best remember that."

"How do you know it's them?" I asked.

"Well, the deputy is in a deputy uniform, so it's not much of a stretch to reach the conclusion he is a deputy." The contempt in Ramsey's voice was obvious. He had no love for law enforcement, having been on the wrong side of it a few times too many in his eco-terrorist days, which we both knew were still going on; it's just that Ramsey had gotten better at it and not been caught blowing up construction bulldozers in years. I suspected he'd started to smuggle endangered species into areas he wanted to protect these days instead of using dynamite. I didn't ask him, though. As with all things between us, we had an understanding.

"What about the guards?" I reminded him. "How do you know it's them? Are they in uniform?"

"No. But there are three of them and they look paramilitary. Flat tops, cammo, storm trooper boots. They look like they're getting ready to invade a country, not shoot some poor bastard of a bear who wandered out of the national park." Ramsey hee-heed to himself, thinking this was high humor.

"I hope the bear wins. They're heading out to hunt?"

"No," Ramsey said. "They're heading in. They look like assholes, but they know what they're doing and they know how to handle their rifles."

"How can you tell?"

"They're tagging and bagging their catch now."

Oh, damn. That made me a little sick. I've seen pigs slaughtered. I've hunted deer. But there was something downright wrong about killing the magnificent black bears that wandered through the Appalachians. Their fur was so glossy it shone silver in the sunlight and all they really wanted was to stay as far the fuck away from humans as possible. I hated these intermittent open seasons on them, even if they only lasted a few days.

"It's a nice one too," Ramsey said. "Those assholes can put a nice bear rug down in front of their fireplace and roll around with each other on it." This he thought even funnier than his first crack at them.

"I need to find out *where* that fireplace is," I reminded him.

"Keep it in your britches, Hot Pants. And don't you dare move while I am gone."

"Where are you going?" I called as he slipped from the cab, but he ignored me and kept walking.

Damn it. I hated being on the run. Ramsey was having all the fun and there I was, lying with my face mashed against a seat cushion that smelled a little too much like the hounds Ramsey had left at home in the care of a neighbor.

"Here." A man of few words, Ramsey was back within minutes, shoving a fresh cup of coffee and a honey bun in my face. "They were out of doughnuts. Deputy Dawg must have eaten them all. But this'll perk you up."

"You're too good to me. What did you find out?"

"The tattoo is on their forearm, a ploughshare and sword?"

"Yup. That's it."

"All three of the assholes have one. Oh, yeah, forgot this." He pulled a rolled-up newspaper from his back pocket and tossed it on the seat between us. I could not believe it. I was staring straight into Bobby D.'s eyes.

"Are you serious?" I asked, choking on my coffee. I smoothed the paper out. it was just a little mountain rag and only eight or so pages, clearly photocopied in someone's basement. But I was horrified to discover not one, but two, mug shots covering half the front page: mine and Bobby's. Oh, god. Poor Bobby looked like an ax murderer was approaching him with killing in mind, he was that scared, while I looked like I'd just pulled a two-day shift turning tricks at a truck stop.

"Oh, my god," I said. "That's the worst photo of me ever. I have never looked worse in my life."

Ramsey made an indefinable sound. "Might not want to look in the mirror right now," he suggested.

I rattled the newspaper angrily. "I can't believe they bothered to put out a special addition of this low class county rag on account of us. This is ridiculous. Listen to this bullshit: they're saying Bobby is some mafia kingpin and I'm his daughter! Who floated this crap to the press?"

Ramsey shrugged. "Some lady named Bunny. She owns a hotel around here or something. Most of the article is based on an interview with her. Probably just someone else you pissed off."

"That bitch!" I said. "And after I was so nice to the other guests."

"Oh, yeah," Ramsey remembered. "They're in there, too. They said they knew all along the two of you were crooked."

"These people are insane." I scanned the article. "They need to get lives."

"Well, you *are* a prison escapee," Ramsey pointed out. "You can't blame them for thinking you're a criminal."

*"She had beady eyes,"* I read out loud. *"And she was kind of pasty, like she'd been in the slammer."* I was incensed. "I remember this woman. She has some nerve saying anything about me. Her hair was orange, her face looked like the ass end of a baboon and she was splitting the seams of her sweat suit. Plus she was whiter than Marilyn Manson. She had enough face powder on to supply a morgue for years."

Ramsey took the paper from me and stuffed it under the seat. "Focus on the job at hand. There were three guards in all that I could make out. Three guards and one vehicle. Which means they will be easier to follow."

"Did they make you?" I asked as I tore away a corner of the honey bun and took a bite. I almost gagged: it had enough preservatives to keep King Tut fresh for the next six hundred years.

"Did they make me?" Ramsey was incredulous. "Are you serious?"

Oh boy, I'd insulted his honor. Ramsey was a mountain man, born in the hills of North Carolina, and if you ever implied he was, in any way, even close to a city slicker, you were in trouble. You had to let him think you considered him something along the lines of Davy Crockett's older brother, maybe on steroids and with some scary automatic weapons to boot, and let it go at that.

"Forget I asked," I said. "What's next?"

"They're waiting for some asshole to weigh his big scary bear, and then they have to check in with theirs and they'll be off."

"Big scary bear?" I repeated, thinking of my stint alone in the woods the night before. Oh my god. I could have been killed while stuffing my face with stolen sausage gravy. How low was that?

"I'm being sarcastic," Ramsey explained. "Some asswipe killed what looks like my niece's teddy bear. It weighs all of fifteen pounds. What the fuck is the matter with people? Now he's going to stand around the water cooler for the next three weeks talking about how his life was hanging by a thread and he was inches from being eviscerated, when he… wait, the asswipe is done and now the three assholes are stepping up for their turn at the scales."

"Ever think about going into television announcing?" I asked.

"Now that's a damn bear to bag." Ramsey was watching the whole thing like he was tuned into his favorite television show, absently chewing his honey bun, without noticing it was actually a petroleum byproduct, and sipping at his coffee. "Wonder which one of those assholes actually tagged it."

“My guess is the meanest looking one,” I said.

“Mean?” Ramsey snorted with contempt. “Those guys are posers. Sure, they probably did a few tours in Iraq, they’re probably hot shit sharp shooters or paratroopers or ex-special ops or some shit like that. But could they spend one night on a mountain like this without crumbling? I think not.”

I perked up at that. “I spent a night on the mountain,” I proclaimed proudly.

His contempt practically oozed over me. “One night? Girl, I spent three months living off the land not fifty miles from here.”

“Did you see Eric Rudolph while you were on the run?” I asked him.

“He’s an asshole, too.” Ramsey abruptly turned on his truck and revved the engine. “Hold on. They’re pulling out.”

Any fear I’d had that Ramsey might change his mind about helping me evaporated. Ramsey had decided the guys were, well, assholes, and he was going to help me bring them down. God bless testosterone.

* * *

FOLLOWING THEIR TRUCK was like being trapped on an endless water slide that twisted and turned without mercy. The road wound around and around the mountain and Ramsey was driving like he was on methamphetamine. It was hell experiencing it all six inches from the cab floor, where the gas fumes wafted in my face. I finally sat up and cracked the window so I could breathe.

“You’re taking a chance on being seen,” he pointed out.

“If I don’t sit up and get some fresh air, I’m going to puke in your lap. You drive like a maniac.”

"Just trying to keep up." He braked abruptly and the truck fishtailed, spinning within inches of a sheer drop-off. I gasped and clawed my way back to Ramsey.

"Down girl," he said, swatting me away. "I've got to concentrate."

"Oh my god, I am *so* not coming on to you."

"Hold on," he mumbled as he took a turn too fast. The tires slipped on the gravel of the shoulder and the entire truck shuddered before Ramsey wrestled it back onto the road.

Words failed me. So I prayed. It had been a long time since I'd asked God for help. Well, asked and meant it. I meant it then, though, as I prayed with all my heart that we would survive the chase down the mountain. I lost years of my life on that one.

"Do we have to stay so close?"

"Yes," Ramsey said abruptly. "If they turn, we're sunk. We could never find them and then — whoa. Where'd they go?" He looked in the rearview mirror. "Like I said."

"They turned off the road?" I asked.

"Right behind us. Hang on and we'll figure this out."

We reached a deserted scenic overlook. The tourists were still lingering over their coffee. "You're sure they turned off?" I asked.

"I'm sure," he said. "But we can't just follow them in by truck. So get ready to follow them in on foot."

"We're *hiking* in after them? Last night wasn't enough walking?"

Ramsey stared at me without comment.

"What?"

"Tell me what you want to get out of this. You call the shots."

"I want to know where the hell this secret society of guards lives, and if they killed Tonya Blackburn and took her son. Mostly, I want to know if they have the boy."

"Okay, then," Ramsey said. "Follow me and keep the noise down or you might get shot in the ass. The woods are thick with amateur bear hunters and they are the biggest bunch of peckerwoods I've ever seen in one place, 'cept for that Hootie and the Blowfish concert in my back forty that one time. That was not worth the rental, let me tell you that."

"I got news for you. It's the same damn bunch of pecker-woods. They just got older and fatter and bought guns."

He ignored me and grabbed a rifle from under a tarp in the back of his truck.

"Where's mine?" I complained.

He laughed. "I'm not giving a firearm to a convict."

"I hate you," I said as I tucked my stolen shirt into my jeans and tried not to think about my underwear, which had already gone through the equivalent of the Battan Death March and was now being asked to carry me further. It occurred to me that maybe it was the bears themselves I ought to be worrying about, specifically the male ones.

"Did you bring me a change of clothes?" I asked Ramsey hopefully.

He laughed again. "My jeans have gone through a lot," he said. "But fitting your ass into them is just not going to happen."

"Fine. But if I start to stink, just remember, I might attract bears."

"Bring 'em on," Ramsey declared. "And remember this: you are with the master. Watch and learn from the master. As of now, you are invisible."

He meant it, too. He got back in the truck and surveyed the area. He found a spot a few yards down the road with just enough room to pull the truck into along the edge of a narrow wooded buffer. Within minutes, he'd snapped an armload of branches free and had arranged them in front of the truck to create a blind. You'd have to be standing within a few feet to ever notice it.

"The blue of the truck looks like the sky behind it," I said. "That's ingenious."

He flashed me a smile. "That's how you do it." He stashed his car keys in the hollow of a tree. "In case one of us doesn't make it," he explained. Then he hunched over and darted into the underbrush and I swear to god he disappeared in front of my eyes. I don't know how the hell he did it. He became the trees and the brush and the light and the leaves, barely visible even from a yard away.

"How do you do that?" I asked.

"Pick an animal," he told me. "Then become it. Keep up."

Okay, I could do that. I became a black bear, only they pretty much trundle, which wasn't far from my natural gait, and they were, after all, in season. Why not pick an animal without a bulls-eye on its ass? I tried imagining myself as a possum, but that led to a lot of scuffling over the leaves. I finally imagined myself as a huge doe slipping gracefully through the forest. That did the trick. Openings started to appear before me and my eyes began to pick out the subtle pathways leading me around the thick strands of laurel. Soon Ramsey and I were flowing through the woods, him in the lead, always taking us slightly up the mountain and always in the same direction. It was hard work, though, he moved fast, and I soon started to sweat. Ramsey was leaner and tougher than me and he was evidently imagining himself as a cheetah with a rocket engine up its ass. But it was still a hell of a lot more efficient than my frantic tramping of the night before, so I kept my head down and my mouth shut as we picked our way to a ridge a couple miles in from the road.

"What are we looking for?" I asked.

"That," Ramsey said. He pointed down. As my eyes adjusted to the light, I could make out a dirt road that had been neatly cut through the forest. “That’s the road they took in. We’ll follow it from the ridge line.”

We made our way along the edge of the ridge, clinging to trees when the red clay started to crumble beneath our feet. “Aren’t we easy to spot from below?” I asked.

“We’re safe. I can spot every vehicle coming from either direction for at least half a mile,” Ramsey explained. “Just look for plumes of dust and listen for the engines.”

I put my faith in him and followed some more. The road below led deep into the forested interior of the mountain, twisting and turning in parallel curves with the ridge. I stopped to catch my breath and Ramsey lingered, his eyes never leaving the dirt road below us.

“Aren’t we in the national forest?” I asked.

He shook his head. “It’s about four miles that way.” He pointed west. “But whoever owns this land bought it for the privacy. You’ve got the national forest curving around to the south, west and north, and the highway forms a natural barrier to the east. You’ve pretty much guaranteed no one will ever build on your doorstep with this acreage. It must have cost a lot. It’s the perfect place for a compound.”

“You think that’s what this is?”

“When was the last time you saw three men in perfect shape with identical haircuts and tattoos hanging out together?” he asked.

“In Fayetteville last Saturday night.”

“Well this isn’t Fayetteville and there’s not a military base within three hundred miles of here. What this is, my friend, is a genuine paramilitary, gun-toting, U.S. government-hating, people’s militia compound.”

I looked at his smug grin and realized I’d been a fool. “You knew about this place all along,” I accused him. “You knew where those men were headed.”

"Not exactly. I had to wait until they turned down the road to be sure. But, hell yeah, I knew this place was here. A raccoon can't fart in the Carolina hills without me knowing about it."

I shook my head in disgust. "You just wanted me to think you were some kind of tracking genius."

"I *am* some kind of tracking genius," he said. "Now, who do you think has the money to buy a place like this? Because that I don't know. Mountain land is not cheap, and it's especially not cheap when it's next to a national park."

"Maybe it's been in the family for generations," I suggested. "Remember, these are mostly men from Bartow County." A thought hit me. "They grew up in these hills. They could be above us right now. Maybe they've been following us when all the time we thought we were following them."

Ramsey's laugh was full of mountain man disdain, which is to say it sounded like he was swallowing a whistle. "A Bartow County man hasn't got dick on a Buncombe County man and never will," Ramsey bragged. "Now come on, you're slowing down the pace and we've got a quarter mile to go."

Ten minutes of hard trekking later, we heard distant voices accompanied by a strange arrhythmic thumping. Ramsey gestured for me to follow him deeper into the woods above. We followed a steep rock line and took shelter in a stand of trees along its outer edge, where we had a clear view of a full-sized basketball court carved out of the side of the mountain. It was smooth concrete, regulation-painted and full of men running and jostling for position.

Was I surprised to find a full-size, perfectly paved basketball court in the middle of nowhere filled with sweaty players? Not really. We were still in North Carolina, after all.

"No wonder they're all in such good shape," I said. "They are burning some serious calories."

"You see your boy down there?" Ramsey asked. "There are a couple of youngun's on the court." His eyes had narrowed and I had the uncomfortable feeling I was perched next to a human hawk looking for a human mouse.

"You seriously think I could recognize Trey Blackburn from this distance? We don't even know if these men took him. Maybe he ran away." I thought of Tonya's bloated body stretched out in that cramped room of the trailer. "Maybe he doesn't even know about his mother yet."

"You say's he's about fifteen, tall, kind of tan looking?"

"Yes. With curly black hair and he's supposed to be a really good basketball player."

"Then they've got your boy," Ramsey said firmly. "Because that kid is running rings around the others." He pointed down below but all I could see was lots of sweaty men, half of them shirtless, running up and down a court. Not that I minded the view.

"I'll take your word for it," I mumbled, but my stomach had dropped at the news Trey was near. Would I have to be the one to tell him his mother was dead if he didn't already know?

"We're not going to be able to approach him right now," Ramsey said, rather obviously, I felt. "We're going to have to make camp and wait for our chance."

"Are you fucking kidding me?" I asked. "I have to stay on this mountain for another night?" My underwear was starting to fuse to my skin. Another day and I'd have to peel it off me with pliers like you do when you're skinning a catfish.

Ramsey glanced up at the sun. "Depends on if I can get him alone this afternoon. Maybe after lunch. But we've got a couple hours to kill. We may as well relax and save our strength."

"What strength?" I complained. "By the way, I'm starving."

* * *

LIVING OFF THE LAND is a teensy weensy bit different when you're with a man like Ramsey Lee. Within an hour, he'd constructed a cozy shelter in the corner of some overhanging rocks, far from the melting snow, with huge sweeping branches that hid the niche from any human eyes and a giant bough waiting to cover the top once we'd finished basking in the sun. He had a small smokeless campfire going and was brewing coffee. I had hardly finished my first cup when he was back with the body of something small and skinned skewered on a spit. He put it over the fire.

"I can't believe you killed Thumper!" I said. "Though just for the record, I'm hungry enough to eat Bambi."

He smiled and unscrewed a small bottle filled with a reddish powder and sprinkled some over the rabbit carcass.

"What's that?"

"Butt Rub," he said. "I put it on everything I eat with legs."

"Seriously?"

"Seriously."

"What the hell else do you have in that backpack of yours?" I asked.

"Everything you need to succeed." He laughed, thinking that was funny.

"Chocolate?"

He pulled out a Hershey's bar and tossed it to me without comment.

Man, but it was so good that the endorphins sent me into a basking stupor. I woke just long enough to accept lunch on a stick, which was delicious, and then, warmed by the sunlight from above, I leaned my head back against a rock and fell asleep, god knows for how long. All I know is that I woke with the sting of too much sun on my cheeks and Ramsey shaking my shoulder.

"Maybe in the morning," I mumbled, swatting him away.

"Wake up!" he said sharply. "I'm not one of your ding dong boyfriends. We got company."

I opened my eyes and stared up straight into the face of Tonya Blackburn's son, Trey.

That was enough to send adrenaline spiking through every vein in my body. I must have looked a little panicked because Ramsey put a reassuring hand on my shoulder. "Down girl," he said. "All I've told him is that his mother sent us to find him."

"Grandmother, really," I stammered.

"Meemaw?" the boy asked. His voice had that unexpectedly deep quality of a young man, tinged with the hint of a higher-pitched crack here and there that betrayed his anxiousness. "I thought she'd forgotten about me."

"Sit down, kid. We need to talk."

# Chapter Fourteen

I won't lie: it was hard. Trey knew his mother had died, but he didn't know how she had died. The men in the compound had taken him from the trailer as they were still talking to Tonya. They had told Trey they were law enforcement, and that they were taking his mother back to jail for violating parole. Two of them had questioned Trey in a car outside the trailer while another two questioned Tonya inside. Trey had never even seen his mother again. Instead, one of the men had come out with a few of his things and told him his mother was being taken into custody and that one of their cars would be taking her back to prison. But they were going to take him to a camp for boys instead of placing him into the social services system. They lied further, promising Trey that they'd find out who his father was and see he got to live with him eventually. It was only after he'd been in the compound for a week and had started to feel as if he belonged among the other boys being groomed, they said, for careers in the military or law enforcement, that they'd told him that his mother was dead. From an overdose in prison, they'd said, and Trey had accepted it as the truth. God knows, he'd seen enough evidence of his mother's destructive drug habit in the past.

So it was hard to tell the kid his mother had actually been murdered, and that the men he was living with and trusted had done it, and that his grandmother was dying and on her way out and wanted to see him before she went.

Trey didn't say much to any of this. He just folded his long arms and legs in on himself and sat cross-legged around the afternoon fire and listened with the resigned air of someone who has heard way too much disappointing news in his young lifetime. It broke my heart to see him so far from childhood already and it broke my heart see how very much like Burly he looked. He was slender and tan, with dark eyes and angular features made more prominent by his lack of hair — it had been completely shaved off, like a boot camp recruit. But he was still a beautiful boy, one who had been forced to live a not-so-beautiful life, retrieving his mother from street corners and cleaning up her puke at an age when other kids were being driven to soccer practice or chatting with their friends on-line.

I don't remember what I said exactly and I sure don't remember what little Trey said in return. What I do remember is how grateful I was that Ramsey was there. He didn't have any kids of his own; indeed he had few people in his life at all. But Ramsey was, at heart, a gentle person, and I think he saw a little of himself in Trey. Most important of all, Ramsey was a man, and that was what the kid needed, someone as close as possible to a father. That was the role Ramsey assumed and he played it well, always saying, at just the right juncture, the things Trey most needed to hear:

*"Your mother didn't die of an overdose. They just made it look that way. She was staying clean for you when she died."*

*"I don't think all the men here were involved, just some. I'm sure the others care about you very much and would be angry if they knew."*

*"Whatever your mother did, she did it to try and help you. Casey says your mother saved every newspaper clipping about you she could find and that she bragged about you constantly. She was proud of you, Trey."*

*"Whatever these men are telling you about your mother and the world outside this compound? I can tell you it's not true. I know*

*lots of men like these men. They're just scared because they see the world is changing and they don't want to change with it."*

*"I know what they're telling you. They want you to become one of them. But your grandmother? She's your blood, and she's poured every ounce of energy and money she has into making sure you're found, and nothing is more important on this earth than your own blood, I don't care what these men are saying."*

Ramsey made it possible for the kid to survive bad news, and he made it sound like, no matter what happened, Trey would not be alone. Which was probably why Trey had not yet bolted down the mountain by the time it came to give him the one piece of good news I had for him: that we knew who his father was and that his father wanted to see him.

He was stunned at the news. "My father?" he asked. "My real father?"

I nodded. "He didn't even know you existed," I explained. "That's why he never came to see you."

"Why didn't my mother ever tell him about me?"

"I can't answer that," I said. "I think she just assumed he wouldn't want to know, that he wouldn't help out if he did. He's white and, well, the world was a lot different back when they were together."

"So he's an asshole?" the kid asked, sounding more than a little like Ramsey.

"Your father is a good man," I said quickly. "He's a really, really good man. He hasn't had an easy life. He's in a wheelchair because of an accident and he always will be, but he's smart and he's kind and he's handsome — you have his smile — and he takes good care of people. He likes to take care of people. It makes him feel useful. And he wants to take care of you. He's made me promise to bring you back safely."

Ramsey was staring at me oddly. I guess I'd sounded more enthusiastic about Burly than he'd thought possible. I was not known for singing the praises of my ex-boyfriends. But in defending Burly to his son, I had stumbled onto the truth of what had happened between Burly and me. He really did want to be needed. His new girlfriend needed him. I did not. The one thing in life Burly could not abide was feeling useless. What had happened to us wasn't personal. It just was.

As soon as I realized that, a lot of feelings I had been carrying around about Burly just sort of evaporated and drifted up into the thin blue sky above Silver Mountain, leaving lightness in their place. I felt unbelievably free.

"Your father is actually a bit like my friend Ramsey here," I said, smiling at him. "They both like their independence."

The boy was silent, staring first at the fire, and then at Ramsey. It had been too much for him to hear all at once. He was overwhelmed.

Below us, a bell began to clang.

"I've got to go," the boy said.

"You can't go," I told him. "I want you to come with me."

He froze, confused.

"Not yet, Casey," Ramsey said gently. "We need to find out which of these men were there when… when the boy last saw his mother. And we need to know more about what's going on down there before we take him or it could turn into a bloody mess. We need to be smart about this."

"What are you talking about?" I asked indignantly. "The kid might tell them that we're up here — "

Trey interrupted me before I could go on. "They killed my mother," he said furiously. "Do you think I want to stay with them? I'm not going to say anything. I just want to go home and see my Meemaw. I want to meet my father."

"Fine. Go back down there. Just act normal," I told him, as if marching around with an AK-47 over your shoulder was normal for someone his age. "We'll come for you."

"What are you going to do?" he asked.

I started to tell him what my intentions were, but Ramsey put his hand on my arm. "We're not sure yet," he interrupted. "It may be we don't want to get into what happened to your mom with these men, at least not yet. The important thing here is to get you home to the people who love you, like your grandmother. Me and Casey will talk about how that's best done. Just get down there before they miss you and don't say anything about our being here, not even to your friends."

The kid was gone in a flash, hurrying down the mountain. I wondered if we'd made a mistake letting him know about us.

"Think he'll tell them?" I asked.

Ramsey shook his head. "I think he's too afraid to talk to them at all. And too curious about seeing his father to screw that possibility up. He might also have known something was off about his mother's death, he had to man up early in life and he's a smart kid. But I didn't want him to know our plans just the same." He flashed me a grin. "Just in case you thought I was being too bossy."

"No, you're right," I said. "What are we going to do next?"

He told me and I didn't like it. I didn't like it one damn bit.

* * *

"YOU ARE SO DURN STUBBORN," Ramsey said in exasperation. "I am only asking you to wait until dark. Let me go down first and find out what we're up against: how many men are living there and what they're armed with. It's not smart to take the kid without knowing who the hell is going to be following us."

"If you're so smart, why haven't you thought of disabling their vehicles so they can't follow us?" I countered.

"That's a good one," he conceded. "We'll do that before we take the kid, but we need to wait until it's dark and most of them are asleep. The last thing we want is for someone to discover a slashed tire, or the kid missing, and sound the alarm. We got one road out of here, whether we stroll down the middle of it or follow beside it through the woods. They could easily cut off our escape."

"So I basically have to sit here with my thumb up my ass while you get to do the fun stuff?" I summarized.

"Damnit, Casey. Just let me do what I do best — sneak around. No offense, but you got the grace of a water buffalo."

"And why would that offend me, pray tell?"

He ignored my sarcasm. "Look, let's compromise. If I'm not back in an hour and a half, come after me. It means something's gone wrong. Can you keep it in your pants for that long? Ninety minutes is all I'm asking."

"Give me your binoculars first," I demanded.

"What binoculars?"

"Oh, don't give me that. They're in that bottomless backpack of yours. Cheater."

He threw the binoculars at my head, but I caught them neatly and fiddled with the dials until I had a crystal clear view of the compound below. "Okay," I conceded. "You have ninety minutes. But remember — I'm watching."

"Oh, yeah?" He spit on the ground. "Watch this."

And, with that, he was gone. He melted into the trees and as hard as I tried, I did not spot him again. I was pretty sure he'd reached the compound because while the minutes passed as slow as molasses, they did pass. First a half hour went by as I brooded over the injustice of being sidelined. Then another half hour passed as I considered the rankling possibility that I had grown too old, too fat and too far removed from my country days to be of use to anyone unless I held a gun in my hand. I was no better than those yuppie bear hunters. I had become a poser, too.

I picked at that for awhile, contemplating the possibility that I had reached my expiration date, then decided that at least I still had my intelligence. And there was a lot to be said for that. I had one of those sneaky minds that can think of a thousand different possibilities. Especially when it comes to how and why people behave badly. And I wasn't often wrong. While the wheels in my head never seemed to stop turning, I'd never been called stupid or sought refuge in stupidity. Age could not take that from me.

I mulled that over for a little while, wondering if we were actually being intelligent about our situation. I mean, here we were, two of us against god knows how many of them, one rifle against a Russian country's worth of weapons, and one skilled tracker, Ramsey, taking on what could be dozens of homegrown boys who'd lived on this mountain their whole lives.

Plus, I was a wanted escapee and half the men below were no doubt either prison guards or law enforcement.

There was only one logical conclusion: *we were being idiots.* Ramsey wanted to snatch Trey and run, because that's what he had done his whole life: bucked authority, circumvented the law and gotten away with it. But the chances of our meeting with success and not being caught, or being apprehended later without a whole hell of a lot of trouble were chances that I pegged at slim to none.

"What is the most important thing here?" I asked myself. That Ramsey and I go in as Rambo and Rambette, or that the boy be returned to his grandmother before she died? I couldn't stay on the lam forever, and Bobby D. needed bailing out of jail, and the more I kept avoiding getting the situation straightened out, all the worse it would be.

The truth was, we needed help. So maybe, just maybe, the intelligent thing to do here was to acknowledge that Ramsey was right: I was too stubborn. I was also defensive and annoying in my need to do it all myself. I wouldn't trust a man as far as I could throw him, and I had my first husband to thank for that. But here I sat, in stolen clothes, with no food or weapons, trapped on the side of a mountain, laboring under the delusion that I could take on the entire world and whip it with one hand tied behind my back.

The bottomline was simple: I either trusted Shep or I didn't. I hadn't tried to get through to him since my prison break and he had troubles of his own. But there was no one else who would begin to know where this compound was, who would understand the importance of why Trey needed to be reunited with his grandmother before it was too late and who would believe me when I told them Tonya Blackburn's killers lived in the compound.

Still I hesitated. I waited the fully ninety minutes I'd promised Ramsey and then I waited thirty more, counting off each second, it seemed, as I waited for Ramsey to return so I could run the idea of calling Shep past him and not take the whole decision on myself.

But Ramsey never returned.

After two and a half hours of watching the sun drop lower and lower into the sky, I finally did what I should have done from the start. I pulled out Bobby's cell phone and dialed 911, figuring it had to connect me to the sheriff's office. There was no other game on the mountain.

When a pleasant female voice answered, I asked for Shep and was quickly told that he was on a leave of absence.

"I know all about that," I interrupted. "And I also know he's checking his voice mail. So, please, just put me through and then page him and tell him he has an urgent message that he needs to listen to before all hell breaks loose on his mountain."

"Who is this?" the woman asked sharply. "Is this is a prank?"

"I wish. But it would take too long to explain. Please, just put me through, then find him."

She put me through and once I heard the beep of Shep's voice mail, it all poured out: the compound in the hills and where I thought it was, finding Trey, the boy's story about the four men who came to visit his mother and how they took him away and he never saw her again. I voiced my suspicion that a few of Shep's own deputies might be involved. And I told him we were going in to take Trey, no matter what, but we were outgunned and outmanned, so he could choose to help us or not. It all poured out of me like one of the waterfalls tumbling over the rocks at the top of Silver Mountain, ending with my ace-in-the-hole, a most unromantic, and perhaps vaguely threatening, "You owe me."

If there was even a chance Shep would ever hear my message, I could not say. I could not say if he'd believe me once he did. Or if someone else would hear the message and simply come out to arrest me and take me back to prison and call it a day. But I can say that I hung up the phone believing I'd made the intelligent choice, under the circumstances.

And then I went in search of Ramsey.

* * *

I CREPT DOWN THE MOUNTAIN, binoculars in hand, stopping every few yards to confirm that the way ahead was clear. Ramsey had chosen our hiding spot well. It didn't take me long to reach the compound. It was a no-nonsense, no-frills collection of one-story clapboard buildings, each built for a specific purpose. The men slept in small bunkhouses, maybe eight to ten beds to a cabin. There were eight of those, all clustered around larger common buildings that I figured to be a dining hall and some sort of recreation center. I didn't see Ramsey and I didn't see anyone through the windows of the cabins. But it was dinnertime and I figured they were all in the dining hall eating. I did see isolated men regularly patrolling the edge of the compound and twice had to dash back into the woods and wait, heart pounding, until they strolled past.

These men did not waste electricity. Most of the buildings were empty and they had left no lights burning. But the dining hall was well lit and I also spotted lights on in a series of three buildings built along the far edge of the compound. They were too big to be storage sheds, but not big enough to be bunk houses. I waited until the closest guard passed me, then followed him around the perimeter, darting from tree to tree, figuring if I had him in my sight, chances were good he had no idea about me. The guard I was following looked like all the others, trim and generically white, but this one also had a rifle slung over one shoulder. He slowed when he drew near the clearing that linked the three outer buildings and called out into the shadows on the edge.

"He talking yet?" he asked someone in the darkness.

"Nope. Probably just some peckerwood wandered onto the property hunting. Grubb says he'll let him go if he can prove it. But he's not to be allowed to see anything on the way out. Says his truck is back on the highway. The guy seems kind of slow, if you know what I mean."

"Yup, I know what you mean. Human sheep." The perimeter guard kept moving, but I stayed put in the woods: they had Ramsey in one of those buildings. I was shocked he had been caught — I'd always thought of him as invincible, and I prayed his "aw shucks, I'm just a dumb ass hunter" act would hold up. I doubted these men took kindly to strangers.

It had grown dark so I took a big chance. I had to know that Ramsey was okay and, if he wasn't okay, I was prepared to go to his aid. He had come to mine.

Once the guard ambled on, I crept up to the back of the buildings and risked peering into the windows. The first was someone's home, and it looked like a pretty nice one. One room, sure, but one big room with a nice bed in one corner, topped with a beautiful wedding ring quilt. The room also had a huge stone fireplace, a kitchenette along one wall, a door leading to a bathroom, and a big table right in the center of the room with eight chairs neatly arrayed around it. Everything was spotlessly clean. It was headquarters for the head honcho, I guessed; the Big Kabuna, whoever he might be, lived here.

The second building was scarier: it was filled with tables littered with weapons in various stages of disassembly or repair, while organized sections of various rifles, shotguns and even automatic weapons leaned against the surrounding walls in a truly awesome display of Second Amendment rights. There were plenty of cabinets, too, and I figured they held handguns. But geeze, if they had this many weapons I fully expected the third building to be filled floor to ceiling with bullets.

It was not. And I didn't want to even think about what the purpose of that third building was, because that was where they were keeping Ramsey. He was sitting in a straight back chair and his arms had been bound behind his back. His feet were lashed to the legs of the chair and two men stood on either side of him, pointing rifles at him in the illuminated glare of a single overhead bulb dangled harshly just above his head. It was the perfect interrogation room — or, more likely, interrogation survival training room — and Ramsey was their prisoner. But who was doing the interrogating? The guards never spoke and Ramsey's back was to me, so I could not see his face. Then I noticed a Japanese room divider arranged in front of Ramsey, blocking one corner of the room. Thin plumes of smoke snaked up in the air from behind it. There was someone else in the room with Ramsey, someone who was smoking a cigarette behind the room divider, someone who clearly did not want Ramsey to see his face.

None of it was reassuring.

I stood there, assessing the layout, counting the guards and weapons in the room, trying in vain to think of a way to rescue Ramsey. I could start a fire, maybe, in one of the other buildings, and hope he escaped in the confusion. If he saw his chance, I knew he'd take it. Or maybe I could break into the second building and steal some guns and then I could… my plans evaporated as a hand clamped down on my shoulder, digging into my flesh. A mocking voice whispered in my ear: "Well, now, sweetheart, are you a lost hunter, too? Because it looks like you've been found."

I brought my right leg up hard behind me, hoping to hit his groin with the back of my foot, but he was expecting it and stepped to one side. I twisted from his grip, elbowing him hard in the gut while stomping on his right foot. But his gut was harder than his grip, he was wearing steel-reinforced boots and he knew more moves than I had ever imagined, even in my wildest *Crouching Tiger* daydreams. Within seconds I was face down on the dirt, one of his knees pinning me to the ground. His mocking tone had given way to fury.

"You just pissed me off," he hissed. "And I haven't been pissed off by a woman since I left my whore of an ex-wife." He grabbed my shirt and dragged me upright, staring me in the face. "You look a little worse for the wear and I don't know what you're up to, but..." he leaned closer and whispered in my ear, "You better hope Grubb doesn't assign me to escort you out of here."

I knew I was truly up a creek without a paddle now. The guy had some serious issues with women.

* * *

HE BROUGHT ME TO THE SAME CABIN where Ramsey was being held, and I don't know who felt more stupid: Ramsey or me. He averted his eyes, pretending not to know me, but I knew that ruse would not last long. What were the chances two unrelated people had been skulking around the edges of the compound on the very same night?

The cabin was warm and, as angry and useless as I felt, I was grateful for that comfort. The guard who had thrown me to the ground pulled a chair up to within a few yards of Ramsey's and shoved me into it. He didn't bother to tie me down. I guess they figured, with two riflemen standing by, I wasn't much of a threat.

They were right.

No one said a word so I just sat there, looking like the captured dumb ass I was. I dared not look at Ramsey, but I could feel his anger just the same. He was hoppin' mad at having been caught. I was mad he'd been caught, too. But at least he hadn't talked, that much I knew, or else Trey Blackburn would be in the room with us.

I looked around. None of the guards would look back at me. Then I noticed a small surveillance camera installed on top of the Japanese room divider that screened the head honcho from view. I grinned at the camera — stress tends to turn me into a smart ass.

"Who are you, the Elephant Man?" I asked. "Are you that hideous to look at?"

His laugh sounded like a dump truck in low gear struggling up an incline: deep and rumbling. "I guess that's a matter of opinion," he said from the other side of the screen. It was an intriguing voice, low and gravelly like his laugh. "You look a little the worse for wear yourself," he continued. "How long have you been living on the mountain?"

I said nothing. He knew anyway. "A couple of my men work up at Silver Top and they tell me a prisoner escaped from there yesterday. From the looks of you, I'm guessing that would be you."

I remained silent, taking my cue from Ramsey.

"I've got nothing against escaped prisoners," the man added. "I might even be inclined to offer them a hot shower."

"Oh god, yes," I blurted out, unable to stop myself.

The man laughed again and, without raising his voice, issued orders to the asshole guard who had thrown me to the ground. "Take her to my personal bathroom and give her some privacy. Give her towels and clean clothes. Then bring her back here."

The guard hated being nice to me, but he didn't lay a hand on me, at least not until we were out in the clearing on the way to the head honcho's cabin. Which meant that whoever was sitting behind the screen had absolute authority over them all.

"No peeking," I admonished the guard after he had hustled me into a modern bathroom with a huge walk-in shower. He shot me the bird and slammed the door.

Hot water had never felt so good, ever, and, believe me, I have needed some damn showers during my thirty-something years. I stood beneath the spray, wondering what I had gotten myself into but unable to care, so intense was my pleasure at finally being clean, at the sensation of hot water swooshing off my body and soap slicking over my skin.

The guard did as he was told and kept a respectful distance at the door of the cabin until I emerged from the bathroom, feeling human again, toweling my hair dry. He'd left me several sizes of jeans and work shirts to choose from, along with clean socks. I had no underwear and would rather have died than put my old pair back on. But I'd gone commando by choice plenty of times before and I'd do it again now. Nothing was going to spoil my pleasure at being clean. I even had fresh socks on my feet.

"Don't I clean up nice?" I asked the guard.

"Shut up," he said. "I would not have dealt with you in the same manner."

"No, but you're not the big cheese, are you?" I taunted him. "Although something tells me you wish you were."

He grabbed my arm and pulled me out the door, dragging me across the dirt clearing to the other cabin. But I noticed he let me walk back into it under my own steam, so no one would know he'd been manhandling me. Like all bullies, he only had the nerve to pretend to be a big man with people he was sure were less powerful than him.

Everyone appeared to be in the exact same position as when I had left. The only difference was that Ramsey shifted ever so slightly and hissed, "Traitor!" under his breath at me when I took my seat again.

"Thank you," I said, more to rub it in with Ramsey then anything else. "That was the best damn shower I have ever had in my entire life."

"We have an excellent plumbing system here. Two of our men make their living in the profession." A plume of smoke spiraled upward from the other side of the screen, rendering him this strange disembodied voice… that smoked.

"What are we supposed to call you?" I asked him. "The Smoking Man?"

He was not an *X-Files* fan. He said nothing.

"You're Grubb, aren't you?" I asked. "One of your men called you that. I think he needs some serious disciplining."

"Leave us," the man said to his men. The two guards with rifles immediately slung them over their shoulders and made for the door. But the man who had failed to appreciate my charms balked at obeying.

"Leave us now," Grubb said louder, his voice taking on an even harsher quality. "I want two of you to guard the door and one of you to guard the back window."

My special friend left — giving me a look heated enough to dry my wet hair on the way out.

"Kisses," I called after him. He slammed the door behind him.

"It is not wise to taunt my men," the compound leader warned me. "I think perhaps you know that."

"If you mean, do I know that your men are complete assholes, the answer is 'yes. I know.' Especially the ones who work at the prison as guards."

Grubb was silent. Ramsey gave me a look that I roughly translated as "Shut the fuck up and play stupid so we get out of here alive." I ignored him. The only weapon I had at my disposal was my big mouth and I intended to use it. If I got any one of the men pissed off enough, he might make a mistake and we might be able to take advantage of it. Besides, Grubb had a code of honor. He had treated me like a gentleman.

"I suppose you know what they're doing at the prison," I said. "I suppose you authorized it."

Grubb remained silent.

"I know all about the drug running," I told him. "I know you use women to sell your drugs to finance this place. I know you force them to do things they don't want to do."

"They are paid well for their services," Grubb said. "Extremely well. They are eager to cooperate. Everyone wins."

"Oh, yeah," I said angrily, ignoring Ramsey's frantic eye signals, which made him look like he was having a seizure. "What about the ones who want a second chance at life with their families when they get out? The ones who want to walk away from breaking the law, but your men won't let them? Do they win?"

"I repeat: our associates are eager and willing. They benefit greatly from our enterprise."

"Does everyone benefit when the guards pull them into bathrooms at the prison and rape them?" I asked. "Do they win when your men kill them and kidnap their children?"

"Explain yourself," Grubb barked, so quickly I flinched. "No one gets raped or murdered under my orders. My men are disciplined. They do not behave in that manner."

Ramsey was squirming so hard his chair was about to topple over. I realized he was trying to kick me into silence with bound feet from three yards away. I shrugged my apology but had no intention of stopping now. I could tell I'd struck a nerve: Grubb did not know all that his men were doing. He had renegades on his hands, men who did not adhere to the compound's code of honor.

"Maybe you need to talk less to me and talk more to your men," I suggested. "Because they are damn sure raping women prisoners, and you have right here in this compound a fifteen year old boy who was taken from his mother after your men murdered her. Yes, murdered her, in cold blood, then made it look like a drug overdose, and left her body to bloat and rot for five days, all because she wanted out of your nasty enterprise."

"We have no one who is not here under their own free will," Grubb said. "Yes, we have young men, but they are all eighteen years old, at a minimum, and quite capable of making their own decisions about where to live."

"You have a fifteen year old boy living here named Trey Blackburn," I insisted. "I was hired by his relatives to find him and I was working undercover at the prison, trying to locate him."

Grubb laughed at me. Meanwhile, Ramsey was resorting to hissing "ssshhh" at me, like I was talking through his movie or something. I was too mad to care.

"I'm telling you the truth," I said angrily. "Call Trey in and talk to him. He'll tell you. Your men lied to him. They said his mother was going back to prison, but she's dead. I can give you her name and where she lived and you can make a few calls. My story is easily verified. Her murder is under investigation now."

Ramsey was shaking his head like I was the biggest idiot on the planet, but I didn't care. I'd gotten a very strong feeling about the man behind the room divider. Yes, he headed up a compound of kooks, at least they were kooks to us, I'm sure they considered themselves true patriots. But he ran a tight ship, and when he let me take my shower, he'd ordered his men to give me privacy and, well, he seemed like a man who treated women with respect, as peculiar as that sounds under the circumstances. I was certain he had not known of everything his men were doing in his name.

"Look," I continued. "Can't we talk face to face? This is ridiculous."

Ramsey rolled his eyes like I was the biggest idiot on the planet.

"I don't think so," Grubb said calmly.

"Why not?" I demanded.

This time Ramsey lost it and spoke. "Why do you think, Casey? Gol-durnit, you're as stubborn as a dead mule. He doesn't want us to be able to identify him and that's just fine with me."

"Oh." I tried to recover with some dignity intact. "Look," I said to Grubb, "I understand you are running a business here."

"Not just a business," he interrupted. "I am facilitating the evolution of the human race. If people want to poison themselves, let them. Have you never read the works of Charles Darwin?"

"Fine. You're only giving evolution a hand. And maybe some of the women who get out of Silver Top are more than willing to make a few bucks by selling your drugs. But your men aren't sticking with using those women for their distribution chain. They're *forcing* women to work for you. They're blackmailing them by threatening to have their parole revoked, and they're threatening their families with harm, and they damn sure are indeed forcing prisoners to have sex with them."

"My men are disciplined," Grubb repeated tersely.

"Then ask some of your men, men you trust beyond question, if they think my story is bullshit. I'll bet you anything they'll tell you I could be telling the truth. They'll tell you that not everyone who lives on this compound is honorable, not everyone follows your code."

In the silence that followed, as Grubb thought over what I had said, Ramsey caught my eye. His eyes kept darting to his right so I followed his gaze. There, mounted on the wall, was a neat row of knives, each one nestled carefully in its place. They ranged in size from daggers to machetes, and I had a feeling they weren't just there for show. But I was glad they were there when I checked out Ramsey's bindings more carefully. His feet were tied to the chair with nylon rope and his hands were so firmly trussed behind his back it would take some serious sawing with one of those knives to set him free.

"What you say is disturbing," Grubb said from behind the screen. He had thought it over and decided my words might have some merit.

"Look, all I want is to take the boy home," I said. "I'll let you deal with the men who murdered his mother. I'm sure the boy can point them out to you."

"That is not necessary. I know who they must be." He paused. "Excuse me a moment. Do not move while I am gone. My men are watching. You will be shot if you attempt to escape."

Grubb moved too quickly for me to see him. He was only visible for a few feet between the edge of the room divider and the front door, and he had a green hoodie pulled low over his face. All I knew was that he was tall and well-built.

The moment he left us alone, Ramsey started in on me. "What the everlovin' hell do you think you're doing?" he asked.

"He has a code of honor," I said. "He's not going to kill us."

"He doesn't need to," Ramsey pointed out sensibly. "I am sure any one of his men would be happy to do it for him."

"He wouldn't let that happen."

"He wouldn't know," Ramsey hissed. "All he has to say is 'take these people out of here' and his men will take us out, all right. That's the way it works. No witnesses. No surprises. No survivors. No chances taken."

"I'm sure you exaggerate."

"I'm sure I don't," he insisted angrily, just as the door opened again. Grubb was back, but he was behind the screen before we could catch so much as a glimpse of his face.

"What did I miss?" he asked smoothly. "Lover's quarrel?"

Ramsey's bitter laugh put that theory to rest.

"I wouldn't touch him with a ten-foot pole," I said, for my part. "And, trust me, he does not have a ten-foot pole."

Grubb laughed. "So you do know this man?" he said. "How is it you two are together, wandering the mountains?"

"I called him from the woods after I escaped," I explained grudgingly, not liking to be reminded I owed Ramsey a debt. "He helped me get away from the guards and the dogs and told me where to go to keep safe until he could get to me. Then he drove all night to get me." I was suddenly ashamed of my earlier outburst and added, "He's a man of loyalty and principle, just like you."

Hey, it's not everyone who can mend bridges with old friends and suck up to new ones all at the very same time.

"He did all that long distance?" Grubb asked. "That takes some skill. I could use a man like him."

"I'm not joining your damn army of fruitcakes," Ramsey said. "I don't rebel against the rigid stupidities of one world by following the rigid stupidities of another."

There was that low, gravelly laugh again. "I take it you're not a joiner?" Grubb asked.

"Damn straight," Ramsey said, spitting on the floor.

Without warning, a horrible scream cut through the night air. It sounded like a wildcat was getting a hot poker jammed up its ass. I about shit in my drawers at the sound and Ramsey looked as scared as I had ever seen him look.

"Don't worry about that," Grubb assured us, even as the agonizing screams continued. "I'm just looking into your story and some of the men are reluctant to talk."

I thought there was a slim chance one of his men was standing just outside the cabin, screaming his fool head off just to scare us… but I doubted it. Grubb seemed way too pleased with himself, like he was welcoming this chance to show the men who was boss. I was suddenly very glad I had blabbed willingly.

Ramsey didn't seem glad about anything and Grubb noticed.

"I see your capture rankles you," Grubb said soothingly to him. "Don't be embarrassed. The man who brought you in once taught covert operations for the military. He, quite literally, wrote the book on the very techniques you were attempting to use."

Ramsey didn't look mollified, especially after another scream rent the air, only to stop abruptly. Too abruptly.

"Are you going to let us go or not?" I asked. "We have nothing against you. Or against your men. This is your mountain. I acknowledge your right to deal with the situation in the way you see fit. All I want is the boy, so I can take him home to the people who love him. To his people."

"His people?" For the first time, Grubb seemed less than calm. "His people poison themselves with drugs, kill each other over the most minor of offenses, live in squalor and debase themselves daily by attacking their own. We have done him a favor by taking him from 'his people,' as you say."

That made me hoppin' mad. As someone who had few people left, I wondered who the hell he thought he was to be putting down someone's family, especially when he didn't even know them. Corndog Sally worked her whole life, over eighty years, from sun-up to sundown. Who was this man to judge her?

"First of all," I told him angrily as Ramsey stared at me, horrified. He looked on the verge of weeping at what he knew was to come. "You had no right to take the boy away from people who have raised and loved him. No right at all."

"The boy is better off with us. We will raise him as white and give him a purpose in life."

"A purpose? As in his purpose is to destroy his own people by flooding their lives with drugs? What kind of purpose is that?"

"You put a lot of stock into the concept of 'his people,'" Grubb said.

"That's because I have none of my own, and it burns my ass when people who do have others who love them don't get the chance to return the favor. Trey Blackburn has people who miss him, and you have no right to keep him from them just because they have a different color skin from you and your men."

"I have nothing against blacks," Grubb said smoothly. "We do not target them. As I said before, people self select."

"Oh, self select this," I said angrily, shooting him the bird. I held it up high, in front of the camera, as Ramsey groaned in frustration.

Grubb laughed at me. "You are quite the hot head, aren't you? What am I supposed to do with you?"

"Let us go," I said immediately. "Just let us go and let us have the boy. None of us will say a thing. I don't even know what you look like and we'll never be able to find our way back here again."

"Maybe you could not, but something tells me your friend here could."

Ramsey looked a little worried at that one. When he didn't speak up, I felt like I had to say something.

"Look, my friend here is no friend of the law, okay? He lives on the same side of it as you and your men. The last thing he wants to have happen is to get involved with an investigation and have the law crawling up his ass."

"A wanted man, is that it?" Grubb asked curiously.

"I wouldn't exactly say *wanted,*" I said quickly when Ramsey turned to me with such a searing look that I was afraid he might porpoise toward me, chair and all, and start biting the crap out of me. "He's more like a person of interest. In a whole lot of unsolved cases. He's one of the 'usual suspects' you might say. He's the last person who would turn you in, and me? All I want is the boy."

"You ask a lot of me," Grubb said. "And I don't even know your name."

"I don't know yours," I pointed out. "All I know is 'Grubb.'"

"Call me Chuck," he said with a laugh.

"Call me Debbie," I suggested. "Debbie Little."

"Is that your real name?"

"Is 'Chuck Grubb' yours?" I countered.

He ignored the question. "Okay, Chuck and Debbie it is."

"Will you give us the boy and let us go?" I pleaded.

"I need to talk to the boy," Grubb conceded. "And see what his wishes are. I can't promise you anything more than that."

"How long will that take?" I asked.

"You are pushing your luck, Miss Little. I suggest you say no more."

"I heartily echo that sentiment," Ramsey said firmly.

Even I can put a sock in it sometimes. I heard the crackle of a walkie-talkie of some sort as Grubb issued orders to his men.

The two silent guards reappeared immediately, one to grab my arm, the other to cut Ramsey free of his foot bindings and help him to his feet. But they were smart enough to keep Ramsey's hands tied behind his back.

"Where are we going?" I asked.

"Don't worry," Grubb assured me in his deep voice. "You'll be safe where we're taking you."

Or so he thought. Ramsey's warning about the men rang loud in my memory. I was not willing to let myself relax with anyone but Grubb. Who knew how many of his men had gone rogue? Who knew what they might do to me?

I was contemplating this possibility as the guard dragged me out of the cabin and stepped me through the dirt yard toward a path that led into the woods. I didn't like it. We were heading toward the storage sheds.

Worse, to my left, under the lights illuminating the clearing, I could see Trey walking slowly toward the interrogation cabin, his face wary but determinedly brave.

I felt a wave of panic, wondering what the kid might tell Grubb about us if they turned up the heat. Who knew where Trey's loyalties lay after a couple weeks of brainwashing? And he *was* just a kid. He wouldn't hold up for long. This wasn't good.

My escort shoved me out of the clearing and onto a darkened path. I inched away from my guard, closer to the forest's edge.

I was thinking about trying to make a run for it, guards and rifles be damned. But before I could do anything about the impulse, all hell broke loose in the compound and, in a heartbeat, everything in my world changed.

# Chapter Fifteen

An explosion rocked the compound. The ground trembled beneath my feet as a massive boom rolled over the clearing, enveloping me in sound and fury. Seconds later, a fireball shot up into the sky from the other side of the property, near where I'd seen the storage sheds.

The men reacted instantly. They poured from the dining hall and recreation building; they ran shouting from their bunkhouses and appeared from the shadows, all converging on the cabin where I'd seen the weapons being stored. Forgotten, I stared as they formed a brigade line in under a minute and started distributing rifles and shotguns as fast as they could, hand-to-hand, each of them taking two or more before disappearing into the shadows. There were dozens of men, all fit and well-trained, all eager to seize the moment their leader had warned them would come. They were under attack and they were fighting back. This was what they had been groomed for.

It had to be Shep. He had gotten my message and notified the feds. Shots rang out from the other side of the compound, enough for an entire war.

"Casey!" Ramsey yelled at me. "Get a knife!"

I dashed back to the interrogation cabin and grabbed one of the knives from the wall. Ramsey was waiting right outside the door and I sawed through the nylon rope binding his hands.

"Leave me some fingers," Ramsey reminded me.

"Got it," I said as the rope fell away. Ramsey grabbed my elbow and pulled me into the darkness next to the cabin.

"Stay here," he said. "Don't move or I'll shoot you myself."

He darted into the clearing where Trey still stood, paralyzed by what had happened, looking every bit his fifteen years old and nowhere near ready to cope with the crisis unfolding around him.

We were not the only ones to have noticed his fear. I saw a tall man on the far side of the clearing dressed in black jeans and a dark green hoodie. It was the compound leader, Grubb. He spotted Trey at the same time I did. He pushed the hood off of his face and I could see him clearly in the moonlight — older, weathered, rugged, handsome. Clint Eastwood in *High Plains Drifter.* A man who lived inside himself, a man who had seen it all. Grubb saw Ramsey coming and gauged the distance between him and the boy. My heart started to pound. Grubb had a gun in his hand and plenty of time plus the skills to shoot. I thought I saw him raise the gun, or maybe I just imagined it, but just then another explosion racked the compound. Grubb looked around instead, as if searching for someone he knew. I realized with a start he was looking for me.

I stepped out of my hiding spot and raised my hand, knowing somehow that it was what I should do. Grubb spotted me, raised his own hand in farewell, and sprinted toward his men.

I dashed forward and reached Trey just in time to hear Ramsey tell him, "If you don't want to spend the next twenty years of your life in the system, follow me." He grabbed the boy's arm and we pulled him into the darkness of the woods, Ramsey in the lead.

"Keep your head down and don't stop moving," Ramsey yelled at us. "There's a lot of firepower down there. We need to get around the roadblock, they'll have one up along the road, and then I'll make the call about whether it's safe to take the road out. If I say so, we'll take the chance. We've got to get to the truck before they find it. For now, just put your head down and run."

We ran. We ran up the mountainside and clawed our way to the rocky ridge, then clung to tree after tree as we moved as quickly as we could along the ridge line, spurred on by shouts and smoke and gunfire below. I had no idea what had happened. I didn't know if a storage shed had blown, if the FBI had lobbed in tear gas bombs or what. Hell, Canada could be invading for all I knew. The only thing I knew for certain was that I had to get my ass to Ramsey's truck and that the next twenty minutes would likely determine the rest of my life.

We had Trey between us and once he got going, he did not hesitate. He followed Ramsey like a gazelle, leaping from one clear spot to the next, slinging himself around trees I had to cling to and crawl past. He did not ask questions. He just put his head down and followed. The kid was a survivor.

Below us, blocking the private road, we could see a dozen or more vehicles pulled up in formation. The cars were empty and mostly official government sedans. I also saw a few sheriff's cars parked among them. It was Shep, indeed, and he had reinforcements. My bet was that his friends were not just Alcohol, Firearms & Tobacco but probably Homeland Security as well.

We cleared the staging spot safely, saw a couple of armed men with "ATF" emblazoned on their vests checking the woods on either side of the cars and kept to the forest above them. Somewhere along the way I fell and skinned the flesh off my palms. It didn't slow me down. Adrenaline kept me going. I heard a rustling in the brush to my left and I wondered if our fear was contagious, if other creatures in the forest had sensed our flight. I imagined them running along beside us, deep in the shadows, showing solidarity for our cause. It helped keep me running.

I did my damnedest to keep up with Ramsey but it was impossible. Soon I was alone, with only the edge of the ridge to guide me. Just as I became fearful that I had somehow lost them, I crashed into Ramsey in the darkness. He was waiting beside an immense Douglas fir, patting Trey on his back, urging the boy to catch his breath.

"How much farther?" I asked between gasps for air.

"Half a mile or so," Ramsey told me.

"I can't do it," I said. "I just can't." My lungs felt as if the air had been sucked out of them with a vacuum cleaner and a deep pain in my abdomen told me I was going to pay for not working out while in prison.

"You can do it," Ramsey said confidently and, I swear, the bastard was barely winded. "We're going to take the road out the rest of the way."

"Is that safe?" Trey spoke for the first time. "I want to see Meemaw." His voice broke and Ramsey patted him on the back again, this time gently.

"It's safe," Ramsey predicted. "I'll take the lead and keep an eye out for approaching vehicles. If you see me go down, I want you to hit the ground like you have never hit it before. Dive into the drainage ditch on the side. This time of year it'll be filled with leaves. Bury under. Don't even breathe. I'll give a whistle when it's time to run again."

As if that would calm us! Just hearing his strategy was enough to paralyze me with fear, but when Ramsey slid down the incline, I gave Trey a gentle push to get him going and slid down after him. Once we hit the smooth dirt of the graded road, we sprinted along in the darkness, the moon high and bright above us. It seemed benevolent and supportive, guiding us toward escape. I began to think we had a chance. The road was solid and predictable and I felt like a long distance runner closing in on the home stretch. I could go on like this forever.

"Down!" Ramsey shouted as lights flickered across the tops of some trees ahead. "Get down now!"

We dove for cover in the drainage ditch and I buried under the leaves. They were damp from melted snow and sticky with pine resin. I held my breath and prayed. An engine roared past at top speed. Then a bigger roar rattled my fillings as another vehicle zoomed past, followed by another and yet another.

The silence that followed was eerie. I could hear my heart beating in my chest. Dust swirled up from the road and my mouth was choked with leaves and pine needles.

But we had done it.

Ramsey jumped to his feet, triumphant, and whistled for us to follow him.

As he led the charge to the end of the private road, it was as if I had stepped through a wrinkle in time. I could see it all in my mind's eye as clearly as if I was there, rifle in hand, tattered flag leading me forward — Ramsey, or perhaps his great grandpappy, leading the charge out of the hills of Tennessee down onto the plains of Georgia, taking on the Union soldiers though they were outnumbered and outgunned, Rebel madmen triumphant at having survived the slaughter at Vicksburg, determined to never give up the fight, fueled by a false sense of their own immortality.

No wonder we had made it through the last few days. Ramsey was one of the chosen. The blood that ran through his veins had been blessed by the mountain gods, or perhaps even Aries himself. I would be safe with him.

I returned to the present the moment my feet hit the blacktop of the highway, all too aware that we had to escape while we could still hear gunshots echoing across the acres behind us. It was harder to gauge what was happening from so far away, but smoke wound in swirls upward toward the moon. The steady pop-pop of rifles was interspersed with the rapid tat-tat of automatic fire, all punctuated by occasional explosions. Grubb and his men were making their stand. I hoped it was all they had wanted it to be, for I had realized something profound when I witnessed them leaping into battle. They didn't really have any ideology. They had no plans for global domination or a new world order. What they really wanted was much more simple: a chance to prove themselves, a chance to assert their independence, a chance to repudiate and transcend the mundane lives that circumstance had forced upon them. They had spent years preparing for battle, wanting battle, and now they were getting their wish. The battle was upon them.

Ramsey was fishing in the darkness for his keys, searching the hollow of the tree nearest his truck. "I'm pissed about my knapsack," he said sourly. "It was waterproof."

"I'll buy you a new one," I promised as I fought to regain my breath. "I'll make Burly buy you an entire North Face store."

He snorted in contempt. "That store is for assholes," he said. "Let's go."

He held up the truck keys in triumph and we piled into the cab, following Ramsey's orders: "Casey, open the glove compartment. We still got cash and plastic?"

"Check," I said.

"Trey, scooch over and take the middle spot. I don't want to get any nearer to that woman than I have to. She's trouble with a capital 'T' and I do believe I am done bailing her ass out."

"Bailing me out?" I cried indignantly as I squeezed into the crowded cab. "I'm the one who saved your ass."

"Yeah," Ramsey said as he ground the gears and backed up onto the highway. "Casey here talked our way to freedom. She ended up boring that poor commander into letting us go. It's a wonder we escaped with our hearing intact."

"Ramsey Lee," I said furiously. "I'll have you know —"

"Hey!" Trey said. "Take it easy, would you? I'm stuck in the middle here."

The kid had a point. I had to laugh. "Okay, I admit it. We did it together," I conceded. "And I can't believe we did it. We did it!"

I rolled down the window as Ramsey picked up speed, tearing down the mountain highway like the hounds of hell were on our tail. "We did it!" I screamed out into the wind. "You can't touch us! We did it!"

I rolled the window back up and turned to my companions in triumph. Trey was sitting stock still, staring at me, eyes wide. He turned to Ramsey and, with the air of a man who is so above it all when it comes to women, he asked our fearless leader, "Is she always like this?"

"Oh, you have no idea, son," Ramsey answered. "You have no idea at all."

* * *

I HAD PROMISED TREY I'd take him straight to see his grandmother but I feared that I had promised him something I could not deliver. Corndog Sally had been going downhill fast last time I had seen her. Who knew if she was even still alive? If it was too late, I would never forgive myself.

The fear gnawed at me for over an hour as we sped down the gentle slope of the highway that led from the foothills to the center of the state. As soon as I was sure we weren't being followed, I told Ramsey I had to make a phone call. Our cell phones had been confiscated by the men in the compound, so we'd have to go low-tech. "It'll have to be a pay phone," I told him.

"For which you will need to borrow change," he guessed.

"I'll pay you back," I said. "But I don't actually know where we should take the kid from here so I have to make the call."

Trey had fallen asleep between us. He looked younger when he was sleeping. You could still see a hint of roundness in his jaw and his expression was as innocent as a toddler's. It moved me that he could hold on to even a whisper of innocence after all that had happened to him, both before and after his mother had been killed.

"It's not going to be easy finding a pay phone," Ramsey predicted and he was right. It had become a cell phone world sometime between the death of leggings and the birth of iPods. We finally found a truck stop that let you call anywhere in the state for a buck and a quarter — you just had to talk fast, since all you got for your money was three minutes. While Ramsey distracted the kid with an offer of hot chocolate topped with whipped cream, I dialed Marcus's number and prayed he would answer.

By then it was after midnight. Marcus was the only one I knew who'd still be awake and was in a position to help me. I pictured him in his silk bathrobe and matching slippers, fumbling for the telephone.

"I need your help," I said, before he could start yelling.

It didn't stop him. "Where the hell have you been?" Marcus shrieked. "Do you know what you've done? Bill Butler has gone so far out on a limb for you that he's dangling from the edges of it, clinging to vines, while the Perry County cops jump up and down on it trying to drop him into the snake pit."

"I have two minutes air time left," I pleaded. "No time for mixed metaphors."

"The police think you killed Tonya Blackburn. I've been interrogated by them twice just for being a 'known cohort' of yours. Imagine that? One moment I'm a respectable civil servant, the next I'm a 'known cohort.' Plus, Bobby left some incomprehensible message about you being in prison somewhere and he's going into the joint, too?"

"Stop," I pleaded. "I need to know where Corndog Sally is. I found her grandson and I've got to get him to her while she's still alive or everything I've gone through over the past few weeks will have been completely in vain."

"I'm going to have to call more than Sally," Marcus said. "My job is on the line. And, by the way, that junkie kitten you foisted off on me? It shredded my silk drapes. Shredded them. He was swinging from them like Tarzan on crack. I came home from work and they were nothing but ribbons fluttering in the wind."

"I'm sorry, I really am," I told him. "But I've got a bad feeling about Sally and it's getting worse. Please find out if she's at in the hospital or at a hospice or what. Last I saw her, she was being taken away in an ambulance and was headed to a hospice, but I don't know the name."

"Fine," Marcus said wearily. "Who am I to stand in the way of a dying woman's last wish? I'll call you back."

"You can't," I explained. "We have no cell phones."

*"We?"* he asked.

"Me and Ramsey Lee. We got captured by white supremacists in this compound in the mountains and they took everything."

It is a credit to our long friendship that this explanation did not give Marcus pause. "That skinny guy with the smelly dogs that look like they have permanent hangovers?" Marcus said, horrified.

"They're called bloodhounds."

"I thought that was all over on account of his mother pulling a shotgun on you. You recycling boyfriends now?"

"His mother pulls a shotgun on everyone," I said impatiently. "And it's still over between us." Suddenly, the need to make what we had gone through real washed over me. The words poured out like vomit, even though they sounded insane, even to me:

"I called Ramsey after Bobby broke me out of prison and had a heart attack in the woods and Ramsey came to my rescue and helped me find this old timey music festival and I saw a wild boar, it was a sign, and, really, no one else could have — "

"Stop your world, I want to get off," Marcus interrupted. "You have fifteen seconds left. And I can only take so much."

"I'll call back in an hour," I said. "By then we'll be closer to..." But the disconnect kicked in and all I heard was a dial tone.

I'd save my remaining quarters for the follow-up call and pray Marcus came through.

* * *

MARCUS CAME THROUGH. We'd stopped at the last Krispy Kreme before the doughnut wilderness kicked in, with about an hour and a half more to go until we reached Raleigh. I'd sensed a tightening in Trey as we drew closer to his future. His right knee had started to jerk up and down in a nervous, subconscious staccato. I felt for the kid. He was walking into the unknown: a father he had never known, a future he had no inkling about, a beloved grandmother who might or might not be alive. His whole life hung on what he found waiting for him in Raleigh. But there was nothing I could have said or done to help him, so I gave him his privacy and kept my trap shut.

Once we hit the Krispy Kreme, while Ramsey and Trey were deep in a discussion about whether to be purists and get nothing but original glazed or mix it up with a couple lemon- and cream-stuffed doughnuts, I walked a half block to a pay phone on the corner, as out of place in these times as a gas-lit lamp from the Sherlock Holmes era might be.

Even though we were in the middle of a rural hamlet north of Burlington, in the dead of the night, there was a skinny white kid waiting by the phone for his drug supplier to call him back. He took one look at me and scurried down the sidewalk without even being asked to beat it. He either figured I was a cop — or I was still carrying my prison mood around with me and it showed.

Marcus was waiting for my call. He'd tracked Sally's whereabouts through ambulance and hospital records, then found a cell number for Sally's snooty daughter, Alicia, and confirmed we were on our way. Sally was alive, though barely, in a hospice outside Knightdale, a small bedroom community on the other side of Raleigh.

I knew why Sally was holding on and I also knew that as soon as she saw him, Sally would let go. I was bringing Trey to his future, but I was also bringing death to Corndog Sally.

I thanked Marcus and trudged back to the truck, feeling the weight of what was to come on my shoulders. Sometimes life gives you an awful lot of power over others and I wasn't the type of person who liked that. I barely wanted responsibility for myself.

"Where's my dozen?" I asked as we climbed back into the truck. Ramsey started laughing, but Trey looked alarmed. "Relax, kid," I told him. "All that prison starch went straight to my ass. I'm going to restrain myself and only eat three."

Good thing they'd bought two dozen. The kid wolfed those doughnuts down like he hadn't eaten in months. I don't know why, but seeing him eat like that made me feel like he had a shot at a normal life one day soon after all.

"Will my father be at the hospice?" he asked me once he'd finished polishing off thousands of Krispy Kreme calories.

"Probably," I said, knowing Marcus would have called Burly the second he hung up from talking to me. For all I knew, Marcus had also called in the FBI and the National Guard. The truth was, I had no more idea of what I was walking into than Trey did. I just knew more about the possibilities that awaited us.

An hour later we entered a crowded waiting room in the Good Shepherd Hospice of Wake County to find a good chunk of my life waiting for me. Marcus. Burly. Bill Butler. Thank god Ramsey had stayed in the truck to await further instructions. It was weird enough as it was.

In the early morning hours, no one looked good. No one looked happy, either. In fact, no one even looked awake. They were sprawled out in the chairs of the visitor's room, snoring together like a cave full of hibernating bears.

*My god,* I thought. *These are the men in my life?*

Marcus had claimed a loveseat that was too short for his lanky frame. His legs were draped over one arm of it and he was emitting a cacophony of snorts as loud as a Hell's Angels gang roaring past. Bill Butler had propped his feet up on a chair across from the one he lolled in. He had his head thrown back and his arms sprawled to each side like he was waiting to be nailed to a cross. His snores were loud enough to shake the photos on the wall. Burly, in contrast, sat upright in his wheelchair, eyes closed, face still, his snores positively delicate in comparison. My heart did a little fandango when I saw him. I was bringing him a son.

"Is that one my father?" Trey whispered as he stared at Burly.

"Yes. Fortunately for you," I added after Marcus gave a snort that sounded like a wart hog mating and Bill Butler answered with an asthmatic wheeze.

"He's younger than I thought," Trey said, voice trembling. "He looks pretty cool." He was putting off the moment of meeting him, I knew.

"You have his smile and features, for sure. Look at that beautiful face." The words were out before I could stop them — but they were true. Burly was still beautiful to me and I knew time would never change that.

He felt me thinking of him. Without so much as another muscle twitching, Burly opened his eyes and stared straight at me. I felt the shock in the core of my heart. Then he turned his gaze to his son and it was as if heaven itself had illuminated his face from within. *This is what joy looks like,* I thought.

Burly was used to his body's stillness and had long since adapted to it. I think he sought refuge in it at that moment, as he processed whatever he was feeling.

Trey stared back, unsure of what to say and probably even more unsure of how he felt. The two men, father and son, gazed at one another with a look so raw I felt that it was not mine to witness.

I turned away to give them privacy, turning back only when I heard Burly speak.

"Come here, kid," he said. "Let me look at you." Trey inched closer and Burly took his hand. "I'm so sorry about your mother," he told Trey quietly. "She was a beautiful woman, inside and out."

"Sometimes," Trey whispered. You could barely hear him.

"I didn't know about you," Burly said. "I would have been there for you if I had."

As Trey pulled his hand away, nodding his understanding, I saw the tattoo: a black ploughshare and sword carved into the skin above his wrist. He'd have a reminder of what had happened to him for the rest of his life.

Trey stared at the rug, unsure of what to say to his father. I ached for the boy. Despite his get-tough training among self-styled commandos, I could tell he had no confidence in the moment, that he didn't want to say anything for fear he'd say the wrong thing and lose what he'd just gained.

"We'll catch up later," Burly promised, knowing to let the moment go. "Right now, your grandmother needs to see you. Your aunt will take you to her."

I realized that Tonya's seemingly perfect sister, Alicia, had been watching from the doorway. She seemed different somehow, less severe. A little beaten down by the circumstances, perhaps. Fatigue had wiped her of her brittleness. I almost felt sorry for her.

"Hello, Trey," she said, making just enough eye contact with Burly to tell me she'd been seduced by his charms or, more likely, the charms of his money. "Meemaw's waiting to see you. I'll take you to her."

They left and I sat down next to Burly, wondering what would happen to me once Marcus and Bull Butler awoke and the wheels of justice started turning. I also wondered if being arrested could possibly be worse than sitting there listening to their godawful snoring.

"Lord," I said to Burly. "Thank god I don't sleep with either one of them."

Burly's mouth twitched as he fought back a smile. "You're one to talk. You should hear yourself when you get going."

I punched him on his shoulder. "I do not snore."

"Only when you sleep," he conceded. Then he looked at me and said one of the most important things a man has ever said to me. "I'm sorry, Casey," Burly said. "I always loved you for being you, but I'm not sure I ever made it easy for you to be you. You were always so far away from me. You were always going places I couldn't go." He tapped the side of his wheelchair. But then he left his regret behind. Burly had never wasted time on things he could not change.

"Thank you for bringing my son home to me," he said. "I will never be able to thank you enough. And I will never forget it. I hope you know that, no matter how far apart our lives take us, I will always love you more than anyone else I know, Casey. You have to believe me when I say that, because it's true."

Then he kissed me — and I knew it was a final good-bye. And it was okay. He had a son to worry about, a new life ahead of him that was full enough without me. Besides, I'd felt something shift between us when I brought him Trey, a balancing out of grudges and hurts and joys and triumphs, the beginning of something new that was more about respect than love. It was all I needed to let go.

I didn't say anything back to him, though I knew I'd always love Burly in return. I can't say things like that. I might feel them, but the words don't come out. I was spared the humiliation of responding with a lame, "Me, too," when Ramsey interrupted us. I guess his concern for Trey had countermanded his fear that he might be arrested if he left his truck.

Ramsey stopped in the doorway and stared in open-mouthed horror at Bill Butler and Marcus. "Good god," he proclaimed as he kicked Marcus's feet to the floor, sending him struggling sleepily upright. "Those sounds are not natural." Then he kicked Bill's trademark cowboy boots, causing Bill to jump up and reach for a gun that wasn't there.

"What the hell?" Bill complained.

"You don't want to know, man," Ramsey told him. "And I'm pretty sure you need to get that deviated septum checked."

Ramsey glanced at me. "How's the kid?"

"He's going to be okay," I promised.

He walked across the room in that long-legged stride of his and shook Burly's hand. "Good to see you, man. You've got a great kid in that boy."

Burly's face came alive. "Thanks for all you did," he said to Ramsey. "For taking care of Trey and Casey like that."

"Casey?" Ramsey laughed. "I didn't do a damn thing for her. She saved my ass, in fact. You know that girl. Stubborn as a dead mule. She's got to do it all by her own self or she's not going to do it at all."

What a liar — but I loved him for it.

"Miss Jones?" Alicia McCoy stood in the doorway. "Could I talk to you alone for a moment?" A hint of her brittleness was back. She was probably going to bitch about my fee or something. Well, I'd be damned if I'd accept a penny from her money-grubbing ass.

I followed her down the hall until we reached a private spot. The hospice was a lot like a hospital in the common areas. It was white, scrubbed and foreboding, the bedroom doors closed against the inevitable noise of funeral home directors coming and going in the night. I knew the rooms were filled with love and families and personal belongings and reminders of lives that were soon to be left behind. But the public areas were reminders that failing human bodies were nearby. And maybe it was kinder that way.

Alicia surprised me. Her back was stiff, her jaw looked like it might crack from the effort of managing a meager smile and her conciliatory tone was more than a little patronizing. But she was clearly attempting an apology. "I'm sorry if I misjudged you before," she said. "And I thank you for bringing Trey home to us. If I seemed cold and uncaring, it's just that I've spent a lifetime watching Tonya let my mother down. I have seen my mother filled with hope that things might be different, that my sister might change, only to go to a place as dark as any she ever had to visit once Tonya let her down again. My sister told so many lies, took so many years off my parent's lives, and for what? Getting high? She died before I could forgive her and I'm not sure I ever can."

"It doesn't matter," I said. "It doesn't matter to Tonya anymore whether you forgive her or not. And trust me, it doesn't matter to me how you choose to go through life. If you want to hold on to that, it's your shoulders carrying the weight, not mine and certainly not Tonya's. But I will remind you of one thing — Trey is not his mother."

"I know that," she said quickly.

"You have no children of your own?" I guessed.

She looked away, not meeting my eyes.

"Don't worry," I said. "You won't have to take care of him. He's got the best father a boy could ever have and he'll never want for anything for the rest of his life. You could even keep all that money Tonya sent to you over the last year, the money she told you to put away for Trey's college tuition. He won't need it now."

Alicia looked up, surprised. I had guessed right. "Don't worry," I said. "I won't tell anyone. Not even Trey, who deserves to know how much his mother cared about him."

"That's not fair," Alicia said. "I love that boy. I would never have taken his money. I would have said something."

Yeah, right. She'd be buried in a coffin lined with dollar bills, diamond rings on her fingers and gold wound round her neck. And it wouldn't take her any closer to heaven.

"It's not about the money," I explained. "It's about family. If you love Trey, then you'd better start showing it. You're the only one who can give him part of his mother back. You're the closest thing left on this earth like her."

"Tonya and I had nothing in common," she snapped.

"I doubt that very much. And if you love Trey, you'll find the part of you that bound you to your sister and make sure he gets a chance to see it."

She was silent and that was fine with me. I'd had enough. I'm not one to judge people, at least not for more than a passing moment of entertainment. I had never been prepared to judge Tonya Blackburn and the way she chose to numb her life with drugs. I hadn't walked in her shoes and I wasn't going to condemn her for the path she'd taken. We all have our demons and not all of us are strong enough to kick the demon's ass. I thought Tonya had done pretty good, considering, especially at the end when the odds were stacked against her and she had tried to protect her son. So I did want to defend her to this rigid, unforgiving woman beside me — but when I saw that Alicia's eyes had filled with tears, I realized that she had tried to confront her demons in a different way, burying them under a mountain of money and houses and clothes and cars. And she was only now figuring out that all of that wasn't going to be enough to keep her particular demons at bay.

"Look," I said more kindly. "Forget forgiving Tonya. She's gone. Maybe what you really need to do is forgive yourself and stop trying to pretend the two of you weren't connected. I've lost family, too. When they die, a little piece of you goes with them. You can't will that feeling away. You have to go through it and learn to live with it."

But Alicia's composure had returned, and her facade along with it. "Thank you, Miss Jones," she said crisply, as if we had just completed a business transaction. But I knew she'd heard a little of what I'd said and that when she needed it the most, she might remember some of my words.

A door opened down the hall and Trey came out, looking grave for his young years. "She wants to see you," he told me.

"Me?" I asked, surprised.

Trey nodded.

As I turned to visit Corndog Sally for what would surely be the last time, I saw him hug his aunt and hold her tight — and I knew, with an unexpected jolt of relief, that they would be okay after all. Grief over Sally would bring them together.

* * *

CORNDOG SALLY was not long for this world. That much was obvious. Her flesh had wasted away, leaving little but bone to support the papery skin that had faded to a dull brown dusted with gray pallor. But the eyes that stared out at me from her shrunken face were as bright as black diamonds. Her voice was raspy, but it was clear that her mind was strong.

"Miss Jones," she said, crooking a finger and beckoning me closer. The room smelled like disinfectant, medicine and decaying flesh. In other words, it smelled like death. I stepped closer and placed my hand as lightly as I could on her arm. It was cold.

"Did I keep my word or what?" I asked. "I'm guessing Trey's grown since you last saw him."

"In more ways than one," she croaked. "Don't think I didn't notice that tattoo of his."

"Maybe a reminder will be good for him," I said gently. "He'll make thoughtful choices from now on."

"That boy was always wise for his age. He had to be." Sally started to cough and I waited until she could speak again. There was a rattle in the back of her throat and I knew what that meant.

I'd brought Trey back just in time. "I'm not worried about my boy now and I want to thank you for that." She squeezed my hand. "I knew you were a person who kept their word. There aren't many of us left in the world."

I was close to tears and found I could not answer.

"You know why I called you in here?" she asked me. The ghost of a smile flickered over her face.

"You want to re-negotiate my fee?"

She tried to laugh but only ended up choking and I decided to hold the jokes from there on out. "No fee for me," she finally said. "Your boyfriend is going to take care of all that."

"Burly's not my boyfriend any more," I corrected her. "And he'll probably take care of your entire family. God knows, he's got the money to do it."

"I'm leaving them plenty of money," she said. "But he's a good man. I feel regret that Tonya did not think she could bring him home when they were together. That was my fault."

"No," I said firmly. "That was the world's fault. You need to let that go."

"Funny you should say that," she said gently. "I called you in here to tell you that the one thing I've learned about life is that you have to let go of the things that are already gone, especially when it causes you pain to hold on to them."

I knew she was talking about Burly. "I let him go," I promised. "Thanks to you. We're even now and I can let him go."

"Something new will take his place," she promised me. "Just you wait and see."

"Thank you," I whispered to her.

"Thank you," she said in a fading voice. "And now I'm going to tell you something you have earned the right to know."

"More wisdom of the ages?"

"Not really. But I know you'll sleep better at night knowing."

I was intrigued. "Go on," I told her.

"When I was a little girl, I had a redbone hound that never left my side. That dog slept with me, ate with me, walked me to school, lay down outside the classroom window on the lawn and waited for me until it was time to walk me back home again. I couldn't take a step without that dog watching over me. He was my guardian angel with fleas."

"A loyal companion," I agreed. "What was his name?"

"Corndog," she explained. "Because he'd eat corn right from the fields. Drove my daddy crazy. That dog would bump a stalk with his rump until it snapped, then pull the husks right off the cob and enjoy himself an ear of sweet corn whenever he felt like it."

"Your nickname," I said, delighted. "That's why people call you 'Corndog Sally.'"

"That's right," she said. "And now you are one of a few people left in the world who know my secret."

"Your secret is safe with me," I promised.

"I have no doubt," she said.

"I'll look after Trey. I'll make sure he stays out of trouble."

"Thank you," she said. "Thank you for that." Her voice started to fade and I knew she was slipping into sleep, and that it was the only comfort she had while she waited for the final sleep. I could not bear to take it from her, so I took one last look at the dark face surrounded by a halo of wild and wiry white hair. I saw a tiny woman, barely hitting one hundred pounds soaking wet with the sweat of all those years of hard work, a woman born into nothing during a time that gave her nothing because she had skin the wrong color and a mind too sharp for anyone's taste but her own. And yet she'd had the strength to survive spirit-numbing poverty and get herself an education and marry a good man and bear his children, then feed them and clothe them and send most of them to college

— and still care about the rest of the world and the people in it without rancor. And after all that, she was able to look death square in the face without flinching.

A remarkable woman indeed.

* * *

WHEN I GOT BACK to the waiting room, the rest of my life had arrived. Judgment was upon me — and my heart felt like it had been stripped and laid bare for all to witness. There was Shep, shaking Bill Butler's hands, looking official in his sheriff's uniform, which meant he'd gotten his old job back and whatever had happened on the mountain after I left had done him more good than harm.

Still, it made me nervous to see so many men I'd slept with in one room like that. I was the 400-pound gorilla in the room, it seems, and in no mood to face the overwhelming and living proof of my somewhat unpredictable taste in men.

Shep's arrival must have made Ramsey nervous because he had disappeared. However he had done it, he was once again here today and gone tomorrow. I'd have to thank him for being such a good friend later.

It was too much for Marcus, too. I was hiding around the corner from the waiting room, trying to get up the nerve to enter, when he brushed past me on his way toward the exit and murmured, "Honey, trust me, there is some serious testosterone in that room."

"Wait," I whispered. "Why'd you have to call Shep?" I asked, knowing only Marcus could have told him where I was. "You ratted me out. Why not call in the FBI while you're at it?"

"Oh, believe me, I was tempted," he said indignantly. "And for your information, your sheriff was already halfway to your apartment in Durham when I called. He was heading your way and I am not responsible for why. Don't ever pull a stunt like this again, you hear me? You disappearing not only put your life in jeopardy, it put my job in serious jeopardy, too. By the way, this is *yours.*"

He retrieved a cardboard box from a warm corner near a heating vent in the hall. "I'm giving you the crack-head cat back. Before he destroys my apartment."

I peeked in the box. The tiny calico was sleeping soundly, flat on his back, all four paws spread wide in an ecstasy of relaxation. "This cat destroyed your apartment?" I asked dubiously.

"It's stoned out of its mind right now," Marcus hissed. "Otherwise he'd be climbing your face."

"What am I supposed to do with it?" I said. "I can't even keep a plant alive."

"That is a problem you are going to have to work out on your own, because I am going home and I am going to sleep in my own bed. I am going to enjoy a nice night of rest without some crazy, flesh-crazed crack-head kitten trying to eat my toes while I sleep."

I started to laugh and that was a mistake. Marcus gets very angry when he thinks you are laughing at him.

"Oh no, you're not," he said incredulously. "After all I did for you? I protected you while detectives from here to Poughkeepsie were looking for your ass. I could have lost my job."

"I'm sorry," I said. "Really, Marcus, I am sorry."

"Oh, go peddle your pussy somewhere else," Marcus said acidly as he sailed out the door. "You owe me. A big one."

"I know," I called after him. But I also knew it would eventually be okay. Marcus gets angry at me regularly, but he also gets over it just as regularly. You just had to let him wallow in his snit fits first.

Bill Butler was the next to bail. He ambled past, hot on Marcus's heels, with little more then a smile that told me I was no longer his problem and he was glad of it.

"Wait," I called after him. "Don't you want to bring your wife a sweet little kitten as a gift?"

He just laughed and kept going.

As I turned with my makeshift cardboard rehab center, I bumped straight into the last man I was prepared to explain things to: Shep. Oh my god, he smelled so clean: like soap and mountain air and freshly ironed shirts. Every hormone in my body stood up and started to sing.

"Hi," I said before I stuttered into silence because, awkward circumstances or not, Shep was focusing those amazing blue eyes on me and when I looked at the crinkles around them, everything else around me kind of faded and I was left helpless and swimming in a sea of estrogen.

"Hi," he said back, perhaps too firmly for someone I had hoped was equally as lovestruck. "Fancy running into you here."

"What's that?" Trey interrupted and I felt a surge of gratitude toward his blessed little teenage soul. Avoidance is a beautiful thing. He peeked down into the cardboard box I was holding. "Where'd you get him?"

"Oh," I said absently, still vibrating from the effect of Shep being so near. "Marcus can't keep him so he needs a home. He's a handful. Truth is, he's kind of an addict. The kitten, not Marcus."

"You can't just give up on it," Trey said, sounding stricken. He cradled the kitten and tickled its tummy, bringing a feline smile to the cat's stoned-out face. The furry little beast looked positively boneless as it draped over Trey's arms, purring mindlessly. I thought of how hard Trey had probably fought to save his mother from drugs and knew he needed the victory that saving the kitten would represent. But would Burly understand?

Trey looked up at Burly, who was watching his son from across the room, and he didn't even have to ask.

"You can keep him," Burly told Trey. "But something tells me he'll be better off as an outdoor cat."

"Absolutely," I said brightly. "Just give him a pine tree and he'll make enough shredded mulch to earn his keep."

"Come on," Burly told his son as he rolled toward the exit doors. "Before Casey sells us another pig in a poke. Let's get you home and I'll show you your bedroom. Then we'll come back to see your grandma again. After that, we've got a lot of paperwork to get started on."

Burly and Trey left, the kitten sleeping soundly once again on its bed of catnip. And I was left with absolutely nothing between me and Shep other than a foot of increasingly warm air.

"Am I officially in your custody?" I asked faintly.

"Yes, it looks like I have drawn the short straw," Shep said cheerfully. "You've been released into my custody."

My heart leapt — no more jailhouse bars for me.

In the silence of the hospice, I could hear my heart hammering in my chest. "What happened?" I asked. "Are you okay?"

"I am," he said, taking off his hat and twirling it in his hands. "I look like a fool for not knowing what was going on underneath my own nose, but I'm cleared. Got my job back. Even got a little glory, thanks to you."

I smiled, unable to speak.

"You got some glory, too," he explained. "I told them you tipped me off about the compound. They're going to look the other way until your paperwork clears the system. Debbie Little may end up with a record, but you won't. Well, other than the one you already got, of course."

"Thank you," I said faintly.

"You need to thank your friend Butler, too," Shep explained. "He's handling Perry County for you. You may have to go up there to talk to the boys a little and set things straight but, otherwise, you're in the clear."

"Trey saw the men who killed his mother," I said. "There were four of them all together."

Shep nodded. "His father's bringing him in to talk to Perry County tomorrow afternoon. They can take it from there."

"How many men did you take into custody on the compound?" I asked.

"More than forty," he said. "A couple wounded, but no one killed, and it was a clean take on our side. Everyone who walked in there, walked out. Textbook case, in fact. They'll be teaching it one day, I suspect. As a counterpoint to Waco."

He stared silently at me.

"What?" I asked.

He handed me Ramsey's cell phone. "I know you took the kid out of there. We found this. It has my number on it. You had help?"

"A little." I had no intention of telling him who had helped me, amazing blue eyes or not.

"You want to tell me how you got out without being seen?"

"Not really."

"Didn't know you were so mountain wise."

"Well, I am now," I said. "I spent a lot of hours on that mountain of yours."

"And it will never be the same for that, trust me," he said with a smile.

"I kind of liked the compound's leader," I confessed. "I don't think he knew what his men were doing to the women. At least not beyond the distributing drugs part."

“You can write him in prison and let him know how much you care,” Shep promised. “He’ll be put away for a long, long time. They had enough assault rifles to defend a small country.”

“I don’t think they’d ever have used them,” I explained. “I think they just needed to know they could have used them.”

“Can’t take that chance,” Shep explained. “All it takes is one real crazy and, boom, you have Armageddon.”

“I’m sorry,” I said. “I know you grew up with those men.”

“Grew up with them in a different world,” Shep said. “Sometimes I can’t seem to keep up.”

“Me, either,” I admitted. “Where do we go from here?”

“Back home. To Silver Top. There’s something you need to do right away.”

“Me?” I felt a flash of panic. “You want me to go back to… Silver Top?”

“Not inside,” he said. “I promise. But I thought you might want to be there when I get your friend out.”

“Oh my god. *Bobby.* How could I have forgotten about him?”

“He’s fine,” Shep promised. “He’s been a pain in the ass for the kitchen staff and tripled the food budget for the month but, other than that, I think he’ll survive. He got his own cell, mostly because no one else could fit in one with him. He’ll be okay.”

“Do you think he’ll ever forgive me?” I asked.

“You’re going to have to ask him that yourself. You got any good-byes to say here?”

“No,” I said. “I’m done saying goodbye.” I smiled at him. He smiled back. The world shimmered, shifted and then settled back down as a better place.

“Let’s go then,” he said. "You want to stop at home first? I’ve got your stuff in the car. The things you left at the lodge.”

"Let's hit the road," I decided. "Bobby sprang me. It's time to spring him."

"One thing I am curious about," Shep said as we left the hospice. "Do I want to know why they found a six-foot Plexiglas hot dog in the woods behind the prison?"

"Definitely," I said. "I'll tell you everything on the way up."

We had reached his car. "Front seat this time," he said cheerfully. "I laid in a supply of Krispy Kremes just for you."

Oh god, what a guy. The fact that I'd stuffed myself with doughnuts on the way down would just have to be forgotten. Could I repay his kindness with rudeness? I think not. I'd just have to eat more Krispy Kremes. It was practically my civic duty.

I climbed inside the car and found a little nest: two pillows arranged, just so, plus a blanket waiting. All for little old me.

"You did this for me?" I asked in a tone of voice I'd normally puke when hearing.

"I confess I do not routinely provide pillows and blankets to the people I transport in this car."

It was too much for me to bear. That man was as sweet as ten dozen Krispy Kremes fresh from the conveyer belt. I scooted over until I was sitting in his lap. He smelled like pine and soap. His cheeks were as soft and his mouth as warm as I had remembered during those lonely nights lying in my prison bunk bed, staring up at the ceiling.

"I really missed you," I said intently. "Was it real?"

"It was real," he whispered.

We kissed. Time passed. We kissed some more.

"I missed you, too," he said when we came up for air. And then he let me know he really meant it.

It was a long time until we pulled out of the parking lot and headed back to Silver Mountain. Once we hit the highway, I plumped up the pillows, pulled the blanket around me, placed my hand on his leg so I'd know he was there at all times and I slept, happier than I'd been in decades.

* * *

BY THE TIME we reached Silver Mountain again, the sun had climbed halfway up the morning sky and not a trace of snow remained to remind me that the stunning beauty of the mountain could turn cruel in the span of hours. The last forty-eight hours seemed as far away and surreal as a barely-remembered dream.

I had learned all I needed to know, for now, from Shep in the last few hours of the drive: he had put his career on the line for me when he got my message. He had believed me, the feds had believed him, and we had both lived, careers intact, to tell the tale.

Now it was time to spring Bobby. We'd stopped at *Bojangles* before we left the foothills and I'd bought a peace offering of six chicken-and-biscuits plus a side tub of gravy and four extra biscuits. I knew Bobby ate to control his outlook on life and I knew he'd need a jumpstart that morning.

So would I. When we turned into the parking lot of Silver Top Detention Center, it all returned in a rush: the inability to breathe, the feeling the sky was going to crash in on me at any moment. Not even Shep could have calmed the panic and he didn't even try. He took one look at my face, pulled into a parking space and ordered me to stay put.

"I'll have him out in fifteen minutes," he promised. "You wait here for me and I'll make it worth your while."

I started to say something smartass back, but Shep's phone rang and, by the tone of his voice, I knew it had to be something big. "Now?" he asked his caller, with a glance at me. "No, actually

I'm at Silver Top now. Just give me fifteen minutes. I want to get another informant out of there first, so he doesn't get hung up by this." He frowned. "Yeah, okay. Give me a warning call five minutes out." He ended the call and stared at me, expressionless.

"What?" I asked defensively.

"Nothing. I'm just trying to figure out how to play you so you don't get all stubborn on me."

"How about not playing me at all?" I suggested.

"Fine. If you dare to so much as move more than ten feet from this car, I'll skin you alive. I'm going in there, and bringing your friend out, and then the two of you are going to stay here with the car, without so much as moving a muscle, while I help the state and federal boys finish up some business."

"You're taking them down *now?*" I asked jubilantly. "I know the guards work in three-day shifts, Shep. There are men in there who have no idea what went down on the compound. Tell me you're going to arrest the rest of the guards involved in the drug ring right in front of all the prisoners, then handcuff them and goose step them out."

"You want me to set fire to them while we do it?" he asked.

"No. I just want the women in there to know that it's over, that what those men made them do was wrong, and someone gave a crap and stopped them, and that they won't have to do it anymore."

"Well then," Shep said. "You shall get your wish. But first, I'm going to get your friend."

The prisoners on the male wing of Silver Top had been let out for morning exercise. As Shep strode toward the front gate, I searched the men's exercise yard for Bobby D. The male prisoners all wore dark blue jumpsuits — except for one dressed in bright orange who lumbered like a neon mountain trapped in a glacier's push. It had to be Bobby D. There could not possibly be another prisoner of his size in the entire state. But what the hell was he doing dressed in a color usually reserved for Death Row inmates?

Ignoring Shep's orders to say within ten feet of the car and willing to taunt my claustrophobia, I crept a few parking rows closer to get a better view of Bobby D., prison kingpin in action. I couldn't see much, though, so I returned to the car and rummaged around until I found Shep's binoculars under the front seat. He was smart enough not to leave a gun there, but I did find a clean pair of socks and a new box of condoms next to the binoculars. Woohoo! I like a man who's prepared for anything.

My god, but the magnified view of the prison yard was entertaining. Bobby D. had jumbo charm to go with his jumbo size. He moved from group to group, fist bumping inmates, shaking hands, slapping fellow prisoners on the back, bullshitting his way to King of the Prom. I could only imagine the stories he had told, most of them no doubt centered around owning millions of dollars worth of houses and yachts and promises of providing prisoners with rich rewards if they didn't jump him in the shower — none of which he actually owned and not that I could imagine Bobby D. being able to bend over, much less an inmate being able to hold on to his slippery bulk long enough to complete an assault. From what I could see, Bobby actually seemed to like being in the joint and that surprised me. He was a ladies man to the core and usually avoided hanging with the dudes. I had to admire his flexibility.

It didn't take Shep long to process Bobby's discharge. Within ten minutes, a guard had approached and, amidst hoots and jeers from prisoners who were convinced he had done something wrong, Bobby was escorted from the yard. I figured he'd stop and change into his regular clothes before he left, but I was wrong: five minutes later, he was happily shaking the hands of the front gate guards as he left the prison behind, beaming like Santa Claus who'd swapped his red threads for a bright orange jumpsuit. He even had a sack with his possessions in it slung over his shoulder.

I scurried back to Shep's car and was casually leaning against the hood by the time they reached me. "Sustenance?" I asked, holding out the box brimming with *Bojangle's* biscuits.

I am sure Bobby would have thanked me had he not been too busy unwrapping biscuits and shoving them in his mouth.

"Why the orange jumpsuit?" I asked. "Surely you didn't get Death Row for helping me escape?"

He glanced up and crumbs tumbled out as he spoke. "It was the only thing that fit. It's real comfortable. I might get me a couple for lounging around the house."

"Stylish," I said. "You could wear one of those fake ball and chains around an ankle when you go to the grocery store. When you hit the junk food aisle, the clerk could call out, 'Dead man shopping!'"

Bobby ignored me, but Shep thought it was hysterical. And that made me happy.

"More calories?" I asked politely. I offered a gallon-sized Pepsi to Bobby. He grabbed it and slurped in contentment.

"Thank you," I said to Shep, remembering my manners, even if Bobby D. had forgotten his. "Thank you for everything."

Shep was too busy watching Bobby D. to answer. That often happened when people witnessed the phenomenon of Bobby eating for the first time. He was the only person I knew in the entire world who ate utterly and completely without guilt. He shoveled it in with gusto, humming and groaning in pleasure, savoring every hit on his taste buds, experiencing eating as one massive sensory rush. It should have been obscene, but honestly, I envied him his pleasure.

Four chicken biscuits later, Bobby attempted conversation: "It's good to see you, babe," he said to me. "You're looking swell."

"Thanks. I was worried. I thought I'd lost you back there in the woods."

“Me, too,” Bobby confessed. “I was sure my bum ticker was kicking in. I had this stabbing pain in my chest, you know? Turns out this corkscrew on my key chain had popped open. Almost punctured a lung.”

Yeah right, the corkscrew would have had to be three feet long to get through Bobby’s layers of fat.

“I saw you sacrifice yourself to the dogs,” I said. “You’re a true friend, Bobby D.”

He waved a hand dismissively. “You would have done the same for me, babe.” But then his face clouded over as he remembered something. He spoke to Shep. “They’re not confiscating my hot dog gun permanently, are they?” he asked anxiously.

“I’m sure it’s safe and sound in an evidence envelope somewhere,” Shep answered. “I’ll make sure it gets back to you.”

*A sense of humor, too?* I was utterly and completely in love.

“I saw you in the prison yard with all of your pals,” I told Bobby. “How do you do that? Making friends wherever you go?”

“Some people just have charisma," he confided. A biscuit later, he added: ”I’m thinking of going to law school. Lot of those guys in there need a good lawyer.”

“You think?” I asked as he tackled the final chicken biscuit. I’d thought of trying to snag one myself but didn’t fancy having my hand bitten off.

Shep’s phone rang, and he was on his way, striding toward the prison gates before he’d even answered it. He shot me a glance and this time I knew to stay put without being told. As Bobby dug into his biscuits-and-gravy with a groan of pleasure, I sat in the front seat of Shep’s car and watched as glossy black sedans slid sleekly past us like sharks on the prowl. They parked near the prison gates and a clan of well-dressed SBI and FBI agents sprang from the cars. I guess looking sharp was an additional “fuck you” to the guards they were about to arrest, a subtle reminder that the finer things in life would soon be completely out of their reach. They had betrayed the code.

I caught a glimpse of startled comprehension on one guard's face as the mod squad checked in. Then I climbed up onto the top of the car and trained my binoculars on the women's wing of the prison, hoping for a glimpse of what was soon to happen.

"What are you doing up there?" Bobby finally thought to ask. He eyed the hood like he was planning to join me but wisely ditched the idea. The car would have flattened like a pancake.

"You missed a lot, Bobby," I told him. "A hell of a lot. But, basically, they're arresting some of the guards."

"No shit? You got 'em?" Bobby's face beamed with pride. "That's my girl. How long are they going down for?"

"A long time," I promised. "Shep says they'll be charged with drug manufacturing, illegal sale of narcotics, sexual assault, interstate transportation in aid of racketeering and spitting on little old ladies each Sunday."

"Not bad," Bobby admitted as he licked the corners of the gravy container, seeking out every last drop. "That sounds like a good twenty years each."

"Some will cut deals," I predicted. "But the ones who used the girls for prison booty will be going down. Shep promised."

"Well, if it's prison booty they want, it's prison booty they're going to get," Bobby predicted. He did not like women to be abused. He loved women in all of their shapes and sizes. "Course, they are likely to be the booty next time around."

"Do you hear that?" I asked him.

We both froze. In the stillness of the day, we could hear a growing roar inside the prison walls. It started out as a low buzz and grew in volume.

"They're making 'em do the perp walk," Bobby guessed. "They're parading them down the block halls."

"Oh, man, I almost wish I could be inside to see it."

But, in the end, I didn't have to go back inside those dreadful, soul-numbing walls. Instead, the prison came to me. The door to the exercise yard on the female wing of the prison opened and hundreds of prisoners streamed out, many of them whooping, hollering and high-fiving one another.

"Hmmm," I told Bobby. "Something tells me more women were forced to play ball than I thought."

"It's just fresh blood," Bobby said. "Something to break the day up. Unexpected entertainment for the masses. Those bastards deserve it, though."

I trained my binoculars on the exercise yard doors and saw Alldread, the female guard who had shot me a knowing glance one day in the hall when one of the guards had emerged, red-faced, from a bathroom, followed by a pretty prisoner. Alldread had let the prisoners out to witness the coming spectacle of the guards being marched to the SBI and FBI cars and I couldn't say I blamed her. She probably wanted the men arrested as much as any of the prisoners, even if she was keeping her face carefully neutral amidst the chaos. I wondered if she had guessed my involvement in their arrest. I probably would never know. And it was okay. If she lumped me forever as just another prison loser rotating in and out of Silver Top, one who had managed to escape but would be back soon enough, that was okay with me. It still put me on the right side of this particular battle.

Some of the women had run to the fence nearest the entrance gates and were crowding each other for a better view. Black, white, short, tall, old, young — you name it. They were as different from one another as a box full of buttons. But, at the moment, they were exulting in a common victory.

A roar went up from the exercise yard as the front gates of the prison opened and an agent pushed the first guard-turned-prisoner, his arms handcuffed behind his back, into the parking lot. The guard stumbled, regained his footing and looked around, confused at the sounds that greeted him. He saw the exercise yard full of jeering women and shrank back, as if afraid they might break through the fence. But the agent behind him shoved him forward, hard, to make room for the next guard being perp-walked out. A fresh cheer went up and it got personal. This guard's name was Dennis, it seemed, and he was a favorite of the crowd — at least when it came to suggestions for his punishment. Some of the women were very creative when it came to kitchen utensils. I thought of the public hangings of old and figured Dennis was getting off easy with this dose of public humiliation.

In the end, four more guards were arrested as part of the drug ring, including a few I was sad to see. They'd seemed okay on the inside. But you can't pick your villains any more than you can pick your true friends.

"Don't know why they don't just turn right around and stick them in the other wing of the prison," I called down to Bobby. "It would save us all a lot of time and trouble."

"And deprive these fine women of their revenge?" Bobby was waving to the cheering female prisoners. They, although clearly perplexed at what a male prisoner dressed in a Death Row jumpsuit was doing lounging in the parking lot, were nonetheless waving enthusiastically back. "Some of them dames are not bad looking," Bobby said, gesturing for my binoculars.

"Get your own peepers," I told him as I searched the crowd, not sure of who I wanted to find. Until I found her. There she was: my former cellmate, Risa Foster, standing away from the rest of the crowd. Her fingers were hooked into the heavy metal of the chain link fence. She was staring not at the guards being dragged unceremoniously to the official cars, but at me. I waved at her, jumping up and down to make sure she saw me. She stared back, hesitantly at first. But as my waving and jumping grew more frantic, her face broke out in a huge smile and she held one hand above her head before she waved it once, just once, in salute. It was the first time I had ever seen her smile.

"She sees me," I told Bobby excitedly, "She sees me."

"Who sees you?" Bobby asked as he peered into the corners of his *Bojangles* box, hoping for a scrap of more breakfast.

"My guardian angel," I explained. "She saved my ass."

"I'm the one who saved your ass," Bobby pointed out. "At great cost to my personage."

"Yes, you did, Bobby D., my truest friend. Yes you did!" I knew I was yelling, but I didn't care. I was overcome by a tide of exultation rising in me. I was *free.* I was standing on the roof of a car, under an endless blue sky, breathing in fresh mountain air, and no one, no one at all, could take my freedom away from me.

"I love you Bobby D.," I yelled down from the roof. "You are my dearest friend, my truest friend." I thought of him, terrified and cold in the woods, surrounded by yapping dogs, sacrificing his Little Debbie cakes for me. "You gave up your freedom for me. You are the best friend a girl could ever have."

"Yeah, yeah, yeah," Bobby replied, unimpressed. "You get a girlfriend while you were inside?"

"Don't ask, don't tell," I answered. "Why do you ask?"

"There's an arm trying to semaphore some sort of message out of a window on the second floor," he explained. "I'm pretty sure she's trying to say 'Are your melons fresh today?'"

"Peppa!" I exclaimed. I focused the binoculars on the second floor windows, counting down until I found my cell. Sure enough, one window over, a sturdy brown arm was dangling outside the bars, waving back and forth in the sunlight. I could not see her face, but I knew it was Peppa. I waved back frantically and almost knocked an eyeball out with the edge of the binoculars.

"You cave that roof in and that sheriff is going to stick you right back inside where you and your melon-squeezing friend can get better acquainted," Bobby warned me.

"He'd never do that to me," I hollered down.

"You sure about that?" Bobby yelled back.

I was sure.

Peppa gave me a big thumb's up. I gave her the same signal back and blew her kisses, letting her know I'd never forget her. That someone outside knew she was there.

The cheering had slowed and become garbled as the women took up some sort of chant. It was hard to hear at first, but then it grew louder, took hold, solidified, grew in volume and became a disciplined roar. I grinned as I realized what they were chanting and fought back the sudden tears.

"Who the fuck is Elsie?" Bobby yelled at me over the din.

"Not *Elsie*," I shouted down at him, the tears streaming down my cheeks. "They're chanting, 'L.D.' That's me: Little Debbie, L.D. They're chanting for *me.*"

And they were. All of those beautiful, forgotten, down-trodden, flawed, struggling, unseen women were chanting *my* name. I stood tall, waving back my thanks, letting their recognition wash over me. It was, hands down, the proudest moment of my life.

"Yo, Beauty Queen!" Bobby was yelling up at me. "Get down off your float. Your boyfriend is heading this way."

"He's not my boyfriend," I explained as I slid down the windshield and hopped from the hood. No sense taking chances — I had, perhaps, bumped into the brackets holding the flashing lights to the roof and I just may have loosened them a teensy little bit.

“You sure he’s not your boyfriend?” Bobby asked as Shep broke away from the agents and headed our way, a grin on his face.

I watched him striding across the parking lot, those long legs eating up the distance between us, the sun glinting off his sunglasses. My heart started to hammer in my chest and it had nothing to do with claustrophobia.

“Oh god,” I said, feeling a little dizzy. “Maybe you’re right.”

“He damn sure looks he’s heading our way for a reason,” Bobby said. “I don’t think it’s me. I’ll just wait in the back seat while you two suck face.”

As Bobby wedged himself into the back seat of the squad car, I leaned against the front grill, waiting for my future to arrive.

“It’s over,” Shep said with a grin. “It’s over.”

“I never want to hear those words come out of your mouth again,” I told him.

“Stay with me for awhile,” he asked as he reached me. He stopped abruptly, standing shyly by my side. He looked up at the sun as if we were discussing the weather forecast. “I got some time off, Thanksgiving’s coming in a couple of weeks, it’s supposed to snow again in a few days and my cabin is pretty great when it snows. Just stay.” He looked down at me and smiled, sending those laugh lines crinkling out from the corners of his eyes. I wanted to lean over and lick them right off his face.

“For how long?” I asked.

“Hell, I don’t know.” He laughed. “As long as you feel like it. I’ll take you for as long as I can get you.”

Well, okay then. Who could argue with that? After all, there was an entire box of condoms under the front seat that needed testing. Just thinking about it was making me as weak as a crack-addled kitten.

“I think I will,” I said. “Who’s it gonna hurt?”

"Exactly," Shep agreed. As he pulled me to him, I caught a whiff of pine and soap. It robbed me of all common sense.

"Just promise me we can keep this to ourselves for a little while," I said. "I don't want everyone on the mountain staring at me every time I step foot out of the cabin door. It makes me feel like such a Jezebel."

"You are a Jezebel." His mouth was so soft and pliant that I had trouble holding my thoughts together. I heard a roaring in my ears and slowly became aware that he was starting to laugh. He didn't stop kissing me, mind you, but he was laughing while he did it. I can't say I minded the sensation.

"What is so funny?" I demanded.

"If you wanted to keep this to yourself," Shep said, "you probably should have gotten in the back seat with your friend."

I looked up and saw them lined up behind the fence: dozens and dozens of prisoners, watching our every move. They were cheering and shouting, yelling at me to kiss him again, hooting and hollering at me to grab his ass. Hell, they were suggesting things not even I had heard of in my prime.

"Good lord," I said to Shep. "Did you hear what that woman just suggested you do to me?"

"I certainly did," Shep confessed. "What say we go back to my cabin and give it a try?"

Well, wasn't he full of surprises? Maybe those days trapped behind bars would turn out to be worth it after all.

"Okay," I agreed. "You're on. But you might want to eat your Wheaties first."

"I'll eat a whole damn box of them," Shep promised. "Just you wait."

# # #

Breinigsville, PA USA
31 March 2010

235289BV00001B/54/P

9 780981 944241